RIGHT BEHIND YOU

A PSYCHOLOGICAL SUSPENSE THRILLER

N. L. HINKENS

Text copyright @ 2021 Norma Hinkens

Published by Dunecadia Publishing, California

ISBN: 978-1-947890-32-9

Cover by: **www.derangeddoctordesign.com**

Editing by: **www.jeanette-morris.com/first-impressions-writing**

1

_____

"**M**oving truck's here!" Jack calls to me from the ladder in our family room where he's attempting to install a curtain rail above the bay window. For a financial consultant who doesn't own a cordless screwdriver, it's proving to be quite the challenge. At his feet, our six-year-old son, Lucas, lies on his belly playing his favorite turtle game on his iPad and singing to himself. Fortunately, he's good at entertaining himself. I was an only child too, but, unlike him, I struggled with the inherent loneliness—which is part of the reason I ended up going down a wrong path in my teens, and burying an unspeakable secret along the way. I'm determined to do everything in my power to make sure Lucas doesn't repeat my mistakes.

Placing the last of the groceries I'd been unpacking into the fridge, I snatch up the moving inventory list and hurry out to the curb, eager to oversee the operation and check that nothing's been damaged in transit.

Jack likes to call me a control freak, but someone has to lead the charge. I'd never have admitted it years ago in my rebellious stage, but I'm a lot like my parents at heart. They were gutsy, make-things-happen kind of people. And they did. They built a software engineering company that sold for a very respectable eight-million-dollars—money I inherited when their small plane went down outside San Antonio six months ago, cutting short the retirement they'd earned after decades of seventy-hour-plus work weeks.

Despite fighting the idea at first, I ended up following in their footsteps and majored in software engineering. And with the infusion of capital I inherited after their death, I've finally been able to set up my own company, Capitol Technologies, in Austin, the city I love and know best. It's only now that I'm back that I realize how much I've missed the vibe and the music scene. I never really settled into life in San Antonio, and it didn't help that all the junipers and cedar trees wreaked havoc on my allergies.

"Hi, I'm Lauren McElroy," I say, shaking hands with a burly, balding man who introduces himself as Chuck. It matches the name embroidered on the navy company shirt he's wearing, so I take it as proof that he's legitimate and not here to rip me off. I've been reading about all the identity fraud that goes along with moving nowadays. Part of me was afraid the truck wouldn't show up at all, so we're off to a good start. Now to validate that all our possessions have arrived intact, primarily my parents' antiques.

I paid a heavy price for their success, so maybe the inheritance is compensation of sorts for the fact that I didn't see much of them growing up. It was mostly just me and my nanny, Kathy, at one end of the burled walnut dining table every night after soccer practice or piano lessons. Until I went off the rails.

An icy shiver runs through me at the grisly memory of how my junior year ended. I've never told Jack about it. It's the one secret I keep from him in our otherwise healthy marriage—well, the biggest secret, anyway.

Chuck tightens his back support brace and gestures to his heavily tattooed partner sporting spiky red hair. "This is Danny. I'll just have you verify a few things and then we'll get started."

While I look over the paperwork he hands me, Chuck unlocks the back of the truck and lowers the lift. Satisfied that our inventory lists match, I shove my copy into my back pocket and turn to watch the movers begin unloading. I'd rather not stand out here in the heat, but there's less chance of them being careless with our stuff if I keep an eye on them from the sidelines.

The rear door rolls up and my anticipation quickly turns to horror. An acidic trail of revulsion creeps up my throat. I blink, as if that will somehow make what I'm seeing disappear like a figment of my imagination. But I can't sweep it away that easily. Oblivious to my mounting dread, Chuck and Danny get busy moving items onto the lift, sweat already trickling down their flushed faces.

"Wait!" I call out in a strangled voice.

Chuck throws me an irritated glance as he and Danny struggle to set down the chest of drawers in their arms.

"That's ... that's not mine!" I say, jabbing a shaking finger in the direction of a decorative scarecrow on a wooden stand, leering down from the back of the truck with a stitched smile. A Walmart price tag dangles from one of its sleeves. A shudder crosses my shoulders at the sight of a stuffed, felt crow sewn on one of its outstretched arms.

"What? You mean this?" Chuck asks, grabbing the scarecrow and scratching his head.

"Yes. It's not ... not on the inventory list," I stutter. "How did it get in there?"

Chuck exchanges a befuddled look with his partner and then shrugs. "No clue, ma'am. We didn't load the truck." He sets the scarecrow back down and shoves it to one side. "Likely got left behind in the last move. If you don't want it, we can toss it for you."

"Of course I don't want it—it's not mine," I snap back. "What I want to know is how it got in there?" I pull the inventory list from my pocket and wave it angrily in the air. "It's not on my docket."

Chuck narrows his eyes at me. I can almost see the gears in his brain whirring as he does a quick risk assessment. Is he dealing with a lunatic, or being set up for a potential lawsuit? "Take it easy, ma'am! I said I'd toss it. It's no big deal."

Danny rubs a hand across his jaw, his eyes zigzagging between me and Chuck, as if betting on which of us will back down first.

I open and close my mouth, but I can't think of a good way to explain myself without admitting to these strangers that the very sight of a scarecrow strikes terror in my heart. I gulp a deep breath, willing myself to calm down when I notice one of the neighbors peering around his front door—wondering, no doubt, what kind of a head case has moved into the neighborhood. "I'm ... sorry for yelling," I stammer. "It's just that this move has been stressful. I want to make sure our stuff didn't get mixed up with someone else's, that's all."

The expression on Chuck's face clears. "Okay, not a problem. We'll go over everything on the inventory list and double check that you got all your items."

"Thank you. I'll run and grab you some waters," I mutter, before bustling off, my heart still pulsing in my throat. I know I'm probably overreacting. It's only a stupid decorative scarecrow. The movers must think I'm demented. I need to take a minute and steady my nerves before I trust myself enough to go back outside and finish overseeing the unloading in a sane and competent manner.

"All good?" Jack calls to me from the top of the stepladder.

Even from here, I can see the rail he's installing is crooked, but I'm not up for that battle right now. "Yup, just fetching the movers something to drink. It's hot out there," I say, forcing the words from my lips as I bolt to the kitchen.

I lean over the sink and splash cold water on my face, heaving several deep breaths. Turning off the faucet, I try to gather my thoughts in some semblance of order. Could the scarecrow have been accidentally left behind in the truck from a previous move, as Chuck suggested? I suppose it's possible, but something tells me that's not what happened. The odds of it inadvertently ending up with our belongings are slim. I have a dreadful hunch it was deliberately placed in the moving truck. It still had the price tag hanging from it —almost as if someone had bought it especially for me.

And there's only one person who would go to such extraordinary lengths to terrify me.

2

After the movers take off, Jack orders pizza and we sit down as a family at our newly installed pedestal kitchen table, exhausted after a long day. But it isn't only physical exhaustion I'm fighting as I take in the bare walls and mentally assess the work still to be done to make this place a home. It's a host of emotions I've mostly managed to keep buried for close to two decades. Now, they're resurfacing, like a skeleton in a horror movie clawing its way out of a grave, ripping my chest open and threatening to tear my world apart.

"Mommy, why aren't you eating your dinner?" Lucas pipes up through a mouthful of Pepperoni pizza.

Jack wipes his lips on a paper napkin and glances across the table at me curiously. "You okay, babe? You're awfully quiet. We should be celebrating now that we've finally moved out of the rental and into our own place."

I stretch my lips into a half-hearted smile and lift a slice of pizza to my mouth, trying not to gag as I take an obligatory bite to satisfy my son's concern for my nutrition. My stomach churns as I will myself to swallow a mouthful of congealed pepperoni and cheese. We've been renting for the past two months, but someone knew we were moving into our house today and sent me a macabre greeting—I'm convinced of it.

Jack leans back in his chair and surveys me. "You're not still stewing over that stupid scarecrow, are you?"

"You don't think it's odd?" My tone is sharp and accusing. Unfairly so. Jack knows I hate Halloween, but I've never admitted to my phobia of scarecrows. There are too many secrets entangled in my fears. I don't want to even think about everything that happened after the night at the pumpkin patch—let alone talk about it. It all devolved into a worse nightmare than I could ever have imagined. "That *stupid scarecrow*, as you put it, wasn't on our inventory list—I double checked. Someone planted it in our stuff."

Jack stops chewing and raises bemused brows. "*Planted* it?" He chuckles. "You're talking about it like it's a bomb or something. It just got left behind, like Chuck said. Happens all the time."

"Then why wasn't it at the back of the truck instead of right at the front in clear view?" I hold his gaze until he gives a defeated shrug.

"I don't know, Lauren. Someone probably took it out when they noticed it had been forgotten, and it was accidentally loaded back in with our stuff. Let it go, will you? Do you have to over analyze everything?"

"It doesn't make sense," I persist. "I think someone deliberately put the scarecrow in the truck after our stuff was loaded."

Jack throws up his hands in defeat. "Okay, so what if you're right and the moving company screwed up? I still don't see what the big deal is. It was a cheap ten-dollar decor item from Walmart. It's not like one of your parents' antique vases got misplaced."

"It's not just a decor item," I say, quieting my voice. "There's ... more to it than that."

I glance across at Lucas whose eyelids are growing droopier by the minute now that his belly's full. I don't want to divulge my fears in front of him and give him nightmares, but I need to make Jack understand why I'm so insistent that this was no accident. "Why don't you take Lucas up to bed while I clean up the kitchen, and we can talk about it afterward?" I suggest.

Jack looks exasperated, but he knows better than to argue with me when I dig my heels in like this. He stands and scoots his chair out from the table. I flinch at the screeching sound on the reclaimed Douglas Fir floor, making a mental note to put felt pads on the bottom of the chair legs in the morning. Everything is so much more jarring with fear heightening my senses. I hate this feeling of losing control. The idyllic evening I'd planned for our first night together in our new home has been marred by the creepy scarecrow turning up with our belongings. If I'm right about it being a warning that I can never truly leave the past behind, then I need to be prepared for a reckoning. Ryder will make sure of it.

After tossing our paper plates and loading the glasses into the dishwasher, I rearrange a few small appliances on the counter and slump back down in my armchair. Inevitably, my thoughts rewind through the decades. I haven't set eyes on Ryder since my junior year of high school. I haven't bothered to look him up online either—or Gareth, or Margo, for that matter. Margo McGowan might have been hard to track down if she'd gotten married and changed her name, but I could easily have looked Gareth

Looney up if I'd cared to. He was the smartest kid in our school, but we gave him a hard time about his unusual last name—that, and never being able to get a date. He had no clue what to say to girls. Which is why he ended up hanging out with Ryder, smoking pot, among other things. Ryder was our gateway to every kind of illicit substance back in the day.

Now that I'm back, I have no desire to get in touch with any of my old friends—if you could even call them friends. I've no idea what paths they took in life, and I don't particularly care. Other than the drugs, and a general dissatisfaction with our lives, we never had much in common to begin with. I lost all contact with them when my parents staged an intervention and relocated from Austin to San Antonio, in part to make sure I was as far from Ryder's influence as possible. But, by then, I was glad to be rid of him.

"Lucas is fast asleep," Jack says, stifling a yawn as he rejoins me at the kitchen table. His dark hair is sticking straight up as if he's been running his fingers through it. "And I'm right behind him. So, let's make this quick."

I give him a tight smile, kneading my sweating palms under the table. It's time I told him about my phobia. It's the only way I can convince him that the scarecrow didn't end up in the moving truck by chance.

"So, I'm guessing you're not going to let this whole scarecrow thing rest?" Jack prompts, propping his elbows on the table in front of him. It's obvious he'd like nothing more than to lay his head down and sleep, but he's doing his best to humor me.

I swallow down my apprehension at the thought of the questions that might arise from my confession. I don't want to tell Jack what actually triggered the nightmares I still suffer from, but I can at least tell him how my fear of scarecrows originated. "Look, I know you're frustrated, Jack, but the reason I was so freaked out is that I have a phobia of scarecrows going all the way back to my childhood. I can't go near them, let alone touch them. At camp one summer, some older kids told me scarecrows come alive at night and chase kids. I was only eight, and, for the longest time, I believed it. Ever since, I've always hated Halloween, especially scarecrows. I hate that disturbing way they stare at nothing, like dolls. Kids used to tease me about it, even in high school. I made the mistake once of confiding in someone that I was terrified of them. Instead of being sympathetic, they used it against me." I tense as an eerie image of a scarecrow flopping a checkered arm at me flashes to mind. Ryder's mirthless laugh echoes through my head and I shut my eyes briefly trying to erase the callous ease with which he tormented me. "That's why I think someone intentionally put it in the truck with our stuff."

Jack rubs a hand over his jaw, looking uncomfortable. "I guess I can understand why you were so freaked out, but I really don't think there's anything to it—stuff gets misplaced all the time. Look, I know this is an emotional time for you moving back to the city where you grew up, but let's not let a little thing like this spoil our new beginning." He reaches for my hand and squeezes it, then gives me an elaborate wink. "Besides, it wasn't exactly a slasher scarecrow. He looked pretty harmless to me."

I prickle at Jack's misguided attempt to get me to laugh. I hate being prodded into reacting in line with someone else's expectations. "What if it wasn't left behind in a prior move?" I say, tossing my head. "What if there's more to it than that?"

Jack leans back and crosses an ankle over one knee, bouncing his foot impatiently. "Like what?"

I chew on my lip for a moment. I don't want to mention Ryder specifically. Jack will have too many questions—like why I never brought him up before, and why we broke up, and if we kept in touch. "I think someone from my past has found out that I moved back to Austin. This is their way of letting me know."

Jack throws me a skeptical look. "If that's the case, your friends have a funny way of welcoming you back."

I turn to look out the curtainless window into the darkness, half-expecting to see the nightmarish face of a grinning scarecrow staring back in at me.

Jack doesn't understand. Ryder's not welcoming me, he's warning me.

3

The next few weeks go by in a blur of activity as I juggle my time between making sure Lucas is settling into his new school and getting my business up and running smoothly in our newly remodeled location. I haven't had time to keep obsessing about the scarecrow in the moving truck. For now, I've relegated it to the back of my mind—labelled in my over-analytical brain as a concerning event but within the realm of possibility of being coincidental. An uneasy compromise for someone like me who doesn't do well with open-ended situations.

"Morning Maria," I call out to my PA as I stride into my office on Monday morning after dropping Lucas off at school.

"Morning, Boss," she replies, promptly setting a cup of black coffee on my gleaming glass desk alongside a stack of mail. Maria's only a couple of years younger than me and she's fast becoming a friend, as well as proving to be an invaluable asset to the firm. I went through an executive PA service to find her and she's worth every penny of her "dowry," as I jokingly call the handsome sum I paid to procure her. *The boss and the bride*, we've dubbed ourselves. I honestly don't know what I'd do without her. She never baulks at a task, no matter how trivial or challenging, and she's put in countless overtime hours working late into the night to help me get the office spaces and cubicles ready for the software engineers I hired. I've had capable assistants before, but no one in Maria's league. I'm lucky to have found her. I only hope she doesn't become involved with any of the engineers and complicate things—she's turned a few heads already with her dark, lustrous hair, Betty Boop lips, and curvy figure. Her intelligence only adds an element of intrigue to her appeal.

"Any pressing issues I need to address?" I ask, perusing the heap of mail in front of me.

"I left a few checks for you to sign that need to go out first thing this morning," Maria says. "Oh, and the locksmith came by and changed the locks on the front door."

I give an approving nod. We had a break-in a few nights ago. The security camera at the front entrance was smashed but, thankfully, nothing was taken or damaged inside the building. The police suspected it was just kids messing around—they informed us there's always a higher rate of vandalism and crime in the days leading up to Halloween. A chill passes over me at the heavy truth of that statement.

"Is my calendar up-to-date?" I ask, taking a sip of coffee.

"Yes, I added in the two additional appointments you texted me last night." Maria replies, consulting our joint calendar on her phone. "If you want to take off early today, I can reschedule our team meeting to Tuesday."

I glance up from the pile of mail I'm shuffling through, a small crease forming on my forehead. Was there something I was supposed to be doing later today? I give a self-conscious laugh, embarrassed to be caught off guard by my ever-efficient PA. I've been leaving more and more in her capable hands of late. "Why? Am I forgetting something?"

She flicks her long, dark hair over one shoulder. "I thought you might want to take Lucas trick-or-treating."

I stiffen, angling my head to hide the fear in my eyes. I've come to dread Halloween each year. So far, I've managed to avoid the whole trick-or-treating tradition, but now that Lucas is in school, he's eagerly anticipating acquiring a monumental candy stash worthy of bragging rights along with all his classmates.

I give a nonchalant shrug and reach for the letter opener on my desk. "Jack's going to take him to a few of the houses on our street. We don't know the area well yet, or where the best places are to go. Lucas is still young so it's not such a big deal."

"Are you kidding?" Maria exclaims. "That's exactly why it's a big deal, picking out your favorite superhero costume, knocking on strangers' doors, ingesting copious amounts of sugar until you crash, drooling chocolate and still dressed to conquer a galaxy far, far away! Anyway, I'm happy to hold down the fort if you change your mind and decide to go with them."

After she breezes out of the room, I set about sifting through the rest of the mail. Systematic as ever, Maria has already gone through it, tossing out the circulars and pulling out anything she can take care of without my input. I approve several bills and check the bank statements, before turning on my monitor. While the computer boots up, I make a quick punch list of everything I need to get done today. Then I start by firing off a couple of time-sensitive responses to emails and wading through the remainder of the items in my inbox. My eyes light on an email from an unknown sender with *Congratulations* in the subject line.

Someone wishing me well on my new venture, no doubt. The business community in Austin has been incredibly welcoming—in the few months we've been open, I've received everything from gift baskets to flowers, and even a few congratulatory phone calls.

I open up the email to discover an interactive card inside. After clicking play, I lean back in my ergonomic office chair, coffee cup in hand. My jaw clenches as a Halloween horror show begins to play. The cup slips from my fingers, and I flinch in pain as hot liquid sears my thigh. Trembling, I scrabble to set the cup back down on my desk and exit out of the email. But it's too late to unsee what I've seen. My mind won't stop replaying a crow with blood-red eyes flying away with the head of a decapitated scarecrow.

I get to my feet and begin pacing the floor. Hot waves of angst wash over me. Just when I'd begun to believe the scarecrow in the moving truck might have been a benign coincidence, I've been emailed evidence to the contrary. I'm being targeted by someone who knows what I'm most afraid of.

An icy finger of fear creeps up my spine. This person knows where I live. And now they know where I work. It has to be Ryder. Who else would do something this deliberate, this twisted, this personal? He's never forgiven me for not being there for him when he got out, but I had no control over what happened. Unbeknownst to him, I was sequestered in central Texas, with no cell phone and no way to contact him. Ryder probably thought I'd changed my number and blown him off. He always said he'd never let me go. And now he's found me again. It wouldn't have been hard with all the publicity surrounding my parents' untimely demise—news of their small plane crash was plastered all over the local news, along with a picture of me.

I flinch when Maria knocks on my door and peeks inside. "Dan Huss from Huss Integrity is here for your mobile application meeting. Oh ... wow ..." Her voice trails off, her eyes flicking over my coffee-splattered outfit. "Did I startle you?"

I wave my hand at her. "No, it was me. That's what I get for trying to type and hold my cup at the same time."

She frowns. "Do you have anything you can change into?"

"I have a clean shirt in the closet. The pants will have to do. At least they're black." I smooth a hand over my hair, trying to collect my thoughts before this important meeting. "Can you show Dan into the conference room and tell him I'll be there in a few minutes? Offer him something to drink."

"I'm on it," Maria says, discreetly closing the door behind her.

The minute she exits the room, I sink back down at my desk and drop my head into my hands. I force myself to take several deep breaths to slow my breathing and calm my racing heart. My gaze settles on a framed motivational quote that Maria helped me hang. *Stay positive, work hard, make it happen.* I can't think about Ryder right now. I need to put my best foot forward and secure this contract. It's a lucrative deal that could feed us work for months—possibly years—to come. Huss Integrity has offices all over Texas and they're rapidly expanding to other states. If we can build the platform they're looking for, it will solidify our reputation in the Austin market. We have the skill level to develop what they need, but we're unknown in this area, and securing a big customer like Huss Integrity would really help us get the word out.

I slip into the tiny bathroom that adjoins my office to

change my shirt and freshen up. *Do it scared, fear's an illusion,* I whisper to my reflection in the mirror as I reapply my lipstick, trying to ignore the sheen of apprehension overlying my complexion.

I clamp my lips together as I head to the conference room, drumming up the steely determination that has got me this far in my career. As soon as I'm done with this meeting, I'll track down Ryder and put an end to his juvenile antics. I'm not the impressionable teenage girl he manipulated at will.

If I can handle powerful men in the boardroom, I can handle a vengeful ex from my past—silence him, if necessary.

4

By the time I walk into the conference room where Dan Huss is waiting, I've managed to get my emotions under control and slipped into my professional persona. I liked Dan's energy right off the bat at our first meeting, and, by all indications, he's already evaluated my initial proposal and is excited about it. Today is all about closing the deal. The meeting gets off to a smooth start, and I waste no time transitioning into the customized presentation I've prepared. "None of our development is offshore," I assure him, "so you'll have the advantage of an immediate local presence to troubleshoot any issues."

"A definite bonus," he agrees, fingering his chin thoughtfully as he studies my laptop screen on the glass table we're seated at. "What about analytics?"

"We have that covered, in addition to a full complementary backend with a built-in capacity for growth," I reply, pleased that I've already anticipated his company's needs. "We'll work with you from start to finish with concept. I can guarantee you'll have an extremely engaged and responsive team at your disposal."

I answer all his questions with ease and the closer I get to the end of the presentation, the more confident I grow that the Huss account is mine for the taking.

"And of course the mobile application will integrate all your social media and search tools, as well as facilitating teamwork and ideation," I add with a flourish as I reach the last slide.

"Your mobile marketing technology is undeniably innovative," Dan remarks, interlacing his fingers and leaning back in his chair. "And I don't doubt your company's expertise or ability to deliver a minimal viable product in a short time-frame." He hesitates, projecting a troubled look. "The issue I'm hung up on is your price. Since we last spoke, I've had a very competitive counteroffer from another company also based here in Austin, Summit Solutions. As you can appreciate, keeping costs down is a priority—our platform will not only be connecting all of our current locations but also needs to cover our expansion plans."

I wet my lips nervously digesting this new information. The last time we met to hammer out the details of a deal, Dan assured me we stood head and shoulders above the other companies he had met with in terms of skill level and value. I was counting on inking a deal today. The idea that a competitor has swooped in at the finish line and undercut our price has caught me completely unawares.

I clear my throat trying to convey an aura of calm at odds with the acidic waves churning in my stomach. "I can certainly take a look at the bid and see what we can do about meeting somewhere in the middle," I offer, trying hard not to sound desperate at the thought of losing such a prized contract.

Dan opens his briefcase and pulls out a sheet of paper. He slides it across the table, and I turn it around to read the terms. My heart sinks. There's no possible way I can match the lowball price, not if I intend to keep paying the competitive salaries of the software engineers I hired.

As if reading my thoughts, Dan gives a sympathetic cough. "As you can see, there's really no way for me to justify your price. They're offering almost an identical set of services for half the money."

I set the offer back down, locking eyes with him. "I find it hard to believe you won't end up with supplemental billing for that price. Our contract is all inclusive."

Dan drums his fingers on the table. "I take it you're telling me you can't match their bid?"

"I'm afraid not," I reply, twisting my sweating hands in my lap, the scent of my spilled coffee wafting up to my nostrils like an untimely omen of disaster. "My engineers are the best in the business and their salaries reflect that."

"Understood," Dan says, reaching for his briefcase. He gives me a tense smile as he gets to his feet. "Perhaps we'll have another opportunity to work together in the future. I look forward to it."

We shake hands and I try to hold back tears as he breezes out of the conference room, oblivious to the wrecking ball he's launched at my fledgling company. While Maria shows him out, I reach for my phone, too numb to think straight. My heart catches in my throat when I see there's a missed call from Dawson Elementary. I play the voice mail message back, but it's only Lucas's teacher asking me to return her call at my convenience—obviously, not an emergency or they would have tried my office or got a hold of Jack by now. I sigh and gently massage my temples. I need to pull myself together and figure out my next move. Should I try to cut costs and counter? I hate to see that amount of business slip through my fingers, but I can't afford to run in the red for months on end either.

Maria returns and leans against the doorframe, eying me with the faintest ripple of her botoxed brow. "You don't look too thrilled. I take it that didn't go as planned."

I grimace. "That's an understatement. Someone came in at the last minute and undercut us—Summit Solutions." I frown, tapping my manicured nails on the desk. "See what you can find out about them. It doesn't seem possible that they can offer the equivalent services for the price they quoted. Something's not right."

Maria straightens up. "If they botched the estimate, maybe there's a way to salvage this deal."

"I doubt it. They can't go back on their price now—not with a written offer. But I want to know everything we can learn about them. They could be a problem if they intend to keep on stealing business from us."

Maria gives a curt nod. "I'll jump right on it."

After she leaves, I take a few minutes to gather my wits and then call the school back.

"Hi, this is Lauren McElroy, Lucas's mom," I say, when the school secretary answers. "His teacher, Gianna Bernardi left me a message and asked me to call her back."

"Oh sure, they should be breaking for lunch right now," the secretary chirps. "Let me put you through to Gianna's classroom."

While I'm on hold, I examine the coffee stains on my pants. They're barely noticeable now that they've dried. I could pass myself off at the school if I need to pick up Lucas. Hopefully he doesn't have an upset tummy or something. I really need to stay here and strategize about how I can make up for losing the Huss Integrity contract.

A soft voice startles me out of my reverie. "This is Gianna Bernardi."

"Hi, it's Lauren McElroy returning your call. Is ... Lucas all right?"

"Yes, he's perfectly fine. Thanks for getting back to me so promptly, Lauren. Actually, I just wanted to fill you in on something that happened in school today. I didn't want there to be any misunderstanding, so I thought it would be best to discuss it before Lucas goes home."

I slowly release the breath I've been holding. It sounds as if this is going to turn out to be a case of some kid's hurt feelings, at worst. Maybe Lucas said something inappropriate. Although, that would be hard to believe—he's such a gentle soul. Still, so long as there's no blood involved, I can smooth things over. After navigating the crisis with Dan Huss, settling a squabble between first graders sounds like a breeze. "I hope Lucas isn't hogging the reading bean bags," I say with a conspiratorial chuckle. "I know how much he enjoys curling up in them every chance he gets."

Gianna laughs. "Not at all. He's such a polite kid; he always waits his turn. Actually, I wanted to talk to you about something else entirely. This might sound strange, but when Lucas went to get his lunchbox at snack time, I noticed some straw falling out of his backpack. I thought it was odd, so I asked him how it got in there. He shrugged and wouldn't tell me at first. I didn't want to make him feel uncomfortable, but I was curious, so I pushed him a little more. I thought maybe he was making something with it. Kids have the strangest reasons for doing things." She gives another laugh that sounds forced. "That's when he told me that a man gave it to him—to bring him good luck in his new house."

I grip the phone like my life depends on it, blood ratcheting its way through my veins. "What ... what man?"

"He didn't know his name," Gianna answers, sounding increasingly nervous.

I swallow hard, envisioning some pervert talking to my son through the chainlink fence around the playground. "Aren't the kids supervised at recess? Where did Lucas meet this man?"

"I was afraid it might have been on the school premises, but ... Lucas says it was your neighbor."

5

I end the call with Lucas's teacher in a daze and shrivel up in my office chair, a tsunami of disquiet building inside me. I rack my brains for a plausible explanation —one that doesn't paint me as hysterical—but it's hard not to make the connection between the straw in Lucas's backpack and the scarecrow. What neighbor could my son have been talking to? And when did this clandestine exchange take place? I suppose it's possible one of the neighbors leaned over the fence in the backyard to say *hi*, or stopped to chat to him while he was riding his bike in the driveway, but why would they give him a handful of straw? There's no logical reason that I can think of. Which brings me to the disconcerting thought that Ryder might have been at my house masquerading as a neighbor. I shiver and rub at the nape of my neck. The very idea of seeing him again makes my skin crawl—like flipping over a stone and releasing a festering nest of pincher bugs.

I pull my computer keyboard toward me and frantically start typing in my browser's search function. I need to find out if there's any truth to the notion that straw brings good luck in a new home. Maybe I'm jumping to conclusions, and this isn't linked to the scarecrow. Why couldn't it simply be a neighborly well-wisher? After scanning through several websites for any relevant information with the desperate air of a mother on a mission to identify some mysterious ailment plaguing her child, the closest thing I can find is an obscure farming tradition about crossing the threshold with a loaf of bread and a new broom.

I wince as I swallow the knot in my throat, my fingers trembling as I skim through the article. It's all symbolism and superstition. It's too much of a stretch to think that this has any connection to the straw in Lucas's backpack. My eyelids twitch with fear, blurring my vision as I browse the article. I can't tear myself away from the idea that it might have been Ryder who approached Lucas. He could have told him he was a neighbor and Lucas would be none the wiser. We've only met a handful of our neighbors, so far, but I can't imagine any of them giving my son a lump of straw for good fortune. The young couple who lives on one side of us work long hours and they're almost always gone camping or back-packing on the weekends. The neighbor on our other side is a divorced doctor and I can't picture her perpetuating some old wives' tale about straw being a good luck charm in a new home.

My first inclination is to call Jack and tell him what happened, but something holds me back. I need to figure out if Ryder is behind this before I decide how to handle it. If I'm way off base, the whole thing could blow up in my face. I consider picking Lucas up early from school and grilling him for information, but I don't want to frighten him, or make him think he's in trouble. Besides, he probably can't tell me much more than what he already told his teacher. I can't just sit here and speculate. I should introduce myself to the rest of the neighbors on my street—find out if any of them talked to Lucas or saw someone talking to him. I can put the loss of the Huss Integrity account aside for now and strategize later —it's not as if we don't have any other business coming in.

My mind made up, I shut down my computer and gather up my belongings before sticking my head into Maria's office. "I need to leave early after all. Can you reschedule that meeting for me?"

"Sure thing. By the way, I have the information on Summit Solutions that you wanted."

"Great, thanks," I reply, taken aback once more at how efficient Maria is. "Email it to me and I'll take a look at it when I get a chance."

Fingers clamped around the steering wheel of my car, I back out of my parking spot in the underground parking structure in a foreboding haze. As much as I'm fighting it, my gut's telling me there's a sinister link between the scarecrow and the straw. It terrifies me to think that Ryder was brazen enough to approach my son. It's a clear message that he's in control—the way things used to be.

On the drive back to the house, I cycle through my jagged memories of Ryder, all of which are painful, none of which are good. Everyone knew he was bad business—but his confidence and good looks were hard to resist at sixteen when he first turned his attention on me. He sensed my loneliness like a predator homing in on the scent of blood, and he manipulated me—introducing me to drugs to take the edge off my pain and feeding my addiction so he could keep me as his possession. I can totally see him sending me that sick interactive Halloween email. He always had a cruel streak—I just chose to overlook it. At the time, I would have overlooked anything for another high.

Margo was besotted with Ryder back then and he enjoyed tormenting her too. Even that night at the pumpkin patch, he'd taken a stab at her. "Hold out your arms and let me take a look at you, Margo McGowan."

She'd simpered at his attention, shooting me a look like the cat who'd got the cream.

"You know what," Ryder had mused. "You won't even have to dress up for Halloween. Hair like straw and clothes hanging off you. You'll make a perfect scarecrow!"

I'm ashamed to say I laughed when Margo flushed bright red. She'd always been insecure about her looks, and it led her into a downward spiral of anorexia. I was never entirely sure if she started doing drugs in a bid to get closer to Ryder or to mask her insecurities, or some combination of the two. In the end, she didn't achieve either goal. Ryder grew increasingly obsessed with me as the months went by, and Margo became more consumed with jealousy. Even Gareth tried telling her it was a lost cause. But she kept clinging to the belief that Ryder would eventually realize it was Margo he wanted to be with. Of course, he delighted in keeping the illusion flickering with just enough life to string her along behind him like a lost puppy. Why not toy with both of us? That's exactly what he did that night at the pumpkin patch.

I remember shivering at the sight of a scarecrow slumped forward in an empty cornfield, a black crow squawking on its shoulder. Dusk had turned the pile of pumpkins into ghoulish silhouettes of corpse-less heads. I kept telling Ryder it was creepy, and that I wanted to go, but he insisted on staying.

"That's why we're here—for the creep factor," he'd drawled, with a mocking smile on his lips as he took a drag of his joint. "Don't you want to see the scarecrows come alive when the full moon's out?"

I'd called him a moron, and tried to laugh it off, but I was shaking inside. I ended up taking a few too many swigs of Margo's vodka to calm my nerves. I thought it was working, until a shadowy scarecrow suddenly lurched upright and flopped a checkered arm at me.

The blood-curdling scream I let loose left me hoarse for days afterward. I ended up tripping over a hay bale in my haste to get away. I can still hear the howls of laughter as Ryder rolled out from behind the scarecrow, clutching his belly as he struggled to his feet.

I shake my head free of the nauseating memories of what happened afterward as I pull into my driveway. I still have an hour-and-a-half before I need to pick up Lucas. I don't want to waste a single minute of it, so I lock my purse in the car and stride back down to the street. The sooner I get to the bottom of who's been talking to my son without my knowledge the better—and that begins by eliminating my immediate neighbors. I'm fairly certain the young couple who live next door aren't home, but I ring their bell anyway and squirm on their front steps for a few minutes before moving on. The doctor on the other side of me doesn't answer her door either, and her Mercedes isn't parked in the driveway where it usually resides when she's home. At the next house, a tiny, gray-haired woman opens the door to me blinking expectantly as if waiting on me to launch into a sales pitch.

"Hi, I'm Lauren McElroy," I say, smiling at her. "My family and I just moved in a few doors down from you."

"Oh yes, you bought the Bartletts' old place. Nice to meet you, Lauren. I'm Sandra Wilson. I would have stopped by to introduce myself, but it's hard for me to get around these days. I have neuropathy in my feet."

I wrinkle my face in an expression of sympathy. "I'm so sorry to hear that. Please let me know if you ever need help with anything—groceries or whatever."

"Thank you, dear. That's very kind."

"I had a quick question for you, actually," I continue. "My son mentioned that one of the neighbors—a man—gave him some straw for good luck in our new house." I give a sheepish laugh. "Maybe it's a tradition or something. Anyway, I was just trying to find out who it was so I could thank them and ask them more about it."

Sandra pulls her sparse, gray brows together appearing to think about it for a moment. "I can't say I've ever heard of that before."

"I don't suppose you have any idea which neighbor it might have been?"

Sandra tugs at the sagging skin on her neck. "I'm sorry, dear, I really don't have a clue."

"Not to worry," I reply. "Thanks anyway, and it was nice to meet you, Sandra. I'll go knock on a few more doors and see if I can track this neighbor down."

She tilts her head toward the house on her left. "Don't bother knocking on that door. That's Stanley Hogg's place. He's home—he rarely leaves the house—but he won't answer the door to you, not on Halloween. He can't stand trick-or-treaters. Can't stand kids any time of the year to tell you the truth. I really can't see him giving your son anything, other than an earful."

I quirk a grin. "You're probably right. Still, it doesn't do any harm to try. He might have seen someone talking to my son. I seem to recall him peering around his door when we were moving in."

Sandra throws me a dubious look. "Don't say I didn't warn you. He's a cranky one, he is. His wife has dementia, and he treats her horribly, if you ask me. On a good day, he'll growl a *good morning* to me—that's about the height of it."

She flutters her fingers in a goodbye gesture, and I make my way next door with some trepidation. This might be a bad idea. By the sound of things, Stanley Hogg would sooner wish us bad luck than good. I press the doorbell, but nothing happens. He could have disconnected it for Halloween. I rap my knuckles on the door as loudly as I can and stand back to wait. Glancing around, I notice very little color in the garden. The flowerbeds are mostly overgrown with misshapen shrubs in need of pruning, and the grass looks tired and dried out, a sad reflection of the grumpy old man who lives here. I knock again and shuffle impatiently from one foot to the other. Maybe he's ignoring me thinking I'm a trick-or-treater. I need to let him see that I'm not in costume. Propelled by an all-consuming determination to find out who's been talking to Lucas, I walk across the lawn to what I assume is the family room window and peer through it.

I've barely had a chance to take in the elderly woman slumped in a brown velvet armchair, her mouth askew in sleep, when the front door scrapes open.

"Hey! What do you think you're doing? This is private property!" the large man filling the doorway yells, flapping an arm in my direction like I'm an annoying insect he can shoo away. Thick, wavy gray hair undulates down from the crown of his head, skimming the collar of his plaid shirt. He could pass for a crazed orchestra conductor—given the right attire—as he gesticulates wildly for me to leave.

I act as though he's waving me over and march firmly up to the door with a fixed smile on my face. He towers above me—he has at least three inches on Jack who stands at six-foot-one. But I don't let that deter me.

"Hi," I say, sticking my hand out in greeting. "You must be Stanley Hogg. I'm Lauren McElroy, Your new neigh—"

"I know who you are," Stanley growls, cutting my pleasantries off mid-sentence.

I continue to smile through gritted teeth. "I believe you might have met my son already—Lucas?"

His thick lips twitch, but he says nothing. My gaze flicks over his shoulder to a gnarled tree trunk propped up in one corner of the shadowy foyer with what appears to be a coat hanging from a branch. Who in their right mind uses a dead tree as a coat rack? Obviously, Stanley Hogg has issues.

Undeterred by his silence, I try again. "One of our neighbors gave my son some straw for good luck in his new home. Was that you, by chance?"

He furrows his brow, his eyes narrowing. "Get off my property before I call the cops."

I raise my hands in a conciliatory gesture and take a step back. "It's okay, I'm not here to complain. I simply wanted to thank you, that's all. I'd never heard of the custom of gifting straw for good luck in a new home before."

His dark eyes bulge, a nerve pulsing in his neck. "If I catch you anywhere near my house again, you'll be clean out of luck—you and your offspring," he snarls, before slamming the door in my face.

6

I 'm shaking with rage as I make my way back down the pathway from Stanley Hogg's front door to the street. Did he really just threaten me for asking a simple question? Or maybe it was because I walked across his sorry-looking grass. How on earth did such an unpleasant man end up in a nice neighborhood like this? I'll have to warn Lucas never to go anywhere near his house. I dread to think what Stanley would do if he caught my son riding his bike in his driveway. On the face of it, it seems unlikely that he would have given my son the straw, but I can't rule him out. His anger toward me was completely unwarranted, and he didn't deny it. What if he was grooming Lucas? You can't be too careful nowadays. He's definitely odd—the secretive sort—and his wife can't be offering him much companionship if she's suffering from dementia. I blow out a frustrated breath, only too aware that I'm fighting an inward battle with my own logic. One that's telling me I'm trying to find guilt where there is none—anything to rule out the possibility that Ryder has reentered my life.

I knock on a few more doors but the only other person who answers is a young mother in stained leggings and flip-flops bouncing a crying baby on her hip. She flashes me an apologetic smile and introduces herself as Carlee. After exchanging greetings, I repeat what Lucas's teacher told me and then elaborate on my concerns. "The truth is, I'm worried because this man said he was a neighbor, but he didn't introduce himself or give a name. It struck me as odd."

"I'm sorry." Carlee pulls a befuddled look. "I have no idea who that could have been. No one gave us anything when we moved in last year. Honestly, it's bizarre—I know it's Halloween and all, but I don't like the sound of it." I can tell by the concern in her voice that I've alarmed her. The chance that there might be a stranger lurking around kids in the neighborhood at Halloween is every parent's worst nightmare.

"Thanks for alerting me," Carlee goes on. "I'll make a point of talking to my kids about it when they get home from school. And I'll be sure to let you know if they've been approached by anyone."

I thank her and make my way back to my house, a gnawing feeling in the pit of my stomach. I'm still debating whether to call Jack and let him know about the stranger. But I just can't bring myself to tell him about Ryder. How can I explain my suspicions without divulging the truth? Jack would never look at me the same way again. Even worse, I'm not sure he would stay with me if he knew the full extent of what happened before my parents finally sent me away.

Seated at my kitchen table with a steaming mug of blackberry sage tea at hand, I open my laptop and resign myself to an hour of proofing contracts before I have to pick

Lucas up from school. Almost immediately, my mind wanders from my work to the questions I need to ask my sensitive six-year-old. The last thing I want is for him to be scared in his new environment, so I'll have to frame my questions carefully. Hopefully, he can give me a halfway decent description of the man claiming to be a neighbor— enough to tell me if it's Ryder or not.

The minutes tick by and I accomplish nothing. I would have been better off returning to the office and tackling some of the paperwork accumulating on my desk in my absence. I gather up my belongings and head out to the car with a mounting sense that things are spinning out of control around me. This is what Ryder does to me—he's like a toxin in my blood.

By the time I pull into the school car line, my stomach is in knots. Is it really possible Ryder has found me and is bent on punishing me all these years later? I plaster a grin on my face as Lucas and his teacher walk toward me, resolving not to dive straight into the topic of the stranger the minute Lucas is in the car. Gianna and I exchange guarded smiles as she releases Lucas's hand.

"Thank you," I call to her as she walks back to the group of students waiting to be escorted to their cars.

"How was school, sweetie?" I ask, as Lucas buckles himself in.

"Good. I played soccer with Brian at lunch, and I scored two goals."

"Way to go!" I remark, sucking in a silent breath at the mention of lunch. "That reminds me, Mrs. Bernardi said something fell out of your backpack at snack time."

Lucas presses his freckled nose to the window and waves at some kids. "Yup, my good luck straw."

"*I* didn't know straw brought good luck," I say, dragging

my words out in a heightened tone of amazement. I glance back at him in the rearview mirror. "Who told you that?"

Lucas swings his feet kicking the back of my seat. I flinch, but don't reprimand him, not wanting to derail the conversation at this critical juncture.

"Um, a neighbor. It's for good luck in our new house."

"That was nice of him. When was this, sweetie?"

"When I was waiting for Daddy to take me to school this morning. He had to go back in the house 'cause he forgot his phone." Lucas tucks his chin into his neck and giggles. "Silly Daddy! Isn't he silly, Mommy?"

"He is indeed. You know, I should probably thank this neighbor," I rush to add, sensing Lucas's rapidly waning interest in the topic. "Do you know where he lives?"

Lucas gives an indifferent shrug. "Somewhere near us, he said."

A prickling cold riddles the nape of my neck. "Do you know his name?"

Lucas shrugs again, pulling his skinny shoulders all the way up to his chin this time. "He didn't say his name."

I swallow hard, trying to strike a nonchalant tone before posing the question weighing heavily on me. "Did he know ... your name?"

Lucas huffs out a weary sigh. "I don't remember. Mommy, can we please not talk about this anymore?"

I grit my teeth. I can't let it go, not yet. I need more information. If Ryder has gatecrashed back into my life, my son could be in danger. "You're not in trouble for talking to a stranger if that's what you're worried about, Lucas. It's just that—" I break off, scrambling for an explanation a six-year-old might accept for my relentless line of questioning. "It's important to be polite to our neighbors, especially when they welcome us with a gift. You know how we always thank people when they give us birthday gifts? It's the same thing."

Lucas kicks disinterestedly at the seat again, his head to one side as he stares out the window at the Frost Bank Tower in the Austin skyline.

"Can you at least tell me what this neighbor looks like, or what he was wearing, and then we don't have to talk about it anymore?" I ask in a beseeching tone.

"Um ... a very big, long, gray coat. And shoes. That's all."

"What can you tell me about his face?" I ask, suddenly wishing I'd looked Ryder up online, after all. Would I even recognize him? He could have a beard, or mustache, or be bald by now for all I know.

Lucas wrinkles his forehead in concentration. "I couldn't see him too good 'cause he had sunglasses on, and a hat." He pulls his hands down over his head by way of demonstration, clearly bored with the back-and-forth. "On ... his ... head."

"Was it a baseball cap?" I prod.

Lucas shakes his head. "It was like Grandpa's hat. I think he was old too because he had a stick."

I scratch distractedly at my cheek, a shiver passing over my shoulders as I run through the information I've garnered so far. It doesn't sound legitimate. A neighbor would have waited around and introduced himself to Jack. I suppose an elderly gentlemen walking by might stop to chat with a child, but I'm more convinced than ever that this wasn't a chance encounter.

I don't press Lucas for further details during the remainder of the car ride home, but when Jack gets home that evening, I tell him we need to talk as soon as he and Lucas get back from trick or treating. He raises his brows, a trace of exasperation in his eyes. "Is this about the scarecrow again?"

I give him a solemn stare in return. "No, but it might be connected, and it involves our son."

A mildly concerned look flits across his features. "What do you mean?"

"We'll talk about it later," I say, nudging him toward the door where Lucas is eagerly waiting, dressed in his stormtrooper costume and swishing his overpriced lightsaber around my parents' antique console table. I've been having second thoughts about letting him go at all, but I know he'll be safe with Jack. "Promise me you won't let him out of your sight," I whisper, so as not to alarm Lucas. "You know how dangerous Halloween can be."

Jack kisses me on the forehead. "You worry too much. I'll stay right by his side the entire time."

I close the door behind them, my insides curling up on themselves like shriveled leaves as I watch them disappear down the driveway, hand-in-hand. It's not laced candy or reckless drivers I'm afraid of tonight. For all I know, someone could be watching my husband and son leave the house. If they realize I'm here all alone, they might take advantage of the situation.

I sink back down on the couch to wait for my family's return, clutching a faux fur throw pillow to my chest. Each time I'm interrupted by trick-or-treaters at the door, my heart sticks in my throat. What if it's Ryder? I take the time to peer around the curtain to make sure he's not standing on the front steps before I open the door, but could I even tell with all the adults in costume too?

When Jack and Lucas finally return two hours later, they're both amped up on sugar and talking over one another. Jack tackles Lucas on the living room floor and wrestles with him for a bit before conceding defeat. "All right, fearsome stormtrooper, you've worn me out," he says with an exaggerated groan. "Time for you to go to bed now. Get your jammies on and I'll read you a story."

Twenty minutes later, Jack comes back downstairs. I'm sitting on the couch waiting for him with a mug of tea in my hand, still torn about how much to confide in him. "Do you want anything to drink?" I ask.

Jack shakes his head. "No, I'm good, thanks. Still metabolizing sugar crystals. So, what's going on?"

I take a breath, trying to order my thoughts. "Lucas's teacher, Gianna, called me today. She noticed some straw falling out of his backpack at snack time. She thought it was odd, so she asked him about it. Lucas told her a neighbor gave it to him for good luck in his new house."

Jack rubs a hand across his forehead in that measured way of his that always preempts a carefully calibrated comment. "Can't say I've ever heard of that before. Which neighbor was it?"

I blow on my tea, dropping my gaze to my white-knuckled fingers gripping the handle of my mug too tightly. "That's the thing, Jack. I don't think it was a neighbor. I went around and knocked on a few doors and no one seems to know anything about it. There is this one eccentric guy who lives a few doors down, but he hates kids and steers clear of them at all costs. The woman who lives next door to him told me he never leaves the house, so I highly doubt it was him."

"Maybe Lucas made the neighbor up," Jack suggests. "He might have found the straw himself and been embarrassed that it fell out of his backpack at school. You know how self-conscious he is."

I shake my head. "He didn't make it up. He described the man to me."

Jack throws me a disconcerted look. "So what are you saying, you think it was a stranger?"

I take a hasty sip of my tea, unable to meet my husband's earnest gaze any longer. *Not a stranger.* If Ryder's found me after all these years and intends to make good on his threats, it's time my husband knows he exists.

7

I slowly circle the tip of my finger around the rim of my mug as I rehearse in my mind exactly what I'm going to say. I need to impress on Jack just how much of a threat Ryder poses without touching on what happened that awful night. I'll give my husband a truncated version of the truth that will undoubtedly leave him with a sour taste in his mouth but, hopefully, won't make him utterly despise me the way I despise myself deep down inside where no one else can see the shame I hide.

"Honey, are you all right?" Jack places a hand on my knee, his eyes crinkling with concern.

I set down my mug and give a jerky nod. "Yes, sorry— zoned out there for a minute. It's just tearing me up that a stranger approached our son in our driveway."

Jack nods in agreement. "Yeah, whoever he was, he should have waited around and introduced himself to me, or at least given Lucas his name. Still, it sounds like he was old—maybe he had dementia or something."

If only that were the case. I take a heaving breath and force the words through my lips before I can talk myself out of it. "Look, Jack, there's something I need to tell you. I haven't brought it up before because it was a phase of my past that I'd rather forget ever existed, and, for many years, I did just that. But sometimes your past catches up with you no matter how hard you try to make it go away."

Confusion pools in Jack's eyes. He opens his mouth to say something, but I raise a hand to stop him. "Let me finish and then you can ask me whatever questions you want. You already know that my parents were workaholics, and my nanny, Kathy, basically raised me. I barely saw my mom or dad. Even on the weekends, they were always working, or flying out somewhere for Monday morning meetings. Kathy was a really kind-hearted woman, and she tried her best to make me feel loved and wanted, but, at the end of the day, like most kids, I wanted my parents at my sporting events and award ceremonies, not my nanny."

Jack gives my hand a sympathetic squeeze. "I can't even imagine how hard it must have been for you."

I manage a weak smile. He really can't. Jack and his brother enjoyed the kind of upbringing that I dreamed of—a close-knit, two-parent family who went camping or fishing most weekends, ate dinner together every evening, and played board games and cards at the holidays. He's still close with his family and talks or texts with his parents and brother almost every day. Lucas adores spending time with them.

"I hated the fact that my parents were always working," I go on. "I began to rebel in high school. I started hanging around with the wrong kids and doing drugs."

Jack blinks at me, clearly taken aback at this revelation. The shock in his eyes quickly turns to hurt. "Why didn't you tell me about this before? I wouldn't have held it against you. You know how much I love you, Lauren."

I give him a grateful nod, a watery film of unshed tears clouding my vision. He wouldn't be saying that if he knew what I'd done—*what the drugs made me do.* I mouthed those words in the mirror to myself for years afterward in a desperate bid to make myself feel better—to justify it some-how. Not anymore. The older I get, the more sickened I am by what I allowed to happen. I can offer up a dozen different excuses for why it went down the way it did but none of them are worth a dime. I'm responsible for the choices I made.

"I was dating this guy at the time—Ryder," I say, choking back a sob. "He's the one who got me into drugs in the first place. He wasn't a good kid, and he had a cruel streak. He knew about my childhood phobia of scarecrows, and he thought it was funny to try and freak me out with them every chance he got."

"Sounds like a real charmer," Jack counters, twisting his lips in disgust.

I fall silent for a moment, trying to calm the pounding in my chest. Even talking about Ryder again is making me break out in a cold sweat. "To cut a long story short," I continue, "he got busted selling meth on the high school campus and ended up going to juvie." I clear my throat to hide the tremor that's crept into my voice as the most haunting memories I've suppressed—the parts of the story I'm glossing over—filter back into focus. "He made me swear I'd wait for him. He said I owed him that much. He swore we'd be together forever after he got out. Looking back, I realize it was more of a threat than a promise. My parents didn't want me to have anything more to do with him. That's when we moved to San Antonio."

Jack crosses one ankle over his knee, frowning. I can't tell from his expression if he's leaning more toward hurt or anger at this point. "Okay, so where exactly are you going with this?" he asks in a guarded tone.

I wring my hands in my lap. "Remember how freaked out I was about that scarecrow the day we moved in? Well, this morning I got one of those creepy animated Halloween emails. When it started playing, this red-eyed crow flew off with a scarecrow's head in its beak. And then Lucas's teacher called to tell me that some stranger gave our son straw for good luck." My breath hitches. "The truth is, I'm afraid Ryder might be behind everything that's been happening."

The look on Jack's face softens. "Honey, I get that you were scared of Ryder back then, but that was a long time ago. I doubt anyone from your high school is taunting you with scarecrows. People move on with their lives."

"You don't know him like I do," I say with a short, mirthless laugh. "He enjoys frightening people. He knows I'm terrified of scarecrows—I think this is a sign that he's found me. He was obsessed with me—it was bad enough to convince my parents to uproot their lives and move."

Jack massages the back of his neck, his brow rumpling as he digests the import of what I'm saying. "Do you know where he lives?"

"No. I've never tried to look him up on social media or anything."

"Maybe that's where we should start," Jack replies. "It's possible this is all just a coincidence, and he's happily married with a family of his own now."

Before I can stop him, Jack leaps up and fetches his laptop from the kitchen counter. He sets it on the coffee table and types in his password. "All right, What's Ryder's last name?"

"Um ... Montero." The lie falls all too quickly from my lips. His real name's Montoya, but I can't risk Jack stumbling across the story. Even though Ryder was a minor at the time and his name wasn't released to the public, there's a chance Jack might come across an article about it and connect the dots. It wasn't dealing drugs that put Ryder away—it was much worse than that. I've given up trying to absolve myself of the role I played. I should have tried to stop it happening.

Jack's fingers fly over the keys for a couple of minutes and then he lets out a beleaguered sigh. "There are dozens of Ryder Monteros but none of them live in Austin. Tell me if you recognize him in any of these images."

He turns the screen toward me and begins clicking through Facebook pages, but of course Ryder's face doesn't pop up on the screen.

After we've finished going through all the results, at Jack's insistence, he leans back on the couch and scratches the stubble on his chin. "How about we try another angle? What about mutual friends? You must have kept in touch with some of them."

"No. I lost touch with everyone after I moved to San Antonio." I give a hollow laugh. "That's what happens when you're a teenager and your parents cut you off from social media and transplant you in a new city. You move on and make a whole new circle of friends."

I reach for my mug as if I can wash down the lie with a mouthful of lukewarm tea. That's not exactly how it transpired. There was the year I spent in central Texas before I moved to San Antonio. But Jack doesn't need to know about that. I'm ashamed enough of my pedigree as it is.

"What about Ryder's parents?" Jack asks. He drums his fingers on the edge of his laptop, signaling a dogged determination to get to the bottom of this. "Or former neighbors? Someone must know where he's living."

I tug my fingers distractedly through my hair. There's no getting around it—my next step has to be to find Ryder before he pulls his next stunt. "I suppose I could reach out to Kathy, my old nanny. She used to be friendly with the lady who lived next door to Ryder's parents—Jan something or other."

"Great, let's start there." Jack gestures to my phone lying on the coffee table. "Why don't you give Kathy a call right now? No time like the present."

I hesitate, a sick swell creeping up my throat at the thought of tracking down Ryder and confronting him. But Jack's right. I need to address this head on. If my hunch is right and it's Ryder who's harassing me, calling his bluff might just be enough to scare him off. Anything to avoid involving the police. I pick up my phone and locate Kathy's number. I haven't spoken to her since my parents' funeral when she sat next to me and held me throughout the service. We've texted a few times and she told me to feel free to call if I ever wanted to chat. But I never did. Even the sound of her voice triggers a range of emotions—reminding me of how much I've lost, how much was left unsaid, and how much I wish I could undo. Blinking back tears, I press the phone to my ear. It rings several times before going to voicemail and I leave a brief message asking her to give me a call.

"Anyone else you can try in the meantime who might know how to locate him?" Jack asks.

My mind goes to Gareth and Margo, but contacting either one of them will be a last resort. "No one I can think of. Kathy might have gone to bed already. Let's give her until tomorrow."

Jack gives a resigned nod. "How long were you with this Ryder guy anyway?"

I scrub my hands over my face. "Long enough to mess me up. I don't want to talk about him anymore tonight."

"Fair enough," Jack concedes, turning his attention back to his laptop. "Want to watch a show before we head to bed?"

"I'll pass," I say, sinking back on the cushions. "I can't focus on a show right now."

Opening up the email app on my phone, I glance through my inbox checking for anything urgent I need to address tonight. Thankfully, it looks like Maria has already handled most of it. I shoot off a quick response to a query from a potential client, and then click on an email from Maria titled, *Info you requested*. I scan the contents, my pulse beginning to pound harder in my temples.

Summit Solutions is owned by a man called Gareth Looney.

8

M y breath comes in short, hard stabs as the name registers like a dull gong inside my skull. I skim through Maria's email a second time on the off chance that my brain is playing tricks on me after sitting around for hours on end thinking about Ryder and everything that's happened. But no, there's no mistaking the name staring up at me from my phone. *Gareth Looney* is not a name I could easily forget.

Jack glances up at me from his laptop and raises a questioning brow. "Everything all right?"

"I ... I'm not sure. It could be a coincidence but ..." My voice trails off. I know better. It's no coincidence. But what does it mean? My brain scrambles for answers as I stare at Maria's text. *Summit Solutions is owned by a man called Gareth Looney.* Gareth made the counteroffer to Dan Huss—an offer that was eerily similar to mine. Could he have gotten a hold of my offer? Maybe that's what the break-in at my office was all about. The police dismissed it at the time as a prank by kids but what if someone made a copy of the contract I drew up for Huss Integrity? My thoughts are barreling down ever-darkening tunnels. What if there's a connection between this and the scarecrows? Could Ryder have enlisted Gareth to help him destroy my life now that he's found me?

Or maybe I've got it all wrong, and Gareth's behind everything that's been going on. After all, he knows about my scarecrow phobia too. He could have sent me the email. But why? He doesn't have a bone to pick with me—at least, none that I'm aware of. Unless he views me as a threat, which seems unlikely. Austin is a big enough market for plenty of players. I swallow down the bile rising up my throat. The thought that Gareth might be helping Ryder in his sick quest is disturbing to say the least.

"What are you talking about, Lauren—what could be a coincidence?" Jack prompts impatiently.

I tear my eyes away from my phone. "Remember that big contract I was hoping to sign? I thought for sure it was a done deal, but I met with Dan Huss today and he blindsided me by telling me that another company came in at the last minute and undercut our bid by a considerable amount. He showed me their offer. It was structured almost exactly like mine—more or less the same terms for less money. I asked Maria to look into the company—Summit Solutions—and see what she could find out about it. Turns out it's owned by Gareth Looney." I hesitate, making sure I have Jack's full attention. "He was one of the kids Ryder and I used to hang out with. Super awkward but brilliant."

"Are you sure it's the same person?" Jack asks.

"It has to be. It's such an unusual name." I shake my head uncomprehendingly. "I just can't understand why he would do this to me. Ryder must have put him up to it."

Jack closes the lid of his laptop and sidles closer on the couch, placing an arm around my shoulders. "You're making a lot of assumptions. Gareth might not have realized Capitol

Technologies was your company. You only opened up here recently. And just because his offer is similar, it doesn't mean he deliberately ripped yours off."

I grimace, anger at the injustice of it festering inside. "Let's hope for Gareth's sake you're right. First thing tomorrow I'm going to march right in to Summit Solutions and have it out with him."

"It might not be a bad idea to have a face-to-face," Jack agrees in a tone that says otherwise. "But give him a chance to explain himself first before you accuse him of anything. You never know, he might be willing to retract his offer once he knows he was going up against you."

"He'll retract it, all right, if I have anything to say about it," I retort, getting to my feet. "He should know better than to mess with someone of his own caliber."

AFTER A LONG NIGHT of troubled dreams, I stumble out of bed and chug down a double espresso before dropping Lucas off at school and making the thirty-minute drive to the commercial business district where Summit Solutions is located. It's a beautiful day to hike or bike along the River Walk with blue skies stretched end-to-end over the skyscrapers that make up Austin's dynamic downtown of restaurants and live entertainment. Ordinarily, I love the buzz and high energy of the drive, but this morning my thoughts are mired in a sea of uncertainty and apprehension. If Gareth's underhanded business move is connected in any way to the scarecrows, it's time I figured out what exactly is going on between him and Ryder and put an end to it. I shoot off a quick text to Maria letting her know where I'm going and why, and ask her to keep digging to see what else she can find out about Summit Solutions.

I park in a public garage and walk two blocks to the imposing glass and steel building that houses Gareth's company. It's hard not to be impressed by what he has accomplished in the intervening years since high school. As I ride the elevator up to the fourth floor, I go over in my mind how to approach the situation. I should probably give Gareth an opportunity to explain himself first, but it will take every ounce of self-control I have not to tear into him as soon as I set eyes on him.

"I'm here to see Gareth Looney," I say without preamble to the blonde woman seated at the floating mahogany reception desk in the foyer. She acknowledges me with a flicker of her heavily coated lashes. "Do you have an appointment?"

"No." I throw her a cutting gaze. "Let him know it's Lauren Bishop from Bowman Rock High School. I'm sure he'll want to see me."

Curiosity flickers in her eyes. She picks up the phone on her desk, wrapping her manicured talons around the receiver as she examines me more closely. After exchanging a few words with someone on the other end of the line, she pushes her chair out from her desk. "This way, please."

I follow her along a corridor lined with black and white photographs of a very different Austin back in the eighteen hundreds to a spacious corner office with glass walls and a stunning view over the city. Through the glass, I see Gareth leaning back on a plush white leather swivel chair talking on the phone and waving his left hand through the air. He looks upset about something which doesn't bode well for our meeting.

The receptionist knocks on his door, and he straightens up in his chair and waves me in. After abruptly ending his call, he gets to his feet and pushes his silver-accented designer glasses up the bridge of his nose. He's filled out since high school, and expensively attired, but his close-set eyes and beaked nose still lend his features an unpleasant symmetry.

His gaze advances over me like a dragnet. "Lauren Bishop! Well, this is a surprise."

He gestures to the chair opposite him, making no attempt to hug me—a small mercy, for which I'm immensely grateful. The situation is awkward enough without being forced to pretend I'm happy to see him. The only thing that linked us was a past we've put behind us and would much rather forget. At least I assume it's behind him—Gareth could still be using for all I know. "It's been a few days," he says with a crooked smile as I sink into the chair and slip my purse from my shoulder. "How are you?"

I don't crack a smile in return. As far as I'm concerned, I'm strictly here on business. "I'd be a whole lot better if my firm hadn't just lost out on a major contract I was certain we'd secured—Huss Integrity. I imagine the name rings a bell."

A flicker of a frown crosses Gareth's face and then he gives a shallow chuckle. "Of course. I submitted a bid to them. Look, it's nothing personal, Lauren. We're all working hard to strike the next big deal. You're the new kid on the block. You can't expect to ride back into town on the coattails of your parents' success and snatch up the most lucrative contracts without some healthy competition."

I arch an accusing brow at him. "So you *did* know it was my company you were going up against?"

Gareth spreads out his palms in a gesture of helplessness. "I'd already submitted my offer by the time I found out. I saw something in the paper afterward about your grand opening and I recognized your picture. Like I said, it's not personal, it's just business."

"Is that what you call the decapitated scarecrow email? And the Halloween decor?"

There's a beat of silence before he answers. "I have no idea what you're talking about."

"Someone put a wooden scarecrow in my moving van. Then, they sent me an animated Halloween email with a crow flying off with a scarecrow's head—not quite the welcome back to town I was hoping for. Not many people know about my scarecrow phobia. You, Ryder, and Margo came to mind. Perhaps it was a joint welcoming committee prank?"

Gareth purses his lips and shakes his head. "I don't know anything about it. Sounds like something Margo might do. She was always jealous of you. It's petty, I'll give you that, but that's women for you, isn't it?" He flashes me a veneered smile, and a shiver of repulsion goes through me. Margo wasn't the only jealous one. I distinctly remember Gareth's awkward attempts to flirt with me when Ryder wasn't around.

I glare across the desk at him. "I see you've come a long way since your misogynistic youth. Your dating life must be fantastic nowadays. Was it you who broke into my office too? Is that how you got a copy of my offer to Huss Integrity?"

"What?" Gareth narrows his eyes at me. "Who do you think you are, coming in here flinging wild accusations at me? I worked hard for everything you see here. We didn't all have trust funds to launch us. If you can't take the heat, maybe you shouldn't have come back to town."

"What's that supposed to mean?" I ask sharply.

A mocking smile plays on his lips. "I know your secrets, Lauren. Unless you want your customers hearing rumors about your murky past, you'd best move on and suck up your loss." He stands abruptly, walks over to his office door and holds it open for me. "It's a pity we won't be seeing more of each other now that you're back in town, but it appears we're competitors."

I barge past him in a flurry of rage. "If that's how you want to play, game on."

My phone beeps with an incoming text from Maria as I exit the building.

Gareth Looney's up to his eyeballs in debt.

9

Maria perches on the edge of my desk clutching a non-fat latte, a glitter of satisfaction in her eyes. "I got the information from an ex-employee of Summit Solutions," she confides. "She used to do the books until Gareth fired her several months back. She started noticing some things that didn't quite add up and did a little digging. That's when she discovered he was overleveraged and being audited by the IRS. But get this." She slides closer and lowers her voice. "He has a major gambling addiction and he's run through a lot of company funds trying to feed the monster. However good he looks on paper, Gareth Looney's hurting for money." Maria pauses to take a sip of her coffee, leaving a voluptuous red curve on the rim of her cup. "He must have been desperate to secure the Huss Integrity contract and get some money coming in. Maybe undercutting your bid wasn't personal at all."

I give an adamant shake of my head. "No, it was definitely personal. He saw the story in the paper about our opening, so he knew it was me." I hesitate, not wanting to bring up the connection to Ryder. "It's a long story, but I think he's still hanging on to some stuff that happened back in high school."

Maria raises one flawlessly plucked brow. "You two were an item?"

"No, nothing like that!" I exclaim. "He had a bit of a crush on me, but we never dated. I had a boyfriend at the time who was a mutual friend. It's .... complicated."

Maria shrugs. "Well, if you ever want to talk about it, I'm here for you. Otherwise, I should get back to work."

I flash her a thin smile. I know she means well, and I wish I could confide in her, but our friendship would never hold up under the weight of the awful truth. "Thanks for looking into Summit Solutions," I call after her. "I'll take it from here."

The minute she exits the room, I close my eyes and exhale a shaky breath. If Gareth is struggling to pay off major debts, then he might just be desperate enough to do whatever it takes to steal my business—twisted things like throwing my old childhood fears in my face to warn me off. Or worse.

I know your secrets, Lauren.

An icy chill goes through me. What exactly was he referring to? Did Ryder tell him the truth about what happened? My phone rings and I glance distractedly at it. Kathy's name comes up and I fumble to slide the bar across the screen before the call goes to voicemail. "Hey, Kathy, thanks so much for calling me back."

"How're you doing, pumpkin? I feel bad I haven't spoken to you since the funeral. But I know you've been busy with the move and opening up your new firm and all. How's everything going in Austin anyway?"

I take a moment before answering. I don't want to worry her unnecessarily with my business woes. She'll be concerned enough when she hears what I have to tell her. "Pretty good on the whole. A few bumps along the way, but it's normal when you're starting out. We have a spacious new office in a brand-new building and I've hired the most amazing personal assistant. She's efficient on steroids—I think she rents space in my brain. She seems to know what I need before I ask her."

"That's good to hear. I'm really happy for you, Lauren. I know you'll make a success of things, just like your parents. You have their same drive and determination."

I bite back a scathing retort, trying not to let resentment creep into my tone. I don't want to repeat their mistakes and build a career at the expense of my family. "Thanks, Kathy. How have you been?"

"Oh, you know. I still miss Austin, but I'm finally settling into Lubbock. It's so much cheaper to live here. I babysit for some of the kids in the neighborhood from time to time." She tinkles a laugh. "I guess I'm a glutton for punishment, but I'd miss the kids too much if I stopped entirely."

"They're lucky to have you in their lives," I remark.

"I don't know about that. Sometimes I think they'd be better off with someone younger who can keep up with them. I'll be sixty-five next month. But we're not here to blather about me. What did you want to talk to me about? You sounded a little stressed in your message."

"Actually, I wanted to ask you if Ryder Montoya's family was still living next door to your friend, Jan."

There's a long beat of silence before Kathy answers. "Lauren, what are you doing? Stay away from that man. He wreaked havoc in your life—in all of our lives. You're a happily married woman with a child now."

"It's not what you think, Kathy. Trust me, I have no desire to reconnect with him. The thing is, someone's been harassing me since I arrived back in Austin. They sent me a Halloween e-card with a decapitated scarecrow, and they left a wooden scarecrow in the moving van with our belongings. It was the first thing I saw when the doors opened. You know how much Ryder enjoyed tormenting me. I think he's at it again."

"Oh, Lauren, honey, I doubt very much that Ryder has any interest in your life these days. From what I hear, he's been in and out of jail for years on drug-related charges." She lets out a heavy sigh. "I imagine there are any number of crazies out there who might be behind it. The story of your parents' plane crash and their only daughter inheriting everything was all over the newspapers. You're a local celebrity of sorts. Attention seekers are drawn to people like you."

"But how would a stranger know about the scarecrows?"

"It's easy enough to find stuff out about people these days," Kathy responds. "They could be friends on social media with some of the kids you hung around with back then."

I chew on my thumbnail. "It's possible, but I need to make sure it's not Ryder. I'm worried Lucas could be in danger. A man approached him in our driveway a few days ago. He said he was a neighbor and gave Lucas some straw and told him it was for good luck in his new house. But I've talked to our neighbors, and no one seems to know who he is. I'm afraid, Kathy. You remember how Ryder threatened me years ago. Maybe now that he's out of prison and found out where I'm living, he's coming after me. If it is him, I need to put an end to it before he takes this any further."

Kathy lets out a grunt of acknowledgment. "Okay, let me call Jan and see if I can get a contact number for him. I believe his mother still owns the house next door, but I don't know if he's living there anymore. Please be careful, Lauren. He's bad business, always was. I'm sorry you ever got mixed up with him."

"Not half as sorry as I am," I say with a shudder. "Thanks, Kathy. I'll wait to hear from you."

I set my phone down on the desk and pull my keyboard toward me. I try to throw myself into my work, but the screen blurs before my eyes as my mind travels back in time. I don't know why I let Ryder control me the way he did. The only reason I stayed with him was because of the drugs. And he wasted no time getting me hooked on them.

Fifteen minutes later, Kathy texts me a phone number:

(512) 763-2293 Let me know how it goes.

I stare at the digits for a long time trying to build up the courage to call. I don't want to come across as scared or spineless in our conversation. The last thing I want is for Ryder to think that he still has any power over me—he doesn't. Mustering my determination, I punch in the number. It rings three times and, just as I've resigned myself to leaving a message, I hear a gruff, familiar voice. "Who's this?"

"Ryder, it's Lauren—Lauren Bishop."

I catch my lip between my teeth, counting the minutes as I wait for him to respond. Maybe he'll start yelling down the phone at me, cussing me out. Or maybe he won't respond at all—simply hang up without a word.

"What do you want?" he growls at last.

"I want you to stop harassing me."

He lets out a snort. "What's that supposed to mean?"

"The scarecrow in the moving truck. The email with the decapitated scarecrow. I suppose you think that's funny?"

"I don't know what you're rambling on about."

"I think you know precisely what I'm *rambling on* about. And now you have the gall to drag my son, Lucas, into it."

"You've lost your mind," Ryder scoffs. "I didn't even know you had a kid."

"Don't play dumb with me," I say in a steely voice. "I know you were the creep talking to my son in our driveway. Stay away from my family or else—"

"Or else what?" Ryder counters derisively. "You're so stinking full of yourself, Lauren. There's nothing you do that interests me anymore. Do you really think I've been pining for a cash cow all these years?"

"I think you've been pining for revenge, because that's the kind of low-life you are," I fire back.

"We're done here," Ryder says, a menacing pitch to his voice. "Don't call me again."

"I don't intend to. Next time I'm going straight to the police to file a restraining order."

"You have a nice day, Lauren. Say *hi* to your boy from me. Oh, and don't forget to tell him scarecrows come alive at night." He laughs uproariously, and I punch the *end call* button, nauseated at the all-too-familiar sarcasm oozing from his voice. Although I managed to hold it together on the call, there's no denying he's left me all shook up. I can't stay here and continue to work in this state. Grabbing my purse, I exit my office in a flurry of emotions. "I'm going to be working from home for the rest of the day," I call out to Maria in passing. "I have a migraine coming on."

"Oh no!" Maria pouts her cherry red lips in a sympathetic grimace. "Text me if you need anything."

I must have jinxed things with the migraine. My head begins to pound relentlessly on the drive back to my house as I reflect on the exchange with Ryder. I might only have made things worse by contacting him. I'm still convinced he's involved in what's going on, but what if my call encourages him to keep at it? He obviously gets a kick out of tormenting me even after all these years. Maybe I should have gone straight to the police with my suspicions.

Twenty minutes later, I pull into my driveway and open my mailbox to retrieve my mail. There's a folded sheet of paper lying on top. I open it up, expecting to see a flyer advertising lawn care or some such service. The breath sticks in my throat as I read the words.

Mary, Mary quite contrary
How does your garden grow?
With silver bells and cockleshells
And scarecrows all in a row.

Terror surges through me, filling my lungs until I gasp out loud. *Don't let this be what I think it is.* I hurry up the front path into the house and toss my purse on the table in the foyer. My legs grow heavier with every step as I make my way through to the kitchen.

Stretched across the new sod we laid in our back yard last weekend, is a row of headless scarecrows on metal stakes.

10

The paper with the nursery rhyme slips from my fingers and flutters to the floor. My whole body is shaking uncontrollably. I scrunch my eyes shut, praying this is all a bad dream, but when I open my eyes again the headless scarecrows are still leering at me from the lawn. The truth hits me like a sledgehammer. *Ryder!* It's precisely the kind of stunt he would revel in to terrify me. My brain fills with static as I grapple with the reality that he was here, today—on my property. He must have been laughing to himself the entire time I was on the phone with him. No wonder he threw out that loaded comment as his parting shot.

... don't forget to tell him scarecrows come alive at night.

I gulp back my fear as I try to figure out my next move. Should I call Ryder back—show him I'm not afraid of his pathetic antics? Or call Jack? Go straight to the police? I sink down at the kitchen table, my eyes riveted on the row of gaudy scarecrows at the bottom of the garden. One, two, three, four, five ... there's a sixth one laying on the ground. It might have toppled over. Or perhaps Ryder didn't have time to finish the job—he might have heard me arriving back home. A shudder goes through me at the thought that I might have disturbed him in the act of violating my property.

Gingerly, I get to my feet and unlock the back door. My skin crawls as my fingers grasp the handle. I can't help wondering if Ryder has been inside my house as well. Logically, I know he couldn't have got in without a key, but I'm going to search the place later anyway. The last thing I need is to come upon a scarecrow hidden in one of the rooms at an inopportune moment. I'd never be able to sleep in the house again.

I make my way to the bottom of the garden, goosebumps pricking my arms as I approach the line of headless scarecrows. *Keep breathing,* I whisper to myself. I can't succumb to a panic attack now. I need to find out if Ryder has left me any other messages. My eyes dart around the yard, coming to rest on the play structure where a lumpy scarecrow head with stitched eyes and a red slash of a mouth ogles me from the top of the slide.

Clapping a hand to my mouth, I turn and run back inside the house, locking the door behind me. Has Ryder hidden the rest of the heads in the garden too? It's exactly the kind of twisted game he would play. I need to get rid of them before Lucas gets home from school. I grope around in my purse for my phone to call Jack. To my frustration, the call goes straight to voicemail. He must be meeting with a client, or he would have picked up. I pace back and forth across the floor trying to decide what to do. I don't trust myself to drive in this state to pick Lucas up from school. I'm too jittery, too dangerously close to having a full-blown panic attack. Maybe I can ask Maria to pick him up—tell her my migraine is worse. Hopefully, she doesn't view me as a failure as a mother, she's always so competent and put together. I wrap my arms around my body and hug myself. This is not like me. I've been overtaken by old fears that I haven't experienced in decades, and I'm not sure I can fight them off this time.

Resigned to the only option available to me, I pick up the phone to call Maria. It's not as if she doesn't have a million things to do at the office already, and school runs are hardly part of her job description, but, so far, she hasn't refused to do anything I've asked her to do. I'm just about to dial her number when Jack calls me back.

"Hey, what's up?" he asks, his clipped tone conveying that he's trying to accommodate me in his busy schedule.

"Someone's been in our backyard," I blurt out. "They staked a row of decapitated scarecrows across the lawn. I'm almost sure it was Ryder. I called him earlier and confronted him about what's been going on. He made this barbed comment about telling Lucas that scarecrows come alive at night. He knows that's what started my phobia of scarecrows as a kid. Jack, this means he's been on our property."

"And he knows our schedule," Jack adds in a grim tone. "Can you send me a picture?"

"Okay," I say, getting to my feet unsteadily and fumbling with the lock on the back door again. I'm not excited about going back down to the bottom of the garden. But at least this means that Jack's finally taking what's happening seriously. "He left a scarecrow head at the top of the slide," I add, as I make my way outside. "He must be targeting Lucas. He's unhinged. We have to stop him."

"We'll have to go to the police," Jack concedes. "Whether or not it's Ryder, somebody's been trespassing on our property. This has gone far enough."

Tentatively, I approach the scarecrows again and snap a

few pictures, then send them to Jack.

"Wow! These are really disturbing," he says, sounding shocked. "When did you spot them?"

"As soon as I got home. There was a note in our mailbox, a nursery rhyme—*Mary, Mary quite contrary.* Except it ended with *scarecrows all in a row.* Somehow, I knew the minute I read it that he'd been here. I went straight to the kitchen and that's when I saw them at the bottom of the garden."

"Here's what we'll do," Jack says, in a resolute tone. "I have a thirty-minute consultation with a client I'm going in to right now and then I'll cancel the rest of my obligations for the day and head home. Don't touch anything in the backyard. We'll go to the police station together and show them the pictures and then you can tell them your suspicions about Ryder."

While I wait for Jack to return, I tiptoe around the house opening every cabinet and closet door with bated breath, even checking under the beds. I conduct my most meticulous search in Lucas's room. If Ryder is targeting him, I don't want my son unearthing any frightening surprises when he goes to bed tonight.

The noise of the front door opening startles me, and I freeze in my tracks. For one terrifying moment I imagine it might be Ryder, but then the reassuring sound of Jack's voice drifts up the stairs. "Lauren, are you up there?"

"Yeah, I'll be right down." I straighten up Lucas's bed and try to catch my breath before I hurry back downstairs. Jack's already out in the back yard surveying the scarecrows and snapping a few additional pictures.

"They're horrible, aren't they?" I whisper, rubbing my arms vigorously as a shiver crosses my shoulders. "I want them out of here."

Jack works his jaw as he studies the gang of hideous scarecrows. "Believe me, I'd like nothing more than to yank them out, but we'd better wait and see what the police have to say about it first. They're going to need them as evidence, they might even want to dust for fingerprints."

"I just hope they take this seriously and don't dismiss it as another stupid Halloween prank," I reply.

Jack rubs a hand over his jaw thoughtfully. "They could argue that, except this isn't an isolated event. Someone's targeting us. It could be Ryder, or it could be some crazy who read about your story in the newspaper."

I massage my neck, soothing the tension that's been building since I arrived home. "Kathy mentioned that possibility too."

Jack's head swivels in my direction. "You talked to Kathy?"

"Yes, earlier this morning. She got me Ryder's number. She didn't really want me to call him—I think she was afraid I was trying to reconnect with him now that I'm back in Austin. I assured her that wasn't the case, but she was still leery of giving it to me at first. She said he's been in and out of prison since high school."

Jack's eyes widen. "What? Lauren, this guy sounds dangerous. Why on earth didn't you tell me about him before now?"

"I didn't know he'd been in and out of prison," I say, my voice wavering. "I didn't keep tabs on him. I wanted to forget about him. And I did, until now."

"The police need to know about this. He's definitely a suspect." Jack glances at his watch. "We'd better head to the station right away and file a report before it's time to pick up Lucas."

. . .

THE OFFICER we're assigned breezes into the room and introduces himself as Detective Hernandez. There's a permanent V-shaped trench between his unruly brows, and he gets straight to business once we show him the photos and explain what's been going on. "All right, why don't you start with the first incident, and I'll take notes," he says, nodding in my direction.

I recount each event as it happened, beginning with the day we moved in and discovered the scarecrow in the truck. When I'm done, Detective Hernandez looks over his notes and grunts. "Could be a case of neighborhood kids harassing the new family on the block." He taps the end of his pen on the desk and throws us a mildly sympathetic look. "I realize this is unsettling but, trust me, it's mild compared to some of the stuff we get calls about this time of year—alleged murders that turn out to be gory decor with nooses or guillotines plastered with fake blood and guts. Not to mention kids setting stuff on fire or smashing car windows or mailboxes with baseball bats."

I lean forward in my chair. "But what if it's not just kids? What about the animated email and the break-in at my office? I have an ex who was obsessed with me. He knows I'm terrified of scarecrows, and he's threatened me in the past. I haven't had any contact with him since high school— in fact, I just found out he's been in and out of prison for years. He always said he'd find me if I ever left him. My parents died a few months ago in a small plane crash, which was all over the local news. So it would have been easy for him to track me down."

Detective Hernandez presses his lips together with an air of forbearance. "What's his name?"

I take a moment before answering. "It's Ryder ... Montoya."

Jack turns to me, blinking in confusion. "I thought you said it was Montero."

I swallow the ball of trepidation in my throat. I can't lie to him any longer—not in front of the detective.

"No, it's Montoya. I ... misspoke."

Jack's frown deepens. He clears his throat as if to say something but stops himself. I know he'll quiz me about it later.

Detective Hernandez turns to his computer and clicks on the keyboard, the lines on his forehead rippling in concentration. He studies the screen for a few minutes and then glances back over the notes he took. "Well, it appears our man, Ryder Montoya, has quite the rap sheet. Definitely a lead worth checking out. I'll do some digging on his whereabouts and swing by your house later today to take a look at the evidence. Don't touch anything in the meantime."

He gets to his feet and extends a hairy hand to us before escorting us out of the room.

The minute we get out to the parking lot, Jack rounds on me, indignation blazing in his eyes. "Why did you lie to me about Ryder's last name? You didn't want me to find him online, did you?"

"You ... you heard the detective talking about his rap sheet," I stammer. "I was afraid of what you might find out. I'm ashamed I ever dated someone like him."

Jack unlocks the car and climbs in without a word. He turns to me as he plugs in his seatbelt, his lips flattened in a tight line. There's a frigid distance in his eyes that I haven't seen before. "Are there any other secrets you're hiding from me, Lauren?"

11

J ack starts up the car but makes no attempt to pull out of the police parking lot. Instead, he turns back to me and gives me a look that makes me stiffen. "Well? *Is* there anything else you need to tell me, Lauren? Because I don't want to find out later that there's more to this Ryder situation than you're letting on."

"What? No! I told you everything there is to tell about him."

"Yeah, I got the part about him being a loser, a druggie and a felon," Jack says, sounding weary. "You found your way out and he didn't. So why did you lie about his name when I tried to look him up? Are you sure there isn't some big secret you're going to unload on me down the line?"

I let out a gasp. "Like what?"

"I don't know." Jack slaps his hands on the steering wheel in exasperation. "Maybe you got pregnant and gave his kid up for adoption and he's only just found out about it and—"

"Stop it! You're being ridiculous! I would have told you about something that consequential."

"Would you?" Jack asks, his eyes avoiding mine. "Because

I'm not so sure. You were very careful to keep any mention of Ryder quiet all these years. If you had nothing to hide, why didn't you tell me about him before?"

"I told you already—I was embarrassed," I snap back. "You didn't screw up in your teens like I did, Jack. I didn't want you to think any less of me when we started dating. I was afraid you wouldn't want anything to do with me if you knew about my past drug use."

Jack stares fixedly through the windscreen. Finally, he puts the car into gear and pulls out. "All right, if you say so. I just don't want there to be any more secrets between us."

I swallow the grainy lump in my throat as I lean over and squeeze his shoulder. "I'm sorry. You're right, I should have told you everything."

Maybe I still can. I wrestle back and forth with the reckless thought. This is my chance to come clean, but I can't bring myself to do it. Jack would never look at me the same way again. How could he? And the last thing I want is to lose him.

We drive in silence the rest of the way to the school and then sit there staring awkwardly out through our respective windows until Lucas's teacher escorts him over to the car.

"Daddy! Why are you here?" Lucas exclaims delightedly when Jack climbs out to help him into his booster seat.

"I got off work early and I thought I'd come pick up my favorite son," Jack teases with a wink.

"With your favorite wife," Lucas adds with a conspiratorial chuckle. I tense at his words. The familiar banter has a jarring ring to it in the stilted atmosphere in the car.

Jack ruffles Lucas's hair before climbing back into the driver's seat, studiously avoiding meeting my eyes. I know he's deeply hurt, and I can't blame him for pushing me away.

"Can we go get ice cream, please?" Lucas asks, ramming his sneakers into the back of my seat.

"Please stop kicking me," I mutter through gritted teeth. I can hear the anger in my tone, even though it's not Lucas I'm irritated at.

"Sorry, Mommy," he says, sounding chastened.

"It's all right, sweetie," I hasten to add. "We'll get ice cream at home. Mommy has a headache. How was your day?"

"Good. Brian let me play with his new football at recess and Mrs. Bernardi said we're going on a field trip to an apple farm next week." He digs around in his backpack and pulls out a form. "You have to sign this."

I turn around to reach for the paper and freeze when I notice a piece of straw sticking out of his pack. "Sweetie, I thought you took all the straw out already?"

Lucas pouts for a moment before answering. "I saved some."

"But why? Remember I told you it doesn't really bring good luck."

"But the man said it did and he said we were going to need it soon," Jack cries out, his bottom lip quivering.

Momentarily forgetting the tension between us, Jack and I exchange shocked looks.

"You never mentioned that before," Jack says in a measured tone.

"It's okay, Daddy," Lucas soothes, as he tucks the straw carefully inside his backpack. "I'll keep this straw forever so nothing will happen to us."

My mind struggles to remain calm. *We're going to need good luck.* Evidently, the veiled threat went right over Lucas's head. But I heard it loud and clear, as did Jack. Ryder's not done with us—not by a long shot. This is only the beginning.

Back home, Jack sets Lucas up at the kitchen table with a bowl of ice cream and some apple juice while I do a quick inspection of the house and back yard to make sure there are no new unwelcome gifts. Maybe I'm being paranoid, but if Ryder keeps upping the ante, it wouldn't surprise me if his next step is to break into our house.

"Yay!" Lucas yells when he spots the scarecrows at the bottom of the garden. "You decorated our yard, Mommy!"

"Um, actually ... one of our neighbors did," I stutter, giving Jack an apologetic shrug. It's better than scaring Lucas with the truth.

"I love it!" he gushes, stabbing his spoon back into the mound of ice cream in his bowl. "Was it the man who gave me the straw?"

My stomach twists. "Eat up, honey," I say briskly, ignoring his question. I've lied enough today, and I can't stomach any more fabricating. "You need to get started on your homework."

I shudder when I glimpse the stuffed headless corpses taunting me from the bottom of the garden. I can't wait to get rid of them, but Lucas won't be too happy about their disappearance. I'll leave Jack to explain that to him.

I'm rinsing the dishes at the sink when the doorbell rings a short time later. I have a momentary flash of panic when I see Detective Hernandez and another officer standing at the front door.

"I'll get it," I say, signaling urgently to Jack to take Lucas upstairs. "It's probably just someone selling something."

He gives a nod of understanding before turning to Lucas. "Hey buddy, want me to help you build something with your Legos?"

"Sure," Lucas cries, thrilled at the thought of his dad spending time with him on a workday. The minute they disappear upstairs I make my way to the front door.

I lead the officers through the kitchen and out into the back yard. Detective Hernandez walks along the row of scarecrows and takes pictures from all angles, including one of the decapitated head at the top of the slide, while his partner searches around the perimeter of the garden. I assume he's looking for any indication that someone climbed over the fence. But they wouldn't have had to do that. They could have simply opened the side gate and come in the same way our gardener does. We're going to have to put a lock on the gate after this. Jack ordered a security system for the house when we moved in, but the installers are backlogged and keep rescheduling.

Detective Hernandez makes a few notes and then walks back over to me. "I think we have everything we need for now. We'll pay Ryder Montoya a visit tomorrow and have a chat with him."

"He'll deny everything," I warn him. "Aren't you going to dust for fingerprints while you're here?"

"Whoever did this most likely used gloves to drive the stakes into the sod," he replies. "We won't be able to lift any usable prints from the scarecrows."

I clench my fists at my sides, repulsed at the idea of Ryder brazenly hammering stakes into our new sod with a sick grin on his face as he pictures my reaction.

"Can we get rid of them now?" I ask, gesturing with my chin to the scarecrows.

"Sure. We're all done here," Detective Hernandez replies, signaling to his partner. He fishes out a card and hands it to me. "Feel free to call me with any questions or concerns."

I watch the officers drive off, already having misgivings

about involving the police. I'm afraid of what Ryder might tell them about me.

After Jack comes back downstairs, I fill him in on the officers' visit. "They're going to interview Ryder tomorrow. I know he won't admit to anything, but maybe a visit from the police will be enough to scare him off."

"Let's hope so," Jack says grimly, as he walks over to the back door. "I'll get rid of those scarecrows now."

Fifteen minutes later, he comes back inside, helps himself to a water from the fridge, and goes to bed without kissing me good night for the first time that I can remember. I know he needs time to process everything, but it still stings.

When my alarm goes off the following morning, I drag myself out of bed and go through the motions of making Lucas's lunch and getting ready for work, my mind stuck on Detective Hernandez's upcoming visit to Ryder. Maybe today will be the day this nightmare ends. Jack leaves for work before me with a mumbled goodbye, clearly still stewing on the secrets I kept from him. I move through the house like a zombie, running on too little sleep and too many anxious thoughts—worried we're going to be late on top of everything else. Grabbing my briefcase and Lucas's backpack, I pull open the front door and stop in my tracks. A frozen scream wedges in my throat.

An abandoned scarecrow lies slumped across our front steps.

12

I slam the front door shut and jerk back from it, blistering fear circulating through my veins. *Ryder was here again!* I knew it was a mistake to contact him. It's only made things worse—fueled his sadistic desire to control me through fear and intimidation. And now that he knows where I live, there's no stopping him. I need to call Detective Hernandez before he talks to Ryder. I'm already running late to drop Lucas off at this point, a few more minutes won't make much difference.

"I'm ready, Mommy," Lucas announces, standing in the hall swinging his ocean shark lunchbox at his side.

"Okay, sweetie, give me just one minute," I reply, fishing Detective Hernandez's card out of my purse. "Let's go out the back door. I've already locked this one."

I hurriedly shepherd Lucas around the side of the house and into my car parked in the driveway, willing Detective Hernandez to pick up. The last thing I want is for Lucas to spot the scarecrow on the front steps. He'll want to keep it. He was so upset this morning when he discovered Jack had disposed of all the scarecrows in the back yard. We gave him some lame explanation about mice making nests in them, but then he accused us of being mean to the mice and promptly burst into tears.

Right on cue, Lucas exclaims, "Mom, look! A scarecrow!"

"Ssh! Mom's on the phone," I say, reversing down the driveway. "Uh, yes, good morning, Detective. I ... I found another scarecrow on my front steps this morning." I hesitate, lowering my voice, "*He* must have been here again last night."

"Did you move it or is it still there?" Detective Hernandez asks.

"I didn't touch it."

"Good, I'll swing by in a bit and take some pictures. I'm planning on having a chat with Ryder this afternoon. The more evidence I have to lay in front of him, the better."

"Could you ... would you mind taking it with you when you're leaving? I know it sounds ridiculous, but I can't bear to think of it waiting for me when I get back from work."

"Sure, no problem," Detective Hernandez replies. I think I detect a faint note of amusement in his voice, but it could just be me being overly self-conscious. I need for him to take this seriously. These aren't just harmless pranks. Ryder's a convicted felon and he's been in close proximity to my son —close enough to abduct him. I don't know what he's planning next, but the thought of anything happening to Lucas terrifies me. I have no idea what Ryder's rap sheet contains. There's no telling how far into the dark underbelly of crime he's gone, or would be willing to go, to punish me.

"Who are you talking to, Mommy?" Lucas asks.

"Just a friend who's going to move the scarecrow for me. You know Mommy doesn't like them."

Lucas pouts and folds his arms in front of him. "Why can't I keep it? Just this one. *Please*."

"No, sweetie. I need it out of there. Halloween's over now, anyway," I answer cheerily.

"But it can be for Thanksgiving," Lucas protests. "Mrs. Bernardi says scarecrows are good. They keep the harvest safe."

"Tell you what," I suggest, "how about we go Christmas shopping this weekend and you can pick out a really fun snowman decoration for the front doorstep instead."

Lucas peers up at me through his long lashes, his eyes filled with tears. "Snowmen are not fun. Brian has a scarecrow," he mumbles, before turning to stare out the window. He doesn't speak to me for the remainder of the ride to school, and squirms away from me when I attempt to kiss him goodbye.

The minute I pull out of the school parking lot, I try getting a hold of Jack. The call goes straight to voicemail, and I hear the tremor in my voice as I bring him up to speed on the latest development. By the time I reach the office, I've managed to calm down enough to assess the situation more rationally. It's not as if it's going to get any worse from here. Ryder won't be able to make another move after Detective Hernandez confronts him. Once he knows the police are on to him, he'll back off. He won't want to risk any trouble with his parole officer, or the possibility of facing new charges.

Maria throws an appraising eye over me when I walk in. "You look exhausted, Boss. Rough night?"

"Yes, and a rough morning—it hit rock bottom with an epic six-year-old's meltdown over mice. Actually it was over scarecrows." I let out a sigh as I sink into my chair. "Someone staked a row of scarecrows across my back lawn yesterday while I was at work. And there was another one waiting for me on the front steps this morning when Lucas and I were leaving for school."

Maria frowns as she places a steaming cup of coffee on the desk in front of me. "Was it a gift from someone, perhaps? Was there a note or anything with it?"

"I don't know," I say, trailing my fingers despondently through my hair. "To tell you the truth, I barely glanced at it before I slammed the door shut. I was too scared to go out that way. I was afraid someone—my ex—might be watching me."

"Your ex?" Maria echoes in a hushed whisper.

I nod wearily. "That guy I told you I dated in high school. He was obsessed with me. He's been in and out of prison for drug crimes. I'm pretty sure he's been stalking me ever since I moved back to Austin. He knows I've always hated scarecrows—I think he's toying with me."

Maria gives an exaggerated shiver, her glossy, dark hair pooling over her shoulders. "That's terrifying to think he's been prowling around your house at all hours. Have you made a police report?"

"Yes. They came to the house last night and took pictures. I told them about Ryder's criminal record and they're going to interview him."

"Good," Maria says, her narrowed eyes glittering. "That should put an end to his juvenile macho nonsense."

"I really hope so," I agree, reaching for my coffee.

"Any late word from Huss Integrity?" Maria asks.

I clear my throat. "Not a breath. Looks like they'll be going with Summit Solutions."

Maria presses her lips together in a disapproving pout. "That's got to be disappointing after all the hard work you poured into that account."

"It is, but we can't get close to their price. Not with our overhead."

Maria folds her arms across her chest, a contemplative

look on her face. "If only there was a way to prove Gareth Looney was behind the break-in."

"There isn't," I say, more sharply than I intend. Gareth's threat to spread malicious rumors about my past is still ringing in my ears. I can't risk jeopardizing my business reputation before I've had a chance to build a client base. "It would only create bad publicity for us if we accused him without any evidence. We'll redouble our sales efforts and try to secure another big account to replace it."

Maria arches a brow. "It doesn't sound like you to give up that easily. You, above all people, should know better by now than to let a man push you around like that."

I flash her a startled look. There's an edge to her voice that's very telling. Maybe she has a dark past of her own. "Trust me, I don't like conceding, but some battles are not worth fighting, and this is one of them. The last thing we need is a lawsuit starting out."

Maria shrugs and exits my office with an armful of files. I can tell she's disappointed that I folded so easily, but she doesn't understand the full extent of what I'm up against. I get to work making a bunch of cold calls to prospects I've already identified. If I don't continue to feed our engineers a steady stream of work, the rumor mill will soon begin. I can't afford to have anyone jumping ship before we get some serious traction.

I'm on a call with a manufacturing firm that sounds like a good match for our services when Detective Hernandez's name pops up on my screen. My stomach twists. Has he already met with Ryder? I wrap up my current call with a promise to set up a meeting with the president of the company to discuss a detailed proposal, and then call Detective Hernandez back.

"I wasn't expecting to hear from you so soon," I begin.

"What did Ryder have to say for himself?" My chest tightens in anticipation as I wait for his response. Although it's a long shot, some part of me is secretly hoping he might even have arrested Ryder already.

"Mrs. McElroy, I need you to meet me at your house right away."

I grip the phone tighter. *Mrs. McElroy.* What ever happened to Lauren? The sober note in Detective Hernandez's voice is setting off alarm bells. My stomach churns as my thoughts spiral downward. Has Ryder struck again? Has something happened to Lucas? My throat tightens and I struggle to get the words out. "Is ... is everything all right ... is my son okay?"

"Please, Mrs. McElroy. Just get here as soon as possible. And call your husband. He needs to come home too."

13

A n ever-encroaching terror of unknown magnitude thunders like a train in my ears. *Lucas!* Something must have happened to my baby! Why else would Detective Hernandez need Jack and me to come home right away? The loaded urgency in his tone, the unwillingness to divulge anything over the phone—he said as much without uttering a word. *Mrs. McElroy, we regret to inform you ...* My thoughts ricochet in a myriad of frightening directions as I hurriedly shove my things into my purse and dash from the office leaving a bewildered Maria to cover for me as I mumble something about an emergency. On the way to my car, I pull up the number for Lucas's school, catching my heel in the curb in the process and almost tripping. My call goes straight to voicemail, and I call back immediately, more panicked than before. Could it be a school shooting or something? *Pick up! Pick up!* After an agonizing wait, the secretary finally answers. "Dawson Elementary, how may I help you?"

I scrabble to reorient the phone at my ear. "Hi, yes, this is Lauren McElroy, Lucas's mom. Is he ... is Lucas okay? I mean ... it's just that ... Did something happen?" I sound breathless and confused after jogging all the way from my office to my car—hardly the demeanor befitting a CEO. Hopefully she doesn't think I'm high or something. I flinch at the thought, wondering where it came from after all these years of being clean and sober.

"Not that I'm aware of," the secretary responds in an unruffled tone—honed, no doubt, by years of expertise in handling parents exhibiting every emotion on the spectrum. "Let me see, there's nothing here on the incident log. Did Mrs. Bernardi call you?"

"No. Uh ... someone else did," I reply, my panic deflating just enough to make me realize how irrational I must sound. But my fear is valid. "Would you mind calling Lucas's classroom and making sure he's all right?"

There's a beat of silence before the secretary answers, "Of course, Mrs. McElroy. Let me put you on hold for a moment."

I climb into my car and turn on the ignition, struggling to plug in my seatbelt. My strength seems to have evaporated and my fingers won't stop shaking.

"Mrs. McElroy? Are you still there?"

I snatch up my phone from the console. "Yes! Yes, I'm here."

"Mrs. Bernardi says Lucas is absolutely fine. He's having a great morning."

Relief seeps from every pore that's been pumping sweat ever since Detective Hernandez called me *Mrs. McElroy* and ordered me home. Trembling, I sink down in my seat and let out an extended breath. "Thank you. Thank you so much. It was ... a misunderstanding on my part."

"Not a problem, Mrs. McElroy," the secretary says. "You have a great day."

My heart is still galloping beneath my ribs as I back out of my parking spot, but I can breathe again now that I know Lucas is unharmed. I try Jack's office number next. His assistant tells me he's in a meeting, and I leave him a message to call me back ASAP. Whatever's amiss, at least I know now that it doesn't involve my family. I'm beginning to suspect that Ryder might have broken into our house. I was afraid that would be his next step. But I can handle a few smashed windows—it's nothing compared to the safety of my husband and child.

Even if it turns out that Ryder has violated our home and vandalized the place, everything is replaceable. Obviously, he must have gone further than depositing an unwanted scarecrow display on my property this time. Whatever it is, it's merited an urgent call from Detective Hernandez. On the flip side, maybe it will be enough to issue a warrant for his arrest. But he's not going to want to go back to prison. He'll go on the run before he'll let that happen. Which means I'll still be living in fear of him turning up at any moment of the day or night. My throat feels torched at the thought of his hands around my neck—again.

As I merge with the traffic on the highway, I try Jack's number one more time and leave another priority message with his assistant—explaining that Detective Hernandez is waiting at the house to meet with us. Gripping the steering wheel, I picture all the possible scenarios that might await me, and mentally prepare myself for the worst. Crude graffiti sprayed over my freshly-painted Monorail Gray walls, glass scattered throughout the Microplush rug in the family room that Lucas loves to curl up on, or maybe even the contents of my drawers and cabinets emptied out—my personal possessions rifled through and desecrated. I grit my teeth, reminding myself that it's only stuff.

I'm halfway home when Jack finally calls me back. "Hey! I just got out of a meeting. What's going on?"

"I don't know, but it must be bad. It's not Lucas. He's fine —I called the school already. I'm guessing Ryder broke in and vandalized our place. He might have been watching the house this morning—waiting to see my reaction when I discovered the scarecrow. Maybe he decided to up the ante."

"Then they'll have to arrest him for breaking and entering," Jack says, sounding grim. "I wish we had that security system up and running. The first appointment I could get for the installation is next Tuesday."

A wave of guilt washes over me. I hate that I've inadvertently dragged Jack into this mess from my *murky past*, as Gareth calls it.

"Are you on your way home now?" I ask.

"Yeah, just leaving the office. I'll be right behind you."

Fifteen minutes later, I pull onto my street and slow to a crawl. My eyes widen at the pandemonium that greets me. Three cop cars are parked along the curb outside my house, and there's an ambulance backed into my driveway. The back doors are wide open, obscuring the view of my front door. I can't tell from here if there's been a break-in. Why is the ambulance here? Is someone hurt? Perhaps one of my neighbors tried to intervene and Ryder attacked them. I think of Carlee bouncing her youngest child on her hip and my jaw goes slack. I got her all worked up about a stranger in the neighborhood. If she saw Ryder loitering outside my house, she might have decided to confront him.

I catch a glimpse of Stanley Hogg huddled in his doorway watching the commotion, stroking his beard in an agitated manner. He spots me driving by and his expression hardens before he disappears inside. I frown, wondering if he witnessed what happened. Maybe he called it in. My befuddled brain struggles to make sense of the mayhem around me as I roll to a stop and park behind the patrol cars. I climb out on rubbery legs and make my way over to Detective Hernandez who's standing in the middle of the lawn rattling off instructions to another officer, a strained expression on his face.

"What ... what's going on?" I gasp.

Before Detective Hernandez has a chance to respond, there's a squeal of tires and Jack pulls up behind my car. He jumps out and jogs over, his eyes darting uncertainly between me and Detective Hernandez. "What's happened?" he asks, slipping a comforting arm around my shoulders. "Is someone hurt?"

I lean gratefully against his reassuring frame, afraid I'm about to collapse at any minute. It's the first bit of affection Jack's shown me since he found out I lied to him. I hope it's not just a momentary reprieve, a lapse in intention.

Detective Hernandez turns to me. "Mrs. McElroy—"

"Lauren, please call me Lauren," I interrupt. I don't know why it's so important to me. It's not as if it will make the news he's about to deliver any less monumental.

He masks a flicker of irritation before continuing, "I need to ask you a couple of questions. Did you see anyone at your house this morning?"

"No. Jack left for work first, and then Lucas and I took off after I called you about the scarecrow on the steps."

"And you're sure you didn't see anyone hanging around on the street or sitting in a parked car?"

I give an uncertain shake of my head. "No, I don't think so. But I was so freaked out I didn't pay much attention."

"What did you do when you opened your front door?"

"Nothing. I slammed it shut right away. I was half-afraid Ryder might have been hiding somewhere watching for my reaction. I left through the back door."

I glance over Detective Hernandez's shoulder and let out a sharp gasp at the sight of two paramedics wheeling a gurney up to our front door.

Jack and I grip each other tightly. My husband's face is ashen with shock. "What's happened?" he asks again in a hushed whisper.

Detective Hernandez sets his jaw in a tight line. "It wasn't a scarecrow on your front steps. It was a body."

14

An oppressive silence descends over the scene, muffling the voices of the officers milling around. My lungs feel like they're deflating as the air is sucked from them. Maybe I'm losing touch with reality. Maybe none of this is actually happening. I stare in disbelief at the ambulance parked in my driveway, a forbidding receptacle waiting to receive someone's remains. *It wasn't a scarecrow on your front steps. It was a body.* I keep replaying Detective Hernandez's words over in my mind.

I'm still not sure I heard him correctly until I turn to Jack for confirmation and see the stricken look on his face. His complexion has paled even further, if that's possible, and his pupils are wide with shock. I've never seen my husband look so completely at a loss. My stomach churns as the reality of the situation sinks in. *There was a body on our front steps.* I clap a hand over my mouth. What if Lucas had seen it up close? Thank goodness I didn't try to put a brave face on it this morning and march him out the front door to the car.

Detective Hernandez clears his throat. "I realize how

distressing this must be for you both but I'm going to have to ask if you can identify the body."

"I'll do it," Jack pipes up, his voice husky with emotion. He turns to me and gives my arm a quick squeeze. "Wait here."

I nod numbly, watching as Detective Hernandez escorts Jack past the waiting ambulance and up the concrete path to our front door. I bury my face in my hands, a tremor ricocheting through my body. This is a far cry from how I envisioned our new start in Austin. It's all evolved into an unimaginable nightmare and I don't know how to begin to untangle it. Ryder has to be behind this. Who else would have done something this sick and twisted to punish me, and actually think it's funny? Did Ryder find some drug addict in a gutter and dress the body up in a scarecrow costume? Or did he really kill someone? I don't doubt that he's capable of murder. I know what he did all those years ago. And he's spent time in prison since, which, doubtless, only hardened him. I frown, wondering if the dead person is a man or a woman—or if it's someone I know.

My legs are shaking too much to hold me without Jack to cling to. I sink down to the curb and hug my knees to my chest, rocking gently back-and-forth as I sift through my thoughts. The newspaper article on my parents' crash must have stoked Ryder's jealous rage—embers of possession that never stopped burning. A pulse flutters in my throat at the memory of his vitriolic anger, squeezing the life out of me, before relenting with a caustic laugh. I bite down on my lip and cast a skittish glance around. Where is he now? Watching from the shadows? Is Lucas safe? Maybe I should call the school again and check on him. I pull out my phone and hesitate, my finger hovering over Dawson Elementary in my contacts. The secretary's going to think I'm a total nutcase if I call again. They would have tried to reach me or Jack by now if anything had happened. I watch in a trance as an officer makes his way down the street knocking on my neighbors' doors. I can't imagine what they're going to think when they hear the news.

I look up as Jack returns, unaccompanied by an officer. I search his face, but I can't tell anything from his blanched expression. He hunkers down on the curb next to me and rubs a hand over his jaw. "It's a man. I don't recognize him. The police need you to take a look. Do you think you're up to it?"

I give a shaky shrug. "What choice do I have? Did you remind them we just moved here a few weeks back? He could be a neighbor and we wouldn't know it." I choke back a sob and Jack gives my shoulder an awkward rub.

"Come on, let's get this over with," he says in a tone of fatalistic determination. "The sooner you do it, the sooner they can take the body to the morgue."

Jack helps me to my feet, and we make our way to the front door. A beak-nosed officer with a protruding Adam's apple and a wooden expression nods discreetly at us before pulling back one corner of the sheet covering the body. I brace myself to be greeted by the cold, gray sheen of death on a stranger's face, but nothing prepares me for what lies beneath. A strangled gasp escapes my lips. Jack grabs me by the arm and holds me upright like a sack of loose bones as I sway first one way and then the other.

Detective Hernandez steps toward me, an air of urgency about him. "Mrs. McElroy—Lauren, do you recognize this man?"

I can only conjure up a gurgle. I break away from Jack and dash over to the bushes where I hurl the contents of my stomach.

"Lauren!" Jack's hand is heavy on my shoulder. "Are you okay?"

I turn toward him and bury my face in his chest, grateful for his presence, but, at the same time, wishing he wasn't here. How can I tell him? How can this be happening? Before I can choke the words out, Detective Hernandez's shadow falls over us. "I'm sorry you had to see that," he says. "I realize it was disturbing. Are you all right?"

Our eyes meet in a telling exchange. We both know it's a rhetorical question. What he really wants to ask is, who the man is lying on my front steps? He knows I recognized him.

I nod mutely, shivering involuntarily. "Who's the man, Lauren?" Jack prods. "What's his name?"

I take a ragged breath and look pointedly at Detective Hernandez's impassive face. "I ... I can't be certain. I haven't seen him in years, but I think it's Ryder Montoya."

"What?" Jack gasps, wheeling around and gaping at me.

Even Detective Hernandez looks momentarily stunned. A nerve twitches in his craggy face, and I'm vaguely aware of an air of suspicion supplanting the look of compassion that was nestled in his eyes moments earlier.

"He ... he must have been trying to break in," I mumble. "Do you think he ... had a heart attack or something?"

Detective Hernandez frowns. "I can't speculate on the cause of death. Do you know how I can reach his immediate family?"

I shake my head. "I can give you my former nanny's number, if you like. She's friends with the lady who lives next door to his family." After fumbling for a few minutes, I finally manage to dig my phone out of my pocket and read off the number to him.

"What happens now?" Jack asks. His voice has a hollow ring to it, and he avoids eye contact with me. I'm willing to bet he has a thousand questions for me, but he knows better than to interrogate me in front of the police.

Detective Hernandez rubs his jaw. "Under the circumstances, there'll be an autopsy. We'll have to wait on that result before we proceed."

My mind wheels first in one direction and then another. Of course they'll have to do an autopsy. People don't normally die on other people's doorsteps dressed as scarecrows. But that doesn't necessarily mean it's a crime scene, does it? The autopsy's only a formality. I have to believe Ryder likely died of a heart attack or a stroke—natural causes. Stress related to his high-octane, extra-curricular activities. It didn't look like he had any obvious injuries. The police would have spotted a gunshot or stab wounds right up front. I need to stay calm and not jump to the worst possible conclusion. At the back of my mind, there's even a little flicker of relief that it's over at last. Ryder will never again be able to stalk me or mete out his sadistic punishments. Once I put this awful event behind me, I can focus on our new life here without constantly having to look over my shoulder wondering if Ryder is lurking somewhere in the shadows. Or worse—lurking around my son.

Detective Hernandez pulls his brows together and eyes us gravely. "I'm going to have to ask you not to go anywhere in the meantime. We'll need to get your formal statements, and we may have more questions for you once the autopsy report comes in."

Without waiting for an acknowledgment, he pivots on his heel and strides back across the lawn, rattling off orders into his radio.

Jack turns to me, his face harboring conflicting emotions. "Are you sure it was him—your ex?"

I give a jerky nod. "As sure as I can be after all these

years." I don't know why I'm pretending there's any doubt in my mind that it's him. Even in death, I recognized Ryder instantly. He hasn't changed that much, other than the tattoos creeping up the side of his neck—the same swarthy good looks, strong jaw, thick head of hair. A shudder crosses my shoulders. I'm just thankful his eyes weren't open. Not even the glazed look of death would have been enough to stop his cruel gaze from lancing through me.

Jack and I watch in silence as the morgue-bound ambulance pulls away, unaccompanied by sirens or lights—just an eerie feeling of horror mixed with guilty relief. I glance around our street, returned once more to its tranquil state. Thankfully, the local media didn't catch wind of what happened in time to show up with an entourage and make a spectacle of it on the evening news. It's not the kind of publicity my business needs right now. Most of our neighbors are at work, but I catch sight of Stanley Hogg peering around his door again before vanishing back inside. I can't help wondering if he might have seen Ryder hanging around my front door earlier. Maybe he saw what happened to him.

Inside the house, I settle into a chair at the kitchen table while Jack makes us steaming mugs of strong tea. He sets them down on the table and pulls out the chair next to me. "I can't believe this happened on our front steps."

I try to interlace my fingers with his, but he quickly retracts them and reaches for his mug instead.

I take a small sip of my tea, pretending not to have noticed his rejection. "What do you think happened to him?" I venture to ask.

Jack scratches his cheek. "You tell me. Was he still using drugs?"

I forward him a helpless look. "How would I know? I

suppose there's a good chance. He wasn't exactly a model citizen." As the words slip from my lips, guilt hits me like a sledgehammer. Who am I to talk about being a good citizen? I was right there doing meth with Ryder the night it went down. I shake myself free of the memory. As much as I wish I could erase that night from history, I can't unlive the life I led back then.

I fiddle with the handle of my mug. "You know Stanley Hogg, our eccentric neighbor," I say. "I saw him standing by his front door watching everything. I can't help wondering if he might have seen Ryder lurking around our house this morning."

Jack frowns. "I'm sure the police have already interviewed him. They were going door-to-door earlier."

I clamp my bottom lip between my teeth for a moment, remembering the testy reception Stanley Hogg gave me. "He might not have answered the door to them. Maybe I should go talk to him."

Jack eyes me dubiously. "I don't think that's a good idea. It might look odd if you go around knocking on our neighbors' doors."

"Why? What are you getting at?"

He drags his fingers hesitantly across his brow. "We don't know yet if Ryder died of natural causes, do we?"

I stare at my husband for a moment, trying to quell the rising panic inside me. It's not as if I haven't entertained the question myself. If the police rule out natural causes, there are really only two alternatives—Ryder was killed, or he killed himself. Somehow, I can't picture him committing suicide on my front steps in a final twist in our sick relationship.

"The police would have spotted any sign of foul play, wouldn't they?" I say.

"It's unlikely he was murdered," Jack concedes, "But we don't know for sure at this point. And you walking around asking questions about your dead ex doesn't look right. All I'm saying is that I think you should keep a low profile until we hear back from Detective Hernandez."

I stare at him, aghast. "Surely you're not suggesting the police will think I had anything to do with it. Ryder was harassing me—not the other way around."

Jack tugs at his collar, uneasy emotions swirling in his eyes. "I know, but we have to be realistic. If it turns out he was murdered, we could both be under suspicion. You know how it goes. The police will rattle everyone's cage. You have a dubious history with the guy. They'll accuse me of taking him out because he was harassing you. They'll ask me if I lost my temper, if it was an accident, if I slugged him and he cracked his head on the concrete and I tried to cover it up. The whole good cop, bad cop routine. *We know it wasn't intentional, but what did you do, Jack?*"

My lips open and close a couple of times, his words a jumbled mess in my brain. "But you didn't ... do anything, did you?"

Jack huffs in frustration. "Of course not! I'm just making a point. Until we know for sure there was no foul play involved, we—you especially—shouldn't go around inserting ourselves into the investigation."

We finish our tea in silence. Deep down I know Jack's right, but I'm not sure I can lay low until the police get back to us. I can't help thinking that Stanley Hogg sees most everything that happens on our street, and that he might be more willing to talk to me than the cops. I glance down at my phone and gasp at the time. "School's almost out. Will you get Lucas? I'm ... still feeling queasy."

"Sure," Jack says, getting to his feet. He takes our mugs to the sink and rinses them out. "Do you need me to pick up anything for dinner?"

I nod, pretending to think it over. "How about some steaks and salad?" It's not like we don't have food in the refrigerator, but this will buy me some extra time.

The minute Jack's Lexus disappears around the corner, I slip out the front door and make my way over to the Hoggs' house. I ring the doorbell repeatedly—operational again, I note with irritation—before making my way across the unkempt lawn to the bay window. The blinds are down but I rap sharply on the glass several times, hoping to get the attention of Stanley's wife. I don't even know her name, but if I'm annoying enough, maybe she'll persuade her husband to open the door, if only to get rid of me. Just when I've decided to go around the side of the house, the front door cracks open.

"Stanley!" I call out as I dart over to him. "I know you were watching all the commotion earlier. You heard what happened, right?"

He scowls but says nothing.

"The police probably told you already about the body that was found on my front steps," I continue with dogged determination. "We don't know yet if it was a heart attack, or what. Did you happen to see or hear anything?"

Something akin to fear flashes in his eyes. For a moment, I think he's about to slam the door in my face again, but then he leans toward me, his grizzled beard moving up and down as he whispers, "He was dead when they dropped him off."

15

I stare at Stanley in horror, trying to make sense of what he's saying. "What do you mean? Who's they?"

He pulls his brows together, scratching maniacally at his neck. "I don't know. I only saw one guy, but I figure it would take two to carry a body."

A frail voice drifts our way. "Stanley, where are you?"

He throws an exasperated glance over his shoulder before turning back to me, his eyes wild and unfocused. "I would have said something, but I figured the guy was drunk," he wheezes. "All dressed up like a scarecrow—I thought his friends dumped him there as a Halloween prank."

He shakes his head, mumbling something unintelligible to himself. "I have to go. My wife needs me."

Not for the first time I find myself standing on Stanley Hogg's front steps as the door closes in my face. At least this time he didn't slam it. He sounded almost contrite. I didn't get a chance to ask him if he'd told the police what he witnessed. It's critical information. It changes everything. Ryder didn't come to my front door of his own accord. But why did someone leave him on my steps? Did they know about our connection? My mind whirls in confusion. Did someone from the seedy world Ryder inhabited knock him off? Was it an argument over drugs? It makes no sense that he was dressed as a scarecrow. Only a handful of people from my past know the significance of that. And that brings up another disturbing possibility.

My mind turns to Gareth as I make my way back to my house. Could he have had something to do with this? He might have known all along that Ryder was harassing me and encouraged it. Or maybe he hired Ryder to scare me. If they had a falling out—over money, perhaps—he could have had Ryder killed. A sick feeling surges up my throat as another thought solidifies in my brain. Is Gareth trying to pin the murder on me? It's a reckless move, but he might be far more desperate than I realized.

I hurry back inside my house and sink down at the kitchen table, trembling like I have hypothermia. I'm vaguely aware that I'm still in shock, it seems to come in waves. I keep hoping I'm going to wake up from this nightmare. Instead, it's going from bad to worse. That look of suspicion on Detective Hernandez's face when I identified the body has suddenly become a whole lot more significant. I need to figure out who dumped Ryder's body on my steps —and quickly. Jack and Lucas will be back from school at any minute. I'll have to tell Jack that I went over to the Hoggs' house. I can't keep this information to myself. Detective Hernandez needs to know about the stranger Stanley Hogg saw unloading the body. It's the only lead we have right now, and the only evidence that points away from me.

I startle at the sound of the front door opening. Seconds later, Lucas comes running into the kitchen carrying his latest art project aloft—a paper plate face with Googly eyes and a scant head of mud-brown woolen hair.

"Look, Mommy! It's me!" he cries, waving the plate in my face. "Except we didn't have blue eyes, so we all had to have the same ones. And the hair was hard to glue 'cause the wool kept sticking to my fingers and Mrs. Bernardi had to help me get it off." Face aglow, he thrusts the sticky plate into my hands, and I gingerly set it down on the table, wrinkling my nose at the tangy odor. The thick layer of craft glue hasn't quite dried yet and the wool is beginning to slide in the direction of the Googly eyes, creating a unibrow effect.

"Awesome job, Lucas! It looks just like you," I say, beaming at him despite the emotional storm wreaking havoc inside me.

He throws his backpack on the floor and trots over to the refrigerator. "I'm thirsty. What's for snack, Mommy?"

Jack slaps a hand to his forehead. "Oh no! I forgot to go by the store!"

"It's fine, I'll figure something out." I force myself to my feet, briefly meeting Jack's eyes. He raises his brows a fraction as if to ask if I'm okay. But of course I'm not. How can either of us possibly be okay when a body was removed from our front doorstep only an hour ago? I give a half-hearted shrug before turning my attention to my child's nutritional needs.

Lucas gobbles down a sliced banana topped with peanut butter and then runs outside to play in the back yard. Jack sits down next to me and folds his arms on the kitchen table. "I hope we don't have to go down to the station to give our statements. We don't have anyone we can leave Lucas with."

I take a deep breath and turn to him, my mind elsewhere, for now. "I went over and talked to Stanley Hogg while you were gone."

"You did what?" Jack throws me a baffled look, shaking his head slowly. "I don't understand you. We talked about this, Lauren. Don't you get the part about us being possible suspects? You need to let the police do their—"

"Listen to me!" I cry, grabbing him by the arm. "Stanley saw someone dragging a body onto our steps this morning. He thought the man was drunk and his friend was leaving him there as a prank."

A look of horror ripples over Jack's features. "What? Did he tell the police?"

I raise my palms in a gesture of helplessness. "I didn't get a chance to ask. His invalid wife was calling for him. He seemed frightened, like he didn't want to get involved. My guess is that he probably didn't open the door to the police when they canvassed the neighborhood earlier."

Jack drags his fingers through his hair. "We have to let the police know. He might be able to give them a description of the person, or their vehicle."

"I'll call Detective Hernandez right now and ask him if anyone talked to Stanley," I say, reaching for my phone.

Jack gives a morose nod, picking at the skin on his thumb as he stares dejectedly at a spot on the table.

Detective Hernandez answers almost immediately. "What can I do for you Mrs. McElroy?"

I flinch at the not-so-subtle reminder that the discovery of my ex's body outside my house has changed the nature of my relationship with the police. I may or may not be an innocent party in this disturbing development, as far as they're concerned.

Detective Hernandez listens to what I have to say without indicating much interest, but he promises to send an officer around to interview Stanley Hogg. "I'd also like to come by later and take your statements," he adds, almost as an afterthought. "Will you and your husband be home this evening?"

I suck in a breath, an ominous fluttering in my chest. I've already told him everything I can. I hope he hasn't been digging too far into my past. I'm afraid he'll see straight through me if I try to dodge questions about Ryder and why he was incarcerated. He has a shrewdness about him that picks up on things that are left unsaid. "We're not planning on going anywhere," I hear myself say.

For the rest of the afternoon, I'm unable to focus on anything for more than a few minutes at a time. I check in with Maria via text, not trusting my voice to hold up for a conversation. She assures me she has everything under control while I take care of *my emergency,* and I let out a silent sigh of relief that I have the world's best PA in my court, even if nothing else is going according to plan.

Jack whiles away the time working on his laptop, oblivious to my mounting dread at the thought of Detective Hernandez's impending visit. Before I realize it, it's dinner time and I'm rummaging frantically through the refrigerator trying to drum up enough complementary ingredients for a meal. I end up making ham and cheese Paninis which Lucas adamantly refuses to eat. My ordinarily placid child seems to have unwittingly absorbed the tension radiating off the walls. After another epic meltdown, and a bath to cool his jets, Jack tucks him into bed and reads him a story. He makes it back down the stairs just as the doorbell rings.

"Sorry to stop by so late," Detective Hernandez says, with a requisite nod of acknowledgment that conveys no warmth. He gestures to the ruddy-faced officer standing next to him. "This is my partner, Officer Allen."

"You timed it well, actually," I tell him, as I lead them into the family room. "We just put Lucas, our son, to bed."

"How old is he?" Detective Hernandez asks, pulling out his notebook.

"He's six," I reply, smoothing my sweating palms over my pants.

"Although he'll be sure to tell you he's six-and-a-half," Jack adds in a cumbersome bid to lighten the atmosphere.

Detective Hernandez gives a tight grin, signaling the end of the niceties. "Mrs.—Lauren—can you run me through again exactly how you discovered the body?"

I take a shallow breath and begin to recount my movements that morning. "Lucas and I were getting ready to leave for school. I opened the front door and saw what I thought at the time was a scarecrow lying on the steps. It freaked me out—especially as we'd just gotten rid of the scarecrows in the yard the night before. I slammed the door shut and told Lucas we were going out the back instead."

"And what time was that at?"

"About 7:40 a.m. That's the time I usually leave the house."

Detective Hernandez turns to Jack. "What about you?"

"A few minutes after seven," Jack replies. "The scarecrow —I mean the body—wasn't there when I left."

Detective Hernandez frowns as he scribbles down some notes. "That means the body was placed at your front door in the span of a half hour."

"The body?" I echo in a questioning tone. I glance across at Officer Allen, but his face is pointedly expressionless. I suspect his role is to blend into the background unless something untoward transpires. "Do you know for sure Ryder was already dead when he was left at my door?" I ask.

Detective Hernandez fixes a steely gaze on me. "We got

the preliminary autopsy report back an hour ago. Blunt force trauma. The coroner estimates he'd already been dead for about six hours, which means he wasn't killed on your doorstep."

I press my knuckles to my lips, trying to take in the shocking revelation. Stanley Hogg was right. Ryder was dead when they dropped him off—whoever *they* turn out to be.

"I take it you already talked to my neighbor?" I say.

Detective Hernandez gives a curt nod. "He claims he saw a man positioning the body before he jogged off. No vehicle that he could see. He might have had a partner parked out of sight."

"That makes sense," I say, rubbing my forehead. "I didn't hear a car pull away from my house."

"The whole thing is odd," Jack interjects. "One man couldn't have carried the body very far."

"We suspect they dropped the body off during the night and hid it in the shrubbery," Detective Hernandez responds. "Then they waited for the perfect opportunity to drag it onto your front steps."

I shoot Jack a horrified look. The idea that there was a body lying in our shrubbery all night, that we knew nothing about, is nauseating. And not just any body—Ryder's body. Not to mention the fact that his murderer was hiding in the bushes, watching Jack leave, waiting for me to open the front door and discover my ex's body. I gulp down the ball of fear threatening to choke off my air supply. "Was my neighbor able to give you a description of the man?"

"It was vague. He couldn't see much from his front door." Detective Hernandez consults his notes and then clears his throat before changing track. "When did you first meet Ryder Montoya?"

"We dated our junior year in high school," I reply, feeling the heat begin to rise in my cheeks. "He wasn't a good influence. He got me into drugs." I shoot a quick look Jack's way, but he's studiously examining the rug beneath his feet. "My parents wanted to get me away from him, so we moved before my senior year." I'm praying Detective Hernandez hasn't bothered to look up my education record. I really don't want Jack finding out the parts I'm skimming over—not like this.

"Have you had any contact with Ryder since?"

I push the phone call out of my mind. That hardly counts, does it? I'm suddenly unsure of myself, wondering how much trouble I'm really in. How would it look to admit that I called Ryder recently? "I haven't seen him since high school, although, like I told you, I suspect he's been harassing me ever since I moved back to Austin."

Detective Hernandez jots down a few notes. "Can you think of any reason why someone would kill him and leave his body on your front steps?"

I shake my head in a ponderous fashion. "I mean, he kept some pretty shady company. I guess it could have been a drug deal gone bad. Maybe someone followed him, caught him skulking around outside my house during the night—saw their chance and took it."

"That doesn't explain why they returned the following morning and dragged him onto our steps," Jack chimes in. "It seems personal."

Detective Hernandez taps his pen on his knee, before turning his attention back to me. "How do you know Ryder kept some shady company?"

I squirm in my seat, detecting an accusing undertone belying the genial expression on his face. "Well, he used to. When I heard he'd been in and out of prison over the years,

I assumed nothing had changed." I drop my gaze and twist my wedding band around my finger, aware of Jack's penetrating gaze. I can sense his suspicion and I know he's wondering if I've told him everything. I haven't—I can't. There's too much at stake.

Detective Hernandez asks a few more questions and then wraps up the interview. "Thanks for your time. We'll be in touch if we have any more questions," he says, getting to his feet. The minute he and Officer Allen take their leave, Jack rounds on me, a tortured look in his eyes. "What is it about you and Ryder that you haven't told me? I know you're hiding something. How deep did you get into the drug scene, anyway?" He runs a hand over the nape of his neck in an agitated fashion, his voice rising. "I need you to tell me the truth, Lauren. What level of shady company are we talking about? You said it could have been a drug deal gone bad. Is someone going to come after us next? Kidnap our son?"

"Don't be ridiculous. Surely you don't think this is my fault."

"I don't know. You tell me!" Jack retorts. "Did you have anything to do with this? Did you tip someone from your past off to the fact that Ryder was harassing you? Someone who had a beef with him?"

"How can you even come up with something that outlandish?" I shout back at him. "If I'd planned to knock Ryder off, the last place I would leave his body is on my own front steps."

"Then who did?" Jack says, his voice dangerously soft. "Because someone from your checkered past did this, Lauren."

16

The atmosphere in our house is charged with a flammable mixture of hurt and suspicion for the remainder of the evening. Jack and I barely exchange another word before retiring for the night, each of us wrestling with the mistrust and upheaval this whole foul situation has brought about. The following morning he leaves for work before it's light out, eliminating any possibility of being forced into civil conversation with me.

Despite the bright smile I plaster on my face, Maria senses something is wrong the minute I walk into work. "You look like you haven't slept a wink, *again*. Is everything all right? You left in an awful hurry yesterday."

I gesture for her to follow me into my office. I don't want any of the engineers overhearing our conversation—I'm still hoping I can keep what happened from the rest of the staff, not to mention our customers. Closing the door, I sink down in my chair and wait for Maria to take a seat opposite me. She places her elbows on the table, silver bracelets jangling on her wrist, and leans toward me. "You're scaring me, Boss. Did we lose another deal or something?"

I press my forehead to my knuckles and inhale deeply before meeting her gaze. "I wish that was the extent of it. Remember that ex-boyfriend of mine from high school I was telling you about—the one who's been harassing me? He was found dead on my front steps yesterday."

Maria's kohl-rimmed eyes glisten with shock and she shrinks back from me as if I'm radiating contamination. "That's ... awful," she gasps. "I don't know what to say, to be honest."

"I don't either. My emotions are all over the place," I reply tersely. "I'm not saying I'm glad he's dead, but I'm not sorry I won't have to endure the harassment anymore."

Maria eyes me with a curious gleam. "How did it happen? Do you know how he died?"

I let out a heavy sigh. "Blunt force trauma—he was murdered. The police think someone hid the body in the shrubbery overnight and then dragged it onto my front steps before I left to take Lucas to school—they waited until Jack left for work to make sure I would be the one to discover it."

Maria toys with a strand of her hair, a contemplative look on her face. "So ... it was personal. Whoever killed him must have known you were his ex. I mean why else would someone kill him and leave him at your door?"

I shrug. "Who knows? He hung out with a rough crowd. He was into drugs and stuff. Maybe he owed someone money and they followed him to my house. They may not even have known he had any connection to me."

Maria puckers her brow, only a threadlike frown visible beneath the botox. "What are the police doing about it?"

"They took my statement and interviewed my neighbors. One of them actually saw a man leaving the body on my steps. He thought it was someone who'd got drunk and passed out or something, and his friends were gigging him. He couldn't see that well from his door."

Maria gives a skeptical grunt. "I can't believe he didn't go over there to check it out. He should have called you at least to let you know someone was lying on your steps and might need medical attention."

"You'd think, but he's a bit of an oddball," I explain. "His wife's an invalid, and he never leaves his house."

Maria pulls her lips down in a dramatic sweep. "I'm so sorry you had to go through something so appalling. It's horrible to even imagine it. Lucas didn't see the body, did he?"

I suck in a sharp breath. "No! Thank goodness! He's oblivious to what happened. It was all over and done with by the time he got home from school."

The trill of my phone interrupts our conversation and I tense when I see Gareth's name come up on the screen. He must have heard the news. He's either calling to pry or gloat. "It's Gareth Looney. I have to take this," I say to Maria. "Don't mention anything to the rest of the staff."

She gives a knowing nod and slips out of the room, closing the door quietly behind her.

"Gareth, I didn't expect to hear from you again. What can I do for you?" I ask, doing my best to nail a professional tone despite the fact that I'm falling apart on the inside.

"I just heard what happened," he replies, his tone oozing sham sympathy. "That's one crazy story. How are you holding up?"

I grit my teeth trying to land on a cutting response. As if he cares how I'm holding up. He's probably hoping this blows up and sends my business into a tailspin. No doubt, the only purpose of his call is to fish for details so he can further tarnish my reputation when he spreads the story around town. I grip the phone tighter as my earlier suspicions that Gareth might be involved come flooding back. How could he have found out about what happened so quickly? Detective Hernandez assured me our privacy would be respected. "What *news* are you referring to exactly?" I retort.

"Aw, knock it off, Lauren. You know what I'm talking about—Ryder turning up dead on your front steps. I bet that was a relief, huh?"

"How did you hear about it?" I ask, ignoring the dig.

"Margo called me. The police notified Ryder's family and his mother called her."

I silently digest this. It doesn't ring true. Why would Ryder's mother call Margo? "I didn't know she was close with his family," I say casually.

There's a beat of silence on Gareth's end. "She's not, but she deserves to hear it from them, she's the mother of his child, after all."

I almost drop the phone. An image of an anorexic Margo with stringy hair and braces comes to mind. When did she and Ryder get together? "Really?" I reply, in an offhand manner. "I never pictured those two as a match made in heaven."

Gareth chuckles—not a friendly chuckle. It's a cold laugh laced with thinly veiled delight at a joke at someone else's expense. "Jealous, are we?" he drawls. "Margo's come a long way since high school. You should check out her Facebook page sometime. I guess all the plastic surgery paid off, 'cause she finally got her claws into Ryder. You know how jealous she always was of you. She wanted everything you had, including him."

My mind bolts in several different directions at once. Margo and Ryder are a couple. Does that mean she knew

Ryder was harassing me? Maybe she put him up to it once she heard I was coming back to Austin. "When did they get together?" I ask.

Gareth lets out a scathing snort. "About eight years ago, but they only lasted a couple of years before Ryder kicked her to the curb. She was too much to handle—paranoid about every phone call he made. She had a breakdown after he bailed on her. And then she found out she was pregnant. It was the perfect way to keep her hooks in Ryder forever."

I frown, wondering how much of this to believe. "How do you know so much about them?"

"They both called me up from time to time, griping about the other one," he says with an air of casual indifference.

"How old is their kid?" I ask.

"Dunno. He's in school—young. She has pictures of him plastered all over her social media accounts." He hesitates before asking, "What was Ryder doing at your place anyway?"

"He's been ... stalking me—at home and at work," I say, reluctant to elaborate, but curious if Gareth knows more than he's letting on.

He gives a satisfied grunt. "Well, there you have it. That explains the break-in you tried to blame on me. You know he did three years for armed robbery?"

I suck in a shallow breath, considering the possibility once again that Gareth might have hired Ryder to do his dirty work for him. "Sure seems like you had more to gain from the break-in than anyone," I comment. "You needed a copy of my proposal—you were desperate for that deal with Huss Integrity, weren't you?"

"I didn't break into your business—I didn't have to," he responds angrily. "Someone emailed me a copy of your proposal. I figured it might have been a disgruntled employee or something. I had no idea Capitol Technologies was your company—not until I saw the article in the paper."

"How convenient!" I'm not sure whether to believe him or not. It's possible he's telling the truth, but until I know for sure that Gareth isn't trying to sabotage my business, I'm going to have to keep my guard up. At least now that Ryder's out of the picture, he doesn't have anyone to do his dirty work for him.

I end the call and fire up my computer, determined to accomplish something before the day is over, despite the fact that my emotions are floating every which way, searching for purchase like tentacles on a jellyfish. I have to get to work on two new proposals that have been sitting on my desk untouched for the past couple of days—potential new business that we need to lock in before my engineers start to get cold feet. I'm halfway through the first proposal when Maria sticks her head around my door. "There's a Detective Hernandez here to see you."

A swell of anxiety churns in my stomach. He wouldn't have stopped by the office if he didn't have something important to tell me. Maybe they've found out who killed Ryder. They might even have made an arrest, although that's a long shot.

"Any leads?" I blurt out the minute Maria shows Detective Hernandez into my office.

He coughs discreetly. "I can't discuss the details of an ongoing investigation. But I do have a few more questions for you."

I gesture for him to take a seat. "I'm happy to try and answer them. I'm just not sure I can help you with much, other than what I've already told you."

He pulls out his notebook and thumbs through a few

pages. "You mentioned that you haven't had any contact with Ryder since high school. Is that correct?"

I blink as I try to focus my thoughts. No physical contact —if we're playing semantics. But I'm only too aware that this isn't a game. I can't hide the phone call any longer. All the police have to do is pull Ryder's phone records—which they might have done by now. In fact, this could be a trap to see if I'm going to come clean or not. "Like I said, we haven't seen each other since high school. Other than a brief phone call, we haven't been in touch."

Detective Hernandez raises his brows, cuing me to elaborate.

But I know from a heavy diet of crime shows that it's better not to volunteer information. Instead, I interlace my fingers and wait for him to ask another question. I breathe slowly in and out, trying to center myself. I just want this all to go away. The last thing I need is for Detective Hernandez to uncover my *murky past*.

"When was that phone call made?" Detective Hernandez asks, breaking our silent deadlock.

"A few days ago," I respond nonchalantly.

"Did Ryder call you?" Detective Hernandez's expression is inscrutable, but I have the distinct impression he already knows the answer and he's more interested in whether I'm going to lie about it. If he's testing my integrity, my best bet is to preemptively answer the question he's building up to: *what did we talk about?*

"No. I called him," I reply. "I confronted him about the stalking and the harassment and told him in no uncertain terms that it needed to stop—that what we had between us was history."

Detective Hernandez's gaze bores into me. "Was he still

interested in you, jealous of your new relationship, perhaps?"

I fidget in my seat. "I'm not sure. He was always very possessive of me when we were together."

Detective Hernandez cocks his head to one side. "So how did the phone conversation go?"

I let out a shuddering sigh. "Not well. He denied everything, of course. I figured he must have seen the article about my parents' plane crash and that's how he tracked me down."

Detective Hernandez gives a thoughtful nod. "Did he threaten you?"

"Not in so many words. He told me I was full of myself to think he would still be interested in me after all this time. He got angry. I think I just made things worse by calling him up and confronting him." I squeeze my fingers together in my lap. "I dread to think what he had in mind when he showed up at my house."

Detective Hernandez rubs a hand across his jaw, seemingly lost in thought for a moment. "Back to that phone call. It's a little unusual to keep a high school ex's number all these years, isn't it? Especially someone you were frightened of."

"I didn't have his number," I explain. "I had to call my childhood nanny to get it. Like I mentioned before, she's friends with the woman who lives next door to Ryder's family."

Detective Hernandez bunches his brows together. "I'm going to need an address."

I throw him an indignant look before pulling out my phone and jotting it down on a post-it note. "You don't believe me?" I ask, as I pass it to him.

"What I believe is irrelevant. It's my job to verify everyone's statement," he says flatly. He glances at his notes before locking eyes with me again. "Were you aware that Ryder had a child with one of your former friends from high school—Margo McGowan?"

My cheeks heat up and I can feel tiny beads of sweat prickling along my hairline. "I just found out about that earlier this morning."

Detective Hernandez sets down his pen. "I've spoken to Ms. McGowan. I take it there's no love lost between the two of you."

I blink, momentarily taken aback by his bluntness. "She was jealous of me in high school, if that's what you mean. She always had a thing for Ryder. But I haven't spoken to her either since my junior year."

"Ms. McGowan seems convinced that it was the other way around—that you were jealous of her relationship with Ryder. She said you couldn't accept the fact that she had a child with him."

"What?" I splutter, my thoughts splintering. "Of course I wasn't jealous of her. How could I have been? I didn't know they had a kid. I didn't even know they were together."

Detective Hernandez's eyes drill into me. "She claims you did. She says you threatened Ryder when you called him a few days ago."

I give an adamant shake of my head. "She's lying. I didn't threaten him. I told him if he didn't stop harassing me, I would take out a restraining order against him. That's a perfectly legal recourse for what he was putting me through."

Detective Hernandez flicks through a couple of pages in his notebook. "Ms. McGowan also claimed that this wasn't the first time you threatened Ryder."

I stare at him open-mouthed. "That's outrageous. I don't know what she's talking about."

Detective Hernandez taps a finger on a page in his notebook. "You have a phobia of scarecrows, correct?"

I flinch, caught off guard by the sudden change in topic. "I ... yes, I hate them—I told you that already. What's that got to do with anything?"

"Ms. McGowan recounted an incident at a pumpkin patch one Halloween back in your high school years. She said Ryder hid behind a scarecrow and flung an arm out to frighten you. You went berserk—started screaming at him and pummeling him."

He consults his notes. "In fact, according to Ms. McGowan, your exact words were: *I mean it. If you ever pull a stunt like that again, I'll kill you.*"

17

Detective Hernandez leans back in his chair, letting the silence hang between us. Shock radiates through me as it dawns on me where he's going with this. It's a not-so-subtle insinuation that I might have had a hand in Ryder's death—maybe even that I set this whole thing up to make it look like he was killed while stalking my house. But it's a ridiculous proposition. He can't really believe I had anything to do with it. Does he think I made up the harassment too—planted those scarecrows in my own back yard, or what?

I bristle at the thought. Where is this coming from? A burst of anger surges through me when realization dawns. This is Margo's doing. She's the one who's been filling the detective's head with lies about me being jealous of her relationship with Ryder. But she's the one who's nursed a jealous obsession all these years. It was always her. She wanted what I had, and she would have done anything to get it—faking a friendship with me, even starving herself to death if that's what it took to make Ryder notice her. My mind goes back to that night at the pumpkin patch. I don't remember exactly what I said to Ryder—admittedly, I was furious—but, evidently, my words are seared in Margo's memory. A throwaway threat that meant nothing. What teenager hasn't ranted about wanting to kill someone at one time or another?

I knew that night was the beginning of the end for Ryder, and me. Even through the drug-induced fog I was operating in, I'd realized by then that he didn't really love me—didn't know what love was. He reveled in the fact that we were the kind of couple that turned heads on the high school campus, but I was only ever a possession to him—a possession he routinely terrorized. As long as I was hooked on the drugs he supplied me with, I was his butterfly with pinned wings, and he thrived on my paralysis.

"Lauren, is there anything you want to tell me?" Detective Hernandez lowers his voice and leans forward in his chair, as if expecting to hear a confession. But I have nothing to confess and nothing to hide—at least, nothing that relates to what happened on my front steps yesterday.

"I don't know what happened to Ryder, and I wasn't involved in his death if that's what you're hinting at," I huff, folding my arms mutinously. "Like I told you, I haven't seen him in almost twenty years. And I had no desire to. Our relationship was dysfunctional. He was abusive and I was an addict. I have a husband and a child of my own now—a life that I love. The only contact I had with Ryder was that one phone call I made a couple of days ago." My chin wobbles, betraying my emotion. "I wanted him to leave me alone, that's all."

Detective Hernandez taps a finger on his nose and snaps his notebook shut, heralding the end of the interview. He slides his chair out, and I allow myself my first deep breath since he began questioning me. My fears that he was going to arrest me on the spot were evidently unfounded. He's on a fishing expedition, for now. We're all under a cloud of suspicion, just like Jack warned.

I eye the detective warily as he gets to his feet, watching for any indication that he's going to whip out a pair of hand-cuffs at the last minute and read me my rights after all. Instead, he tips his hat to me. "I'll be in touch if I have any more questions. Thanks for your time. I'll see myself out."

The minute the door closes behind him, I lay my head down on my desk and sob silently. My emotions feel like they've gone through a heavy-duty spin cycle. Even though I'm not being escorted to a squad car in handcuffs, Detective Hernandez has made it abundantly clear that he considers me a person of interest. To hear Margo tell it, I hated Ryder, threatened to kill him, and only a few days ago, made an intimidating phone call that could be perceived as another threat. I can see how it looks. A history of drugs and abuse, jealousy, and violence. I could have hired a hitman to kill Ryder, dress him as a scarecrow, and then place him outside my door to make it look like he was stalking me when he was killed.

The idea that I could be tried for murder, with Margo as the chief witness for the prosecution, chills me to my soul. I shiver, rubbing my arms vigorously to shake myself loose of this senseless train of thought. I need to pull myself together. I'm innocent—I have nothing to be concerned about. Bracing myself, I reach for my phone and call Jack to bring him up to speed on the detective's visit. "He might be heading your way next," I warn him, "to accuse you of knocking Ryder off to protect me, just like you predicted."

"You shouldn't have agreed to speak to him without counsel," he fumes.

"He showed up unannounced. I thought he had news for me. I figured they might have made an arrest."

"You need to call a lawyer right away," Jack replies, his voice strained. I picture him pacing across his office floor, scratching his brow as he thinks aloud. "We're both going to need one. Not the same one. We've got to get ahead of this."

"But they haven't accused us of anything," I point out. "They can't arrest us. They don't have any evidence."

"It doesn't matter," Jack insists. "We need legal advice in case things take an ugly turn like they often do in these kinds of situations. If the police can't find the killer, they'll push hard to nail somebody so they can close the case."

I jump at a knock on the door and hurriedly wipe my eyes. "I've got to go, Jack. I'll talk to you tonight."

I end the call right as the door opens and Maria walks in. "I saw the detective leave. Any news?"

I grimace. "No good news. It seems I'm now a person of interest."

"What?" Maria gasps. "You can't be serious!"

I give a defeated shrug. "It was only to be expected, I suppose. The police have to look at everyone. I had a history with Ryder—a volatile one. He threatened me in the past, and I reported him to the police—accused him of harassing me. And then, all of a sudden, he shows up dead on my doorstep. It's the perfect storm."

"What are you going to do?" Maria asks, fussing with her hair.

I suspect it's not a benign inquiry. She might be beginning to question my ability to ride out this storm, and the last thing I need is for Maria to bail on me now. I clasp my hands in front of me and meet her gaze. "Handle it, like it's business. I'm going to hire a lawyer. I can't risk this affecting our reputation. After that, I'll have to wait and see what

Detective Hernandez's next move is. Hopefully he finds whoever did this quickly and puts an end to the investigation before it blows up."

"If you need to go home, I can take over here for you," Maria offers.

I shake my head. "Thanks, but I can't let any more work stack up. I have to finish these proposals."

For the remainder of the afternoon, I manage to hold it together, but my focus wanes and ebbs. I ignore all my calls and let them go to voicemail. I can't face dealing with people right now. While I work, I weigh the pros and cons of contacting Margo. On the surface, it would be the decent thing to do—offer my condolences. After all, Ryder was the father of her child. And if I reach out to her, I might be able to persuade her to retract her statement to the police. Or at the very least to drop her misguided attempts to pin Ryder's murder on me. It's worth a shot. A quick search online gives me all the information I need. Her phone number's linked to her Facebook account. Clearly, she's never taken the time to review her privacy settings, or maybe she enjoys flaunting her endless parade of selfies featuring her overly made-up face and hair extensions to everyone in cyber world.

It takes me a good half hour to prepare myself mentally to call. I'm not sure what kind of reception I'm going to get, but I'm under no illusions that it will be a warm one. The phone rings several times before Margo answers.

"Hello?" she croaks, as if her throat's raw and she's all cried out. Despite my anger, guilt pricks at me. I can't help but feel bad for her—and her now fatherless child. Ryder was all she ever aimed for in life. She followed him around in high school like a sick puppy while we laughed at her behind her back. I'm not proud of the things I did to please Ryder back then.

"Margo, it's Lauren—Lauren Bishop."

She doesn't answer at first, but I hear her breath hitch. I brace myself, unsure if she's going to start screaming down the phone, or simply hang up. "You have some nerve calling me," she says eventually, her tone low and measured.

"Margo, I'm sorry about Ryder. I didn't know you had a child together. I'm sure this must be very difficult for you."

"And I'm sure that makes you very happy," she snaps back.

"Of course it doesn't. It's horrific what happened to him."

"You're so full of it. Ryder was right about you. Just another entitled leech who thinks the world revolves around you. I bet you're thrilled he's dead. All these years later and you still couldn't leave him alone—calling him up and accusing him of harassing you, lying to the police about him. It's you the police should be investigating."

"I *was* being harassed, Margo, and all the signs pointed to him. What was I supposed to think? He always threatened to hunt me down—he just didn't know where I was, until now."

"He had no interest in you anymore," Margo retorts. "He had me, and his son. Until you came back to town. You threatened him, and now look what's happened!"

I chew on my lip for a moment, trying to decide which direction to steer the conversation in. Gareth told me Ryder wasn't even with Margo anymore, but it's a moot point. I need to smooth things over with her, not rile her up. If she keeps putting pressure on the police to look at me as a suspect, they might uncover more than I'd like them to. And I can't risk Jack finding out any more about my past than he already has. I have to offer an olive branch. "Margo, I'd like to see you again and meet your little boy."

After a beat or two of silence she asks, "What do you want from me, Lauren?"

"Nothing. I just want to reconnect and reassure you that I had nothing to do with Ryder's death. We're both grown women now. Surely we can put whatever issues we had in the past behind us."

"Gareth told me you have a son too," Margo says. "What's his name?"

"Lucas, he's six years old."

There's another long silence and then she lets out a relenting sigh. "Meet me for lunch at noon on Friday at The Red Snapper in The Sycamore Mall. And bring your boy."

"He has school—" I don't bother finishing my sentence. She's already hung up. I set down my phone and rub my hands over my face. The conversation was every bit as painful as I anticipated, but at least she's agreed to meet me. Face-to-face, I have a better chance of talking some sense into her and persuading her not to keep pushing a false narrative. I can't help but think she must want Ryder's real killer to be caught and brought to justice—for her son's sake, if for no other reason.

Next, I turn my attention to hiring a lawyer. After Googling several potential candidates and checking out their reviews online, I make an appointment with an attorney by the name of Gabriel Williams. His services require a hefty retainer, which I take as a good sign that he's competent.

After picking Lucas up from school, I drive home only half listening as he chatters on about the cardboard space-ship he's building along with the rest of his class for their solar system module. Inside the house, I seat him at the kitchen table to make a start on his homework, while I flick idly through my cookbooks trying to decide what to make for dinner. I settle on a chicken stir fry, hoping the elementary task of chopping vegetables will return some sense of normalcy to my life. I feel like I've been trapped in a house of horrors, circling the walls unable to find an exit, for the past twenty-four hours. Despite my good intentions, I struggle to complete the simplest tasks, and by the time Jack strides through the door, I've cut my finger twice and burned the chicken, and my nerves are fried.

We don't make much conversation during dinner, and I'm relieved when it's over and Jack takes Lucas upstairs to run a bath. I busy myself clearing the table and set the dishwasher to run before kicking off my shoes and sinking down on the couch. Jack comes back downstairs a few minutes later and takes a seat opposite me. Other than inadvertently brushing past me in the kitchen, he hasn't touched me since asking if I had anything to do with Ryder's death. But I can tell by the long-suffering look he shoots me that he's here to talk.

"I'm scared, Jack," I begin. "What if they arrest me?"

"They won't. The police don't really believe you're involved. They're treating everyone as a suspect—including me."

I throw him a look of alarm. "Did Detective Hernandez pay you a visit too?"

"Yeah, right after he got done with you. He asked me outright if I knocked Ryder off because he was harassing you."

I tent my hands over my nose and mouth. "I'm sorry, Jack. This is so traumatic. I hate that you've been dragged into it."

"Well, we have nothing to hide so we have nothing to worry about, right?" he replies, his tone turning wistful.

My eyes swerve from his penetrating stare and come to

rest on the lamp in the corner of the room. "I made an appointment with a lawyer like you suggested," I tell him.

Jack gives an approving nod. "I hired one too. We need to know what our rights are, and what the police can and can't do."

"This whole thing is so stressful," I say. "Between the move, and starting my business, and now the murder investigation, it's difficult to focus at work. Maria's good about keeping me on track and prioritizing my schedule, but the work's piling up on my desk. I need to get some contracts lined up ASAP or my engineers are going to get antsy. And I want to be there for Lucas, too."

"I realize you need help," Jack says, folding his arms across his chest. "Which is why I've hired your old nanny, Kathy, to help out. She's agreed to come and stay with us for a few weeks—longer if we need her—until we get through this. We don't know anyone here we can trust enough to watch Lucas."

"You hired Kathy?" I say, shooting him an incredulous look. "You do realize she lives in Lubbock now? She retired there after we moved to San Antonio."

"I sent her a plane ticket and I've booked her a rental car through my company that she can drive while she's here. It'll be available tomorrow," Jack replies, looking pleased with himself.

I throw him a puzzled look. "How did you get her number?"

"I didn't. She called me. It was her idea."

18

S hortly before three the following day, I leave work and head to the airport to pick up Kathy. Her friend Jan must have told her what happened—it's the only way she could have found out this quickly. I'm not sure how I feel about her offer to come to Austin to help look after Lucas. It's incredibly generous, and I desperately need the help, but I'm feeling embarrassed. Not for the first time, I've dragged my nanny into a mess involving me and Ryder. Kathy did everything in her power to try and talk some sense into me when she first found out I was seeing him behind my parents' backs. But once I passed my driving test and got my own car, she couldn't keep track of me or my lies.

Despite my misgivings, I feel a huge infusion of relief knowing Kathy's going to be around to help out in the coming weeks. Between Maria keeping me on track in my business world, and Kathy holding down the fort at home, I might finally be able to crawl out from this mess I'm in. Kathy's capable enough to run a household blindfolded, and there's no one I'd trust more with my child. But I'm also aware that she's older now—mid-sixties—so I need to be careful not to overload her.

I park in the short-term parking lot and make my way to the arrivals terminal. I'm fifteen minutes early, but, to my surprise, I spot her standing outside the terminal at the curb. I give her a wave as I draw closer and she waves back, then reaches for the handle of her wheeled suitcase. She's let her hair go gray, but it suits her, bouncing off her shoulders in a chic bob as she walks toward me. At five-foot-ten, she's still an imposing woman.

"Lauren! It's so good to see you again, pumpkin!" she exclaims, her familiar face crinkling into a smile as she wraps me up in one of her famous bear hugs. "Can I still call you that?"

"Of course! It's good to see you too, Kathy," I say, laughing as we pull apart. "Thanks for coming."

She angles her face and makes a tutting sound. "I felt obligated to do something. I'm truly sorry about what happened. I feel partly responsible—"

I cut her off with a dismissive wave of my hand. "Don't even go there. It had nothing to do with you."

She gives a small shake of her head, her neatly styled bob swaying to and fro. "Jan told me the same thing, but I blame myself for giving you his number—knowing your history and what a hothead he was. He never changed his ways. He was always a hard character. Do they have any leads yet on his murderer?"

"If they do, they're not saying," I reply, averting my gaze.

Kathy slants a mistrustful look at me. "Is there something you're not telling me?"

"Let's talk about it on the way." I gesture to her suitcase. "Is that all your luggage?"

"Yes. I always go carry-on ever since they lost my bag on our trip to Hawaii that time."

I give her a flicker of a smile which rapidly extinguishes. It was supposed to be a family vacation, until my parents backed out at the last minute citing a work conflict. I spent five days in Hawaii with my nanny instead—most of it trying to track down her suitcase. I got high for the first time shortly after that trip.

"All right, let's get out of here," I say, leading the way to the parking lot. "Lucas can't wait to meet you. He's kind of shy with new people at first, but once he gets to know you, he'll chatter away like a chipmunk."

Once we're buckled up and underway, Kathy turns to me with a concerned look. "Okay, tell me what's going on with the murder inquiry."

"You asked if the police had any leads," I reply in a grim tone. "Apparently, I'm a person of interest."

Kathy's eyes widen, shock frozen in her lined face. "But why? Just because his body was found on your doorstep?"

My shoulders sag as I slow to a stop at the traffic lights. "That didn't help. Margo McGowan's been feeding the police all kinds of stories about me threatening Ryder and being jealous of her having a kid with him."

Kathy purses her lips. "Who knows if it's even his kid? I did hear they had a fling after he got out of prison. I suspect he just needed a place to stay, and she was more than willing to accommodate him. I remember how obsessed she was with him."

"She still is—it's almost worse now that he's dead. She seems determined to try and pin his murder on me. Maybe she really believes I did it. She told the police I threatened him when I called, and that I have a history of threatening to kill him."

Kathy lets out an indignant humph. "No one's going to take such nonsense seriously. He was the abusive one in your relationship. He almost strangled you that one time—which is why I did everything I could to try and talk you out of seeing him."

"The thing is, I think I did yell something about wanting to kill him one night back in high school," I confess to her, pulling forward as the light turns green. "It was Halloween, and we were at the pumpkin patch. He hid behind a scarecrow and scared me almost to death. Of course Margo told the police about that. She made it sound like it was a serious threat—dangerous even. And then a few days ago, I made that call and threatened him—for lack of a better word—with a restraining order for harassing me, so it looks to the police like I had a motive for murder. Not to mention the fact that his body was found on my front steps."

"I couldn't believe it when Jan told me," Kathy says with a bewildered shake of her head. "That's when I picked up the phone and called Jack—well, I tried your number first, but it kept going to voicemail all afternoon."

"I was ignoring my calls—trying to get caught up on my work." I throw her a curious look. "So Jan still lives next door to Ryder's family?"

"Yes, it's just his mother now. His father passed away of cancer a few years back. Anyway, like I told Jack, I want to do something to help. Your family was always so good to me over the years. It broke my heart when you moved away to San Antonio."

I grimace inwardly. Kathy knows where I really spent my senior year, but she never refers to it directly—it all gets thrown into the *move-to-San-Antonio* pot in any conversation around the topic. "I appreciate you coming out to help, Kathy," I say. "This couldn't have happened at a worse time—

not that there's ever a good time for a murder. It's just that I'm trying to get my business off the ground and I'm struggling to secure contracts. The big one I was relying on to see us through for the next six months fell through. That's another sore spot. I had worked on the negotiations for weeks and we got undercut at the last minute by Gareth Looney—remember him? Looney-goon we used to call him."

Kathy nods. "Of course. He was a very bright kid. I always wondered why he wasted his time hanging out with Ryder and doing drugs."

"Honestly, I think he was bored to death in school," I say. "He was borderline genius."

Kathy shoots me a sideways glance. "I seem to remember he had a bit of a thing for you."

I twist my lips in an exaggerated grimace at the unwelcome reminder of a slobbery kiss he stole one night in a misguided attempt to make a pass at me. I never told Ryder about it because I wasn't sure which of us he would have beaten to a pulp.

"Maybe if you explain to Gareth that you were counting on the deal, he might retract his offer," Kathy suggests.

"I tried. He swore up and down he had no idea it was my company he was competing against, although he did admit someone anonymously emailed him a copy of our bid. I'm not sure whether to believe him or not, but there's nothing I can do about it now."

Kathy fishes a tissue out of her purse and dabs at her nose. "In that case, best to let it go, pumpkin. Focus on your other contracts. I'm here now to help with Lucas and the house, so you're free to attend to whatever business you need to."

"Thanks, Kathy. I'll definitely take you up on that. Actually, I have an appointment with a lawyer later this afternoon, so you timed your arrival well. I'll need someone to watch Lucas. Jack picked him up from school, but he'll be working in his home office for the rest of the day. I know Lucas will love having you here—I've told him so many stories about you." I hesitate and then add, "At least I don't have to worry about Ryder lurking around him anymore. He wasn't just targeting me. He made a point of proving he could get to Lucas too."

Kathy throws me a look of consternation. "What do you mean?"

"Lucas was in the driveway one morning when a man in a gray overcoat approached him. He said he was a neighbor, and he gave Lucas some straw and told him he was going to need it for good luck. It totally freaked me out. At first, I thought it might have been this crazy neighbor who lives a couple of doors down from me—he's kind of a scary-looking character—but then when I put it together with all the other incidents, I realized it had to be someone who knew about my phobia of scarecrows."

"What other incidents?" Kathy asks, quieting her voice.

"Stupid things mostly. Like putting scarecrows on stakes in my backyard and sending me an animated email with a decapitated scarecrow. What scared me the most was that Ryder knew where I lived and worked."

Kathy reaches over and rubs my arm. "It's over now, pumpkin. I'm sure the police will get to the bottom of his murder and Margo's wild accusations will amount to nothing more than hot air. As for that too-smart-for-his-own-boots Gareth Looney-goon, I'd be happy to give him a piece of my mind, if you want. It's not as if he didn't consume enough of my blueberry muffins back in the day for me to have some leverage with him."

I burst out laughing, and we end up spending the rest of the drive home reminiscing about some of our marathon baking sessions. It's comforting to have Kathy here. She's a good soul—a part of my past I cherish, like a familiar blanket on a cold evening.

I can't help but think things can only get better from here on out.

19

"Lucas, this is my nanny, Ms. Kathy, who I told you all those stories about," I say by way of introduction when we arrive back at the house.

"Well, hello there, young man," Kathy greets him, grinning down at him. "And none of that miss stuff. You can call me Kathy."

Lucas stares up at her slack jawed. "Are you taller than my dad?"

Kathy chuckles. "Tell you what, I'll stand next to him, and you can decide. How does that sound?"

"Good," Lucas says approvingly. "But he's on an important phone call right now. Do you want to see what I made in school today?"

I exchange a meaningful look with Kathy. As I'd hoped, Lucas has accepted her unreservedly. He usually takes a little longer to warm up to new people, but he instinctively trusts Kathy, or maybe he's content knowing that I trust her. "How about we take Kathy up to her room first?" I suggest. "She can drop off her suitcase and freshen up and then you can show her all your art projects."

"Okay," Lucas replies, jumping up and down in anticipation.

After I show Kathy to the guest room, I peek in on Jack. He gestures apologetically at the phone in his hand, so I leave him to it and head to the kitchen to grab a bottle of water to take with me to my appointment.

Moments later, Lucas comes racing in, followed by Kathy. "Mommy! Guess what we're going to make!"

I tap my finger to my cheek and give him a crooked grin. "Green beans?"

"No, silly! Chocolate chip cookies."

"Mmm. Sounds delicious."

"They're for after dinner, with ice cream," Lucas adds gravely.

"Perfect. I can't wait. Mommy has to go now but I'll be back in time for dinner." I give him a kiss on the forehead and nod to Kathy. "Jack's just finishing up a phone call. You have my number if you need it. I have to swing by the office after my appointment to check on a few things. I'll try not to be too late."

"Don't worry about us," Kathy responds, with an elaborate wink. "Lucas and I have big plans while you're gone."

GABRIEL WILLIAMS LOOKS like the sort of lawyer who wins cases. Clean, pressed, wrinkle-free, and tanned. He adjusts the cuff of his expensive suit jacket, applying a professional smile as he appraises me in a sweeping gesture. We shake hands and he motions for me to take a seat.

"I've read through the notes my assistant took," he begins, as he retrieves a pen from a marble stand on his desk and flips open a file folder. "Why don't you give me a little more background information and a quick rundown on the current situation?"

I cross my legs and settle into the ebony leather wing-back chair. "As I explained to your assistant, the man who was found murdered on my front steps is an abusive ex of mine from high school. I haven't seen him in the intervening years, but I understand he served time in prison."

Gabriel cocks his head. "Do you know what crime he was convicted of?"

"Drug-related, I think, but I'm not sure of the exact charges."

"Not to worry, I'll have my assistant look into it," Gabriel replies. "So, when did the stalking begin?"

"A few weeks ago when I moved back to Austin. In fact, it began the day we moved in. I found a decorative scarecrow in the moving truck. At the time, I wasn't sure it was inten-tional, but when the scarecrows showed up in our back yard and a stranger gave my son a handful of straw for good luck, I realized it was someone familiar with my phobia of scare-crows. They even sent me an email with a decapitated scarecrow."

Gabriel raises his brows. "Did you save the email?"

"Yes, but I can't trace the IP address."

"It's still an electronic trail." Gabriel glances back at his notes. "What other evidence do you have? Did you keep the scarecrows?"

I pull my lips into a dramatic grimace. "Unfortunately not. I couldn't stand to look at them. I had my husband get rid of them as soon as the police were finished photographing them."

Gabriel taps his fingernails on the desk in front of him, clearly irritated at my shortsightedness. I squirm in my seat, trying not to feel like a reprimanded schoolgirl, while inwardly berating myself for the dumb decisions I made as a teenager that brought me to this point.

"Tell me about the phone call you made to Ryder a few days ago," Gabriel continues.

I lift one shoulder and let it fall. "I didn't want to call him, but I decided I had to confront him. I told him I knew he was behind the harassment and that it had to stop. And to keep away from my son."

Gabriel eyes me with an inscrutable expression on his face. "Did you threaten him?"

I flick an imaginary speck from my sleeve. "Not physically. I told him I would take out a restraining order if he didn't stop. I don't consider it an unreasonable course of action under the circumstances."

Gabriel silently jots down a few notes. "What about the other threat that your friend, Margo McGowan, told the police about?"

I uncross my legs and straighten up in my seat, trying not to look as irritated as I feel. "She's not a friend, per se. We hung out when we were teenagers—did drugs together. She told the police I threatened to kill Ryder one Halloween. A total exaggeration, of course. He jumped out from behind a scarecrow in a pumpkin patch and freaked me out. I lashed out at him, that's all. Whatever came out of my mouth in the heat of the moment, it was hardly a serious threat."

Gabriel flashes me another of his executive smiles. He leans back in his leather swivel chair, bouncing gently back and forth. "I dare say you have nothing to be concerned about. There's certainly not enough here to warrant an arrest. Any case the police try and make against you at this point would be purely circumstantial and wouldn't hold up in court. Nonetheless, you did the right thing to engage my services in the event they ask to interview you again."

He gets to his feet, signaling the end of our session. A weight slides from my shoulders as I grip his hand. "Thank you, Gabriel. You have no idea how relieved I am to hear that."

"We'll keep in touch over the next few days as the investigation progresses. Call me if there are any developments, or if the police ask you to come down to the station."

I drive to my office with the sunroof open feeling almost euphoric for the first time in weeks. Gabriel knows what he's talking about. There's no reason for me to be concerned that Detective Hernandez is digging around. Whatever comes up during the investigation, Gabriel can make it go away—even Margo and her wild accusations.

Maria brings my mail into my office with a conspiratorial smile on her face. "Good news, boss, we secured a two-million-dollar contract today. And several new requests for proposals have come in."

I pump my fist in the air. "Yes! Take that Looney-goon!"

Maria sets the pile of mail down on my desk, her lips curving into a satisfied smile. "Let me know if you need anything else," she says as she breezes out of the room in her three-inch pumps.

Sinking down in my chair, I reach for a courier letter and slit open the envelope. I take a sip of my water before sliding out a single sheet of paper.

The words float up to me from the page like an apparition.

Kathy's not who you think she is.

20

"Are you certain no one saw who delivered this?" I ask Maria.

She gives a helpless shrug, her arms folded in front of her. "I'm positive. I've asked everyone. No one saw a courier service arrive."

"It's not a real courier service," I say, flicking the envelope with the back of my nail. "It's been dummied up to make it look official."

"It might have been dropped off at lunchtime when there was no one around," Maria suggests.

"Wasn't there anyone at the reception desk?" I ask trying to curb the irritation in my voice.

"Faye was there," Maria replies. "She said she left for a couple of minutes to grab a water bottle from the refrigerator. That could have been when the envelope was left on the counter."

I swallow down my trepidation. That means someone was watching for an opportunity. Am I being stalked again?

Maria coughs discreetly and straightens up. "I'll be in my office if you need anything else."

She closes the door behind her, and I lean back and thread my fingers restlessly through my hair. I don't know what to make of the letter, but it has left me shaken on several fronts, beginning with the fact that Ryder is dead. Who else could have sent it? And why? I've known Kathy my entire life, so I don't for one minute believe there's any merit to the message. But it does mean that someone is still out there jerking my chain. It's thrown me back into a chasm of terror I was only just beginning to climb out of.

I was sure the harassment would come to a screeching halt with Ryder's death. Could this be something else entirely? There are plenty of other crazies out there. After the plane crash, I dealt with a few looky-loos driving slowly past the *software heiress's* house as if I was some kind of side show.

I press the tips of my fingers to my temples and rub them in tiny circles to release the tension. My thoughts are spinning faster than I can process them. How would anyone know that Kathy is here in Austin? Did I mention it to Gareth? Or Margo? No, I talked to them before Jack told me he'd hired her. I finger the ominous note thoughtfully. I should call Gabriel and update him on this latest twist. I'm anxious to hear what he makes of it, and whether he thinks I should notify the police.

I call his office and leave a message with his assistant. I'll need to save the letter as evidence, but I don't want to keep it in my purse and run the risk of Kathy seeing it. I take a quick picture as I weigh my options. I should probably stash it in my desk for now. It would distress Kathy to no end to think that someone was still harassing me even after Ryder's death. And it would hurt her to think her name was being dragged through the mud—not to mention terrify her. She might elect to pack up and go home right when I need her most. I shoot Jack a quick text and ask him if he told anyone he was hiring Kathy. Even if he'd mentioned it in passing to his work colleagues, none of them know her, and Jack doesn't know Gareth or Margo, so he wouldn't have talked to them. A chill passes through my bones. I'm teetering on the edge again, just when I thought things could only get better.

Pulling the pile of mail toward me, I glance half-heartedly through the rest of it. I should process it while I have a few minutes, but my mind is all over the place trying to figure out who could have sent the letter, and why. Gareth might have followed me to the airport and seen me pick up Kathy. But what would be the point in sending me the letter? It has nothing to do with derailing my business. Unless he knows what an asset Kathy will be to me, and this is another lame attempt to throw me off my game. If that's the case, he's more desperate than I realized. Maybe it's not only about the crippling debt he's facing—maybe he's deriving a certain amount of personal satisfaction in bringing me down for rejecting his advances years ago.

I shove aside the stack of mail and jump to my feet, slipping the letter into my purse. I can't stand the uncertainty any longer. I have to know if this is Gareth's doing. And the only way I'll know for sure is to have it out with him. I'm confident I'll be able to tell from his reaction, when I show him the letter, if he's lying. He had me almost convinced the last time I confronted him that he wasn't involved in what's been going on, but, with Ryder out of the picture, I don't see who else would have anything to gain by sending it.

On the drive across town, I shoot Kathy a quick text to let her know I'll be home later than planned. It's already after five and I'm sure to be caught up in rush-hour traffic at this point. But I need to get to the bottom of this.

I know I need to be careful how I broach the subject with

Gareth. If he didn't have anything to do with the letter, he's going to think I still have a beef with him about the Huss Integrity contract. He'll be on his guard, wondering if I'm planning some type of revenge move—a lawsuit, perhaps.

He keeps me waiting for twenty minutes when I arrive. I'm not sure if it's legitimate, or if he's sending me a message that he's in control.

"Sorry to keep you waiting," he says, running a hand through his hair in a distracted manner as he leads me into his office.

"Problems?" I arch a brow at him.

"Always," he replies with an exaggerated groan. "But enough about my lousy day." He eyes me warily. "If you're here to chew me up again about the Huss deal, like I told you, I have no idea who sent me a copy of your contract, and, for the record, I didn't know it was your company. It was under your married name."

"Regardless, it was an underhanded move." I cross my legs and scrutinize him. "Is that the way you normally conduct business?"

He shifts uncomfortably under my accusing gaze. "It's not illegal. We all know it's cutthroat out there. I do what I have to do to survive, same as anyone else."

"Sounds like you're desperate," I throw at him, casually.

His eyes glisten at the underlying insinuation. "What's that supposed to mean?"

Pinning a sympathetic smile on my lips, I lean toward him and lower my voice. "I know you're in trouble with the IRS. And when people are at the end of their rope, they do things they wouldn't ordinarily do."

A slow flush creeps up his neck merging with the stubble on his weak chin. When he speaks, there's a distinct wobble in his voice, "I don't know where you're getting your information, but you're mistaken."

I study my nails for a heartbeat, making him sweat. "Maybe you have a disgruntled ex-employee of your own. Your gambling addiction is public knowledge."

Gareth glares at me. "What do you want, Lauren? The contract with Huss Integrity is a done deal. I'm not backing out now."

"That's not why I'm here," I reply. "Let's say, for old time's sake, I'm willing to believe your version about how you got a hold of my bid. Maybe I can even buy into your story about not knowing it was my company, but the part that really bothers me is that you're still trying to pull the rug out from under me." I reach into my purse and toss the letter onto the desk. "With cheap shots like this."

With an air of apprehension, he picks the letter up and frowns as he reads it. "Who's Kathy? What's this supposed to mean?"

"Kathy Welker, my childhood nanny. Don't pretend you didn't know she was here. I picked her up from the airport yesterday."

Gareth rubs the back of his neck. "How would I know that? What's she doing here anyway?"

"We hired her to look after our son while I get my company off the ground. Seems like an arrangement you might be interested in sabotaging seeing as you're doing your level best to make sure my business fails."

Gareth scowls. "I swear to you, I had no idea Kathy was here." He passes the letter back to me. "I didn't write this. You're talking to the wrong person."

"Then who should I be talking to?" I ask, sharpening my tone a notch. "Ryder's dead and you're the only other person who could benefit from hurting my relationship with Kathy."

"What about Margo? She's always had a screw loose. You know that."

I toss him a scathing glare. "And what would her motive be?"

"She's jealous of all your relationships," Gareth says with a dismissive grunt. "Maybe she's doing it to spite you. Or maybe she thinks you had something to do with Ryder's death and she's punishing you."

I stretch my fingers out and then curl them slowly into fists as I consider the possibility. Margo did accuse me of having a hand in Ryder's death. If she and Ryder plotted together to harass me, she might not be willing to quit now that he's dead. Still, it doesn't explain how she knew Kathy was coming into town.

"I need you to call Margo and ask her if she sent that letter," I say, pinning an implacable gaze on Gareth. "It's the least you can do to make up for ripping me off over a multi-million-dollar contract."

Gareth twists his lips. "I suppose I could mention it to her."

"Get busy then," I say.

"What, now?" he asks, his pale eyes widening behind his glasses.

"Yes, now. Put her on speaker. Tell her I was here and accused you of sending the letter before storming out."

Gareth fidgets in his seat, looking uncomfortable. "You want me to lie to her?"

I let out a snort. "Why not? You excel at it."

I stare at him until he fishes his phone from his pocket and pulls up his contacts.

"Margo!" he says, when she answers. "You're never gonna believe who was just here."

I wasn't wrong about Gareth's performance abilities. He's quite the consummate professional when it comes to smooth talking—which makes me question once again his story about receiving an anonymous emailed copy of my bid.

"I don't know," Margo responds, her voice even wearier than before.

"Lauren—Lauren Bishop," Gareth replies. "She showed up ranting about me sending her a letter about her nanny."

"Her nanny? Why would you do that?"

"Exactly! That's what I said."

"What was in the letter?" Margo asks.

Gareth catches my eye and I give a subtle nod.

"*Kathy's not who you think she is.* Whatever that's supposed to mean," he adds with a snort.

"I don't get it," Margo says, her voice pitching up. She sounds genuinely confused. But maybe she's a better actress than I'm giving her credit for.

"I don't either," Gareth says. "I guess Kathy's here looking after Lauren's son for a few weeks. She came into town yesterday—the same day Lauren got the letter. She already accused me of stealing business from her, now she's convinced herself I sent her an anonymous letter. It ... wasn't you by chance, was it?"

"I don't know anything about it." There's a pause and then Margo continues, "Although she did call me up out of the blue and wanted to get together. Maybe she's going to accuse me of sending it too."

Gareth raises his brows at me.

I give a vehement shake of my head.

"I doubt it," Gareth says breezily. "She's just mad at me because she lost out on a deal we both bid on."

"I don't know what she wants with me," Margo grumbles. "I only agreed to meet her because I think she had something to do with Ryder's death. With the money she's rolling in, she could have hired someone to take him out. I told the police as much. Hopefully, they investigate her thoroughly."

My stomach knots as her rant continues. I knew Margo was pushing a narrative about me being involved in Ryder's death, but I underestimated how far she was willing to take it.

"I'm sure the police are crawling all over her," Gareth reassures her, throwing an amused glance my way. "Look, I gotta run. Let me know how your lunch date goes."

He hangs up and slips his phone into his jacket pocket. "There you have it. She didn't write the letter. And neither did I." He pushes his chair out and gets to his feet. "It's been a long day. I'd ask you to join me for dinner, but I know you have *a delightful family* waiting for you at home."

I exit his office with the barbed tone of his comment ringing in my ears. *A delightful family.* Does it bother him that I have a family and he doesn't? He might have had a thing for me years ago, but is he still interested in me? I shake my head free of the thought. If anything, Gareth's more likely consumed with jealousy over my inheritance. By the sound of it, he could use a hefty influx of funds.

It's after seven by the time I finally get home. I pull into the garage and hurry inside the house, eager to catch up on Lucas's day. The aroma of a home-cooked meal wafts my way, and I let out a satisfied sigh as I toss my purse on the kitchen counter. It's so comforting to have Kathy here, a temporary reprieve from my frantic rooting around in the refrigerator every night.

"Where are the boys?" I ask as Kathy turns from the sink to greet me. Her brow furrows. "Jack's upstairs reading Lucas a story. We ate already." Her eyes dart back to the platter soaking in the sink.

"Did everything go all right today?" I ask, taking stock of her strained expression as she swipes a strand of gray hair from her face.

She throws a harried glance in the direction of the door before whispering, "I didn't want to mention anything to Jack before I had a chance to talk to you about it first."

My stomach twists like a rag being wrung out. My thoughts immediately go to the letter I received. Did someone send her one too? "What's wrong?" I ask.

She wipes her hands on a dishtowel. "I took Lucas to the park today after school. We'd only been there a few minutes when I noticed someone was watching him—an older man."

My breath freezes on the roof of my mouth. "Are you ... sure he was watching Lucas?"

She gives a terse nod. "He didn't take his eyes off him."

My pulse thuds in my eardrums. "What did this man look like?"

"I couldn't see his face. He was standing off to one side, partly obscured behind a tree." She hesitates, pinching her bottom lip between her teeth. "Didn't you say the man who gave Lucas the straw was wearing a gray coat?"

21

Kathy and I stare at one another for what seems like an eternity before I manage to choke out an answer. "Yes. It was gray."

"He had a walking stick too. Do you think it could be him?" Kathy asks in a hushed tone.

"I don't know. It's possible." I scrunch my eyes shut in a vain attempt to block the terrifying thought from my mind. Just when I thought the stalking was over, at last, someone is sending me a clear signal that I've got it all wrong. Whoever this person is, they're brazen. They weren't even trying to hide the fact that they were watching my son in a public place. Maybe they wanted Kathy to notice—knowing she'd go back and tell me. They want me to cower in fear.

"At least it means you're no longer the primary person of interest in the investigation into Ryder's death," Kathy remarks, sinking down in a chair at the kitchen table.

My eyes shoot open. I hadn't even considered that angle, but she's right. This man could be Ryder's murderer. I need to call Detective Hernandez right away and fill him in on everything that's happened since Ryder's death, but I can't let Kathy overhear the conversation. If she catches me talking about the letter, she'll be petrified. The person who wrote it might be the same man who was watching Lucas at the park, which means he's watching her as well, and knows she's working for me. My stomach heaves with anxiety at the thought of the potential danger my family is in, and the danger I've inadvertently exposed Kathy to by allowing her to come here to Austin.

"We should call the police," she says, peering anxiously at me. "I thought about calling from the park, but I wanted to wait until I checked with you first to make sure he matched the description of the man who talked to Lucas."

I nod and fumble with my phone, my thoughts spiraling in several directions as I dial Detective Hernandez's number. I can't exactly tell Kathy to make herself scarce—besides, Detective Hernandez will want to talk to her. Once she goes to bed, I'll call him back and tell him about the fake courier letter.

"Lauren, what can I do for you?" His tone is decidedly cool. Clearly, he hasn't eliminated me from his shortlist of suspects. Maybe what I have to tell him will be enough to change his mind on the matter. I put him on speaker and place the phone on the kitchen table. "Detective, I'm here with my nanny, Kathy Welker. She took my son, Lucas, to Sunny Highland Park near our house this afternoon. Shortly after they arrived, she noticed an older man with a walking stick standing along the perimeter watching Lucas. He caught her attention because he was wearing the same outfit as the man who talked to my son in our driveway—a gray overcoat." I take a quick breath and continue before Detective Hernandez has a chance to respond. "He could be Ryder's murderer. Maybe Ryder wasn't his real target, he just got in the way. This man's still stalking me and my family.

You need to assign us police protection. What if he abducts my son? I don't—"

"Hold up!" Detective Hernandez cuts in. "Let me talk to your nanny for a moment. Ms. Welker, can you tell me when you first noticed this man watching Lucas at the park?"

Kathy leans toward the phone. I signal to her that it isn't necessary, and she nods in understanding before sinking back in her chair. "We had only been there about five or ten minutes when I spotted him. He wasn't there when we first arrived, or I would have noticed. I'm very observant of my surroundings, especially when I have children in my care."

"How do you know he was watching Lucas specifically?" Detective Hernandez asks. "Maybe he was just walking by and stopped to watch the children playing."

"I did think he might have been a grandparent or something, at first, but I noticed that none of the mothers were conversing with him. It made me uncomfortable—my nannying instincts kicking in, I guess. That's when I moved back out of his line of sight and pretended to be reading on my phone. All the while, I kept an eye on him. He positioned himself behind a tree, but he kept his head tilted toward Lucas. He would watch him like a hawk until he saw me glance up. Every time I put my head back down, he turned his attention back to Lucas. Finally, I got up and stared right at him. He immediately started walking away from the park in the direction of the street."

"How old would you estimate this man was?" Detective Hernandez asks.

Kathy frowns in concentration. "It's hard to say really. I couldn't see him all that well from that distance. I assumed he was older judging by the clothes he was wearing and the fact that he was carrying a walking stick."

"Did he make any attempt to approach Lucas or talk to

him?"

"Oh no," Kathy replies. "I wouldn't have let that happen. Lucas never even saw him—he was too busy playing with the other kids. I did ask a couple of the other moms afterward if they knew who the man was, but no one seemed to have any idea. One woman said she'd talked to him briefly and he sounded confused. She was worried about him—she thought he might have had dementia or something. She was considering calling the authorities if he was still at the park when she was leaving. Of course he'd already taken off by then. I suspect the whole dementia thing might have been an act."

"All right, that gives me enough to go on for now," Detective Hernandez says. "I'll find out if there are any cameras at that park."

"And if there aren't, what are you going to do about finding him, and protecting us?" I prod.

"We'll put out an all-points bulletin. If we spot him loitering around your home or business, we'll pick him up and bring him in for questioning," Detective Hernandez answers. "In the meantime, I'll assign a patrol car to your neighborhood. Keep your son close at all times. Call me immediately if anything else transpires."

I hit the *end call* button and stare at the phone, still trying to come to terms with everything that's happened.

"Are you okay, pumpkin?" Kathy asks.

I swallow the sob stuck halfway up my throat. "I'm worried about Lucas."

"At least the police are taking this seriously now," Kathy says.

"They'd better be." I let out a heavy sigh and rub my hand over my brow. "I'm so sorry I dragged you into this, Kathy."

She flaps a hand at me. "Nonsense! I offered to come and help. And I'm happy to stay and see this through. I just want this man to be caught so you're not forced to endure this nightmare any longer."

I give her a grateful nod. "We should get some sleep. Maybe tomorrow will bring some better news."

We get to our feet, and she wraps me up in her arms and squeezes me tightly. "Try not to worry. The police will get to the bottom of it, sooner or later. They always do."

I go upstairs with her words ringing in my ears. It's a common enough sentiment, but it's not real life. There are no guarantees the truth will come out in the end. Not in this life, anyway. I know that better than anyone.

When I peek in on Lucas, Jack's gentle snores greet me. He's fallen asleep next to our son, the Dr. Seuss book they were reading lying open on the pillow next to them. Gingerly, I pull the door closed and tiptoe my way down the hall to our bedroom. Once inside, I waste no time calling Detective Hernandez back. "It's Lauren McElroy again. I couldn't say anything earlier with Kathy in the room, but there's something else I need to report. I got an anonymous letter in a dummied-up courier envelope at work today. The message said, *Kathy's not who you think she is.* Which is nonsense, of course. I've known her since I was a baby, but I'm afraid she might be in danger now too. Whoever sent it knows she's working for me."

"Can you drop the letter off with me at the station tomorrow?" Detective Hernandez asks. "I'll need it as evidence."

"I'll bring it by on my way to work." I hesitate before adding, "Do you think it's safe to send my son to school?"

"It's the safest place for him right now," Detective Hernandez answers. "Whoever this man is, he's avoiding crowds and hanging out on the sidelines—watching for an opportunity to strike when you're alone. He's not likely to confront your son at school. If you like, I can put in a call to the school administration and bring them up to speed on the situation. That way they can alert the resource officer and any marshalls on campus."

"That would be great, thanks," I say. "I'll bring that letter by in the morning."

I hang up and make my way back down to Lucas's room to check on Jack. I stretch out my hand to wake him, but he looks too comfortable. I'll probably end up tossing and turning all night and only keep him awake anyway. After backing away from the bed, I pad softly out of the room once more. Gabriel told me to keep him apprised of any developments. But it's too late to update him tonight, I'll give him a call in the morning.

Propped up in bed, I pull the letter back out of my purse and stare at the words: *Kathy's not who you think she is.* It's meant to sound ominous, but, in a way, it has a ring of truth to it. Nobody's ever really who they say they are. We're sanitized on the outside—rotting away on the inside. I'm not who Kathy thinks I am either.

I WAKE the next morning to a loud buzzing in my ear. It takes me a few seconds before it registers that it's the alarm on my phone. I turn it off, and the sound of running water fills my ears. I groan and sit up, rubbing my eyes. Jack's already in the shower getting ready for work. I must have fallen into a deep sleep at some point. The last thing I remember is sifting through childhood memories of Kathy, wondering what it is that I don't know about her.

Jack comes out of the bathroom securing a towel around

his waist. "You should have woken me up when you came to bed," he says in a reproving tone.

"You looked too comfortable to move," I reply, attempting a grin before abandoning any pretense that we're jousting in fun.

He grunts. "I wasn't. I have a crick in my neck now." He yanks open a drawer and lifts out underwear and a T-shirt. "Did Kathy seem all right when you came home last night?" he asks as he pulls on his boxers. "She seemed stressed to me. I hope this whole situation isn't proving too much for her."

"She was ... definitely stressed out," I agree. "We both were."

Jack pauses, his T-shirt halfway over his head and swivels to face me. "What's wrong? Did something else happen?"

I pat the edge of the bed, and he walks over with an exaggerated air of reluctance and sits down next to me. Up close I see purplish stains under his eyes. I know this whole situation is taxing him to his limits.

"Kathy took Lucas to the park after school yesterday," I say. "She noticed an older man with a walking stick watching him. He was wearing a gray overcoat." I pause and blow out a breath. "It matches the description Lucas gave us of the man in our driveway."

Jack's eyes flicker in confusion as he rubs his freshly shaved jaw. "So ... it wasn't Ryder. That means ..." He trails off, frowning down at his bare feet.

"Yes, Jack. It means that someone else is still harassing me—us. I don't know if they were in on it with Ryder, or if they hired Ryder, or what's going on. All I can tell you is that it's not over, yet."

"Did you call Detective Hernandez?" Jack asks, turning to

look at me.

"Yes, he's assigned a patrol car to our street. He's put out a description of the guy, and if they see him loitering anywhere near us, they'll pick him up. He's going to alert the school too, but he thinks Lucas will be safe there."

Jack gets to his feet and begins pacing across the floor, smoothing a hand over his damp hair as he talks. "What does he know about keeping our son safe from this lunatic? We have no idea who we're dealing with. This man's obviously targeting our son—he was in our driveway, and now you're telling me he was at the park, watching him. We need to pull Lucas out of school until this pervert's been caught. Kathy's here, she can take care of him, and make sure he keeps up with his schoolwork. I'm going to call again on the security cameras today—see if I can speed things up. Lucas will be much safer at home, especially with a cop car patrolling the neighborhood."

"I ... don't know, Jack. He loves school and he's making new friends. He might think he's being punished for talking to a stranger if we pull him out—we'll have to give him a reason for why we're doing it. And who knows how long this will go on for. What if they don't catch the guy? We can't keep Lucas housebound indefinitely."

Jack scrubs a hand over his face. "I'm not saying it has to be long term. I just think for the next few days it makes sense to keep him close to home. He couldn't be in better hands than Kathy's. Why don't you call the school and get his work sheets so he has something to do?"

I chew on my lip as he waits for my response. I'm not sure why I'm holding out on the idea. Fear has crept under my skin—and it's not just fear of scarecrows anymore. I'm losing faith in everyone.

What if Kathy's not who I think she is?

22

The following morning I find myself back at the police station turning in the evidence suggesting my stalker is alive and well. Detective Hernandez studies the letter for a moment or two, tapping his stubby fingers on the desk. "They know your nanny's name which implies it was someone who's familiar with your history. On the other hand, if they've been following her and your son around, they could easily have overheard it."

I nod. He's not telling me anything I haven't already considered. I thought about it long and hard last night. The most logical suspect I keep coming back to is Gareth—he knows my history, he knows Kathy, and he has a beef with me, as it turns out. But if I give Detective Hernandez his name, it's going to open another can of worms. I can't be sure how much Gareth knows about what happened that night. He hinted that he knows the truth about my *murky past*. What exactly does he mean? Did he find out that I spent my senior year in central Texas, instead of in San Antonio with my parents? At the very least, he knows enough about my past drug use to tarnish my business reputation here in Austin. But that goes both ways. I have a bad feeling he might have found out something much worse. What if Ryder told him everything?

Detective Hernandez leans back in his chair and scrutinizes me with his perceptive eyes. "You look like you might have someone in mind."

I glance out the window, wrestling with my decision. This could be my only chance to get to the bottom of what's really going on. Maybe I'm way off base, but I can't shake the notion that Gareth's the mastermind behind what's happening. He certainly has the brains to pull it off. And his debts are motivation enough to shut me down before I can take a piece of his business out from under him. He knows I can make things happen in this market if I'm given a fair shake. And that should scare him.

The other more compelling reason to give Detective Hernandez Gareth's name, is to take the heat off me. Margo's claim that I was threatening Ryder means I'm still a strong contender—perhaps the only contender—on the suspect list.

"There is one name that comes to mind," I say, looking Detective Hernandez square in the eye. "Gareth Looney. He was a mutual acquaintance of Ryder's and mine. He's the CEO of Summit Solutions. It's a software company located here in Austin, a direct competitor of mine. I know for a fact Gareth wasn't too happy when I opened my business in the area."

Detective Hernandez raises his brows. "What are you implying?"

"I think he's trying to sabotage my business. My office building was broken into recently. Nothing was taken so the police put it down to vandalism. But a short time later, I found out a major client I had worked hard to secure had gone with Summit Solutions at the last minute. Their CEO showed me a copy of Gareth's offer. It was almost identical to mine other than the fact that he had undercut my price by a considerable amount. In retrospect, I'm convinced that's what the break-in was all about. The contract was lying on my desk in my office. It would have been easy enough to make a copy."

"Did you catch the intruder on your security cameras?"

I shake my head. "They weren't operational at the time. We'd just moved into the building, and we were doing some remodeling."

"Did you raise the matter with Mr. Looney?" Detective Hernandez asks.

I twist my lips as I recall the encounter. "I drove clear across town to Summit Solutions and confronted him about it as soon as I discovered he was the CEO. It was the first time I'd seen him in eighteen years. He denied it of course. He told me if I couldn't stand the heat, I shouldn't have come back to town—which sounds like a veiled threat to me."

Detective Hernandez scratches his jaw. "What motive would he have to steal your business?"

"It was a particularly large contract," I explain. "Gareth Looney is in substantial debt—gambling debt from what I understand—and he's also in trouble with the IRS."

Detective Hernandez throws me a sharp look. I can tell I've finally piqued his interest. At the end of the day, cops are only ever interested in motive and evidence. I've given him the motive; it's his job now to find the evidence. "So you think he might be waging a harassment campaign against you to run you out of town?"

"It's a possibility. He might even have hired Ryder to do some of his dirty work for him. If he's hurting for money, it's possible Ryder never got paid and threatened to expose Gareth. That would have been reason enough to kill him. It might also explain why Gareth left his body on my front steps. By turning the spotlight on me, he could further jeopardize my business." I grimace. "Let's face it, being a suspect in a freakish Halloween murder doesn't exactly tie in with the professional image I'm trying to project at Capitol Technologies."

Detective Hernandez jots down a few notes and then gets to his feet. "I have a court hearing I need to get to, but I'll have a talk with this Gareth Looney. If there's anything to suggest he might be involved, I'll put a tail on him."

As I'm driving away from the station, I can't help questioning the wisdom of what I've done. I might just have stirred up a hornet's nest. But it's too late to undo it. Detective Hernandez has heard enough to make him want to take a closer look at Gareth Looney. And that's a good thing. Even if it turns out he's not behind the harassment, I don't regret making him sweat a little. Stealing the Huss Integrity contract out from under me was a low blow, unethical if not illegal.

I head to Gabriel's office next. I left a message for him earlier this morning and his assistant texted me back and asked me to stop by. I'm hoping he'll agree with Kathy's reasoning that the latest developments mean I'm not high on the suspect list of Ryder's killers anymore. By the time I reach Gabriel's office, I've convinced myself that Gareth killed Ryder, and that he was the brains behind the harassment, if not the perpetrator. What is it he always used to say to me? *Just think, you could have had me instead. Brains over brawn.*

A finger of dread works its way across my shoulders. Gareth always was a slick operator. I imagine he knows how to avoid getting his hands dirty. He might have contacted Ryder when he heard I was coming back to Austin and hatched a plan. By teaming up, they could both get what they wanted—Gareth could make sure I wouldn't move in on his territory, and Ryder would finally get to punish me for leaving him. The only question in my mind is where Margo comes into it? That's what I intend to find out when we meet for lunch. I'm beginning to think all three of them might have been in cahoots.

"LAUREN, it's good to see you again," Gabriel says, getting to his feet and reaching across his desk to squeeze my hand. "What's been going on?"

"Lots," I answer, as I set my purse down and take a seat opposite him. "My nanny spotted someone watching Lucas at the park yesterday—an older man. He matched the description of the man who confronted our son in our driveway. It could have been Ryder's killer."

Gabriel lets out a low whistle as he leans back in his chair and tents his fingers in front of him. "This is an interesting development. Not one that gives you any peace of mind, I imagine, but it does take the focus off you as a suspect."

"I was hoping you'd say that. Speaking of peace of mind, I received another unsettling letter." I pull up the photo I took of the message warning me about Kathy and pass my phone across to him.

He studies it, his expression unreadable. "Is there a possibility the note has merit?" he asks, handing me back my phone.

I shake my head. "Definitely not. Kathy was my childhood nanny. She practically raised me. My parents trusted her with my life. They often left me alone with her when they went on business trips."

Gabriel reaches for my file and flips it open. "I assume you've turned the letter over to the police?"

"Yes. Detective Hernandez agrees that it seems to suggest someone who knows Kathy is behind it, but it's impossible to say for sure. He asked me if I had any idea who it might be. I gave him the name of a former mutual acquaintance of mine and Ryder's who has a competitive software business here in Austin. I happen to know he's struggling with substantial debt and in trouble with the IRS. He stole a contract out from under me, right before my customer was ready to sign—made them an offer with terms almost identical to mine, and then undercut my price."

"Could it have been a coincidence?" Gabriel inquires.

"I don't believe so. There was a break-in at my office a few weeks ago. I think Gareth might have orchestrated it to get a hold of a copy of my offer."

Gabriel arches a brow. "You said he owes the IRS money. How did you come by that information?"

"I asked my extremely resourceful PA to do some digging, and she talked to a bookkeeper who used to work for Gareth. She claims he fired her because she questioned him about the anomalies she uncovered."

Gabriel strokes his jaw. "He sounds like a promising lead. But, from now on, you need to let the police do their job. I don't want you contacting Gareth Looney again until he's been eliminated as a suspect. Can we agree on that?"

I give a curt nod. "Absolutely." I have no intention of going anywhere near Gareth again. He's going to be livid when Detective Hernandez shows up on his doorstep. Gabriel might not be too happy with me either if he knew I was planning to meet up with another mutual acquaintance on Friday—the mother of Ryder's child, no less—who might very well have some involvement in the situation too. I'm hoping to leverage whatever influence I have left with her to find out how much she knows about what's going on.

And whether all of this was her idea to begin with.

23

I've been anticipating my lunch date with Margo with a growing mixture of curiosity and foreboding. I'm desperate to know if she's involved, but I'm afraid things might take an even darker turn if she realizes I suspect her. Friday morning stretches out before me like a never-ending road coiling into an uncharted horizon. No matter how many times I check my phone, time seems to have come to a standstill. I keep going over in my mind the best way to handle the conversation. One option is to go in guns blazing and accuse her of aiding and abetting Ryder in his campaign of harassment. Or I could start out by offering my condolences, acknowledge her as the mother of Ryder's child, show some interest in her relationship with Ryder. Perhaps I should stick to the middle ground—make believe it's purely a lunch date for old time's sake and wait to see what she divulges, if anything. I squirm in my chair at the thought of revisiting my high school memories with Margo —things I'm ashamed of now. Not to mention the fact that I'm pretty sure she secretly hated me back then. She hung out with me, but only because she coveted my life and everything about it, including Ryder. Did she have any idea that he laughed about her behind her back? Scoffed at her efforts to dress like me, mocked her embarrassing attempts to flirt with him when she thought I wasn't paying attention?

At 11:45 a.m. I pull into the Sycamore Mall parking lot and look for a spot to park near the main entrance. My stomach flutters with nerves as I switch off the engine and gear myself up to meet with Margo. I wonder if I'll even recognize her after all the work she's had done. I pull down the visor and study my face in the mirror. Kathy always told me I had the bone structure of a model. But there are creases in my skin that I haven't seen before, and mottled half-moons below my eyes that attest to sleepless nights. Still, it will only serve to bolster my case if I look like the victim of harassment. After applying a swish of lip gloss, I lock my car and make my way to The Red Snapper restaurant located just inside the mall. I'm a few minutes early but I want to have the advantage of watching Margo arrive.

Seated at a booth facing the entrance to the restaurant, I place my phone on the table in front of me. I'm not entirely sure she won't message me and back out at the last minute. Or simply not show up at all. Minutes later, she breezes up to the hostess station. I raise my hand and wiggle my fingers to get her attention. She nods, unsmiling, and says something to the hostess before walking toward me. Dressed in jeans and a tight sweater, it's hard not to notice the exaggerated results of plastic surgery on her thin frame as she sashays her way between the tables. She slides into the seat opposite and smirks in greeting. "I wasn't sure you'd be here."

"I wasn't sure you'd come either," I reply, schooling my tone to neutral. We're already playing a game of cat and mouse, neither one of us wanting to be the first to declare ourselves friend or foe. I force a smile, trying not to stare too hard at Margo's swollen lips. She's bought into the bee stung lip-mania, but it doesn't quite go with her fine features. I can't help wondering if Ryder's drug money funded her extensive sculpting campaign.

A waitress swoops in with a pen and a pad, breaking up our uncomfortable standoff. "Can I get you ladies started with something to drink?"

"An iced tea for me, please," I say.

"I'll take a Diet Coke," Margo adds. "And we're ready to order. I'm short on time. I'll have the Asian Chicken salad."

"Um, a Greek salad for me," I add, reading off the first item I spot on the menu.

The waitress walks off, and Margo and I stare in charged silence at one another.

"You look different—you look ... well," I say, searching for the right word.

"You didn't bring your son," she responds. I can tell by the questioning tilt of her brows that she's asking for an explanation.

"He's in school." I offer her an apologetic shrug. "Perhaps we can get the boys together another time. This way we get a chance to reconnect first."

"Who said I was interested in reconnecting?" Margo asks coldly.

I give a self-conscious laugh. "You're the one who suggested meeting for lunch."

She places her elbows on the table and interlaces her taloned fingers as she leans toward me, a menacing glint in her eyes. "Wanna know why I told you to bring your son?" She flicks her tongue over her painful-looking lips and whispers, "I wanted to see if he looked like him."

I blink, struggling to absorb the significance of her words. "You mean ... Ryder?"

She throws back her head and lets out a harsh laugh at my shocked expression. "Yes, Ryder. Who else would I be talking about? He cheated on me when we were together. I just don't know for sure who it was with, yet."

I swallow, holding up my hands in protest. "Margo, I haven't seen Ryder since our junior year. I'm happily married to Jack, the father of my son, Lucas." I hesitate and then add more softly, "For what it's worth, I'm sorry for your loss, and for your son's loss."

Margo gives a disgusted shake of her head but before she can say anything, the waitress returns with our orders. "Anything else I can get you, ladies?"

I flash her a quick smile. "No, everything looks great, thanks."

She lays some extra napkins down and flounces off to another table.

"You don't seriously expect me to believe you're anything but ecstatic now that Ryder's dead," Margo says, spearing a piece of chicken on the end of her fork with a little more force than necessary.

"Of course I'm not happy he's dead. I'm especially not happy that he was found murdered on my front steps. I want to know who did it just as much as you do." I set down my fork and gaze earnestly at her. "Margo, I know you talked to Detective Hernandez. Was Ryder stalking me? I need you to tell me the truth."

Margo chews her food for a moment and then dabs her lips on her napkin carefully before answering. "Ryder and I weren't together anymore. We barely communicated, only what was essential relating to our son. I have no idea what he did in his free time to *entertain* himself."

Ignoring the jab, I press on. "Did you two ever talk about me when you were together?"

Margo gives an irritated toss of her head. "He never wanted to talk about you. He never forgave you for dumping him when he got locked up. But he didn't keep pictures of you in his wallet or anything like that—believe me, I checked—so he wasn't pining for you if that's what you're getting at."

I gulp down a mouthful of iced tea. "Someone's been harassing me, Margo. Someone who knows about my scarecrow phobia, someone who knew me back in high school. They know who Kathy is too. They've been sending me sinister messages and leaving scarecrows on my property. If it wasn't Ryder, who was it?"

Margo glowers across the table at me. "What exactly are you insinuating? Believe me, I've got better things to do with my life than harass you."

"What about Gareth Looney? Do you think it could have been him?" I take a bite of my salad, my eyes never leaving her face.

She arches a heavily powdered brow at me. "What makes you think Gareth's behind it?"

"He stole a major contract from me recently. Somehow, he got his hands on a copy of my proposal and undercut my pricing. Word is that he has a serious gambling addiction and he's in trouble with the IRS. Which means he has a vested interest in making sure my company fails at the outset, now that we're competitors in the same territory."

Margo shrugs, avoiding my gaze. "I haven't spoken to him in years. I can't imagine him wasting his time on you either." She averts her eyes, picking at her fingernail. "What I want to know is whether you were involved in Ryder's death."

I push a piece of cucumber around on my plate, taking a moment to recover my composure. "I can't believe you're asking me that, Margo. Do you really think I could do something that heinous?"

She reaches for her Diet Coke, anger glimmering in her eyes. "People with money always get what they want. All you have to do is click your fingers and shell out the cash. It's not as if you'd have to get your hands dirty if you wanted to get rid of him."

I push my plate to one side, my appetite gone. "I had nothing to do with Ryder's death and I have no idea who did. That's why I need you to tell me the truth about Gareth. Think about it for a minute. What if he hired Ryder to harass me? Maybe Gareth didn't pay up and he and Ryder got into an argument about it, and Gareth killed him. It would make sense that Gareth would leave Ryder's body on my front steps to try and pin the murder on me. Kill two birds with one stone, so to speak. The bad publicity could destroy my business. Please, Margo. I need you to be honest with me. What's really going on? Are you in on it?"

Margo narrows her eyes. "Whatever you think Gareth did, I'm not involved."

She shoves her plate to one side and digs in her purse for her wallet.

I reach across the table and lay a hand on her arm. "Let me get this. I appreciate you meeting with me. I know it can't have been easy, under the circumstances. And I'm sorry I had to ask such difficult questions. But try and look at it from my perspective. Someone who knows me very well has been terrorizing me with scarecrows. If it wasn't Ryder, you can hardly blame me for wondering if you or Gareth were involved."

Margo zips up her purse and throws it over her shoulder.

"Don't bother contacting me again. I have nothing more to say to you." She clamps her lips together, gets to her feet, and strides away from the table.

I take a moment to compose myself before leaving some cash on the table and darting out of the restaurant after her. I keep my distance in the mall parking lot, making sure she doesn't spot me. I'm not sure what I'm hoping to accomplish, but I get the feeling she was lying to me about her involvement in all of this. Maybe I can follow her and find out where she lives. My heart pounds as I watch her get into a tired-looking blue Volkswagen Jetta a couple of aisles over. She's talking on her phone, oblivious to her surroundings, so I take the opportunity to jog across to my car and climb in. While I wait for her to drive away, I retrieve a baseball cap from the passenger side pocket and don my sunglasses. The minute I see her pull out, I put my car in drive and follow at a discreet distance.

If I can find out where she lives, maybe I can reach out to her again and appeal to her to retract her statement to Detective Hernandez. After simmering down, she might come to realize I'm right to suspect Gareth. Surely, she must want to locate Ryder's killer as much as I do. The traffic is growing heavier, and it takes all of my concentration not to lose Margo as she weaves and bobs her way toward the city center. She doesn't appear to be heading home just yet. At the next light, she turns left and drives into an underground parking lot. I let another car go in front of me and then tail her inside. She swerves into a parking spot, and I drive past her and pull into another space nearby. The minute she disappears into the stairwell, I jump out and go after her. Wherever she's headed, she's in an awful hurry to get there. I dash down the stairs two at a time and out onto the street, looking in both directions to see where she's disappeared to.

To my relief, I spot her jogging across the street, her over-sized purse slapping at her side.

I follow at a distance, dread gnawing in the pit of my stomach when I recognize where we are.

Moments later, my worst fears are realized when she pushes open the door to the building that houses Summit Solutions.

24

I pivot away from the shocking sight and stare blankly at the mannequins in the store front window in front of me. My mind is rocketing a million miles a minute as I try to piece it all together. I can't believe how smoothly Margo was able to lie to me all through lunch. My suspicion that she was conspiring with Gareth was spot on. They've both been feeding me a pack of lies. Gareth likely hired Ryder to help run me out of town, and Margo was in on the scheme from the outset.

No doubt Ryder was only too eager to avail of the opportunity to satisfy his own personal vendetta against me, while being paid for the privilege. And of course Margo, ever the salivating groupie, played whatever role she was told to play —anything to please Ryder. Maybe it was even a pitiable attempt to win him back. No doubt, she also got a certain level of personal satisfaction from helping to take me down, she probably felt it was justified. Her jealousy was on full display at lunch with her dig about my inheritance—something about only having to *click my fingers and shell out the cash.* Just like Gareth's snide comment about *not having a trust fund to launch him.* What she and Gareth don't seem to understand is that I've invested every penny of my money into outfitting my business, and I still have a mortgage on the office building. I need this venture to succeed, or I risk losing everything.

I glance at the time on my phone and suck in a sharp breath. I need to get back to the office and start making some follow-up calls on the proposals I sent out earlier in the week. It's imperative I get some more contracts signed before word begins to leak out that my ex was found murdered on my front steps. I've no doubt Margo and Gareth are already scheming on how to spread the juicy news. One call to the local papers is bound to stir up renewed interest in another titillating chapter in my story. I can see the headlines now: *Capitol Technologies CEO questioned in scarecrow slaying. Death follows software heiress wherever she goes. Freakish Halloween murder leaves locals shaken.*

Back in the parking lot, I unlock my car and climb in, wondering if I should confront Gareth about the visit Margo paid him. If he knows I've caught him red-handed, he'll have to offer up an explanation. I'm lost in my thoughts when a call from Detective Hernandez comes in. "Detective," I say, attempting to sound upbeat. "Good news, I hope."

"I paid Gareth Looney a visit this morning," he replies, getting straight to the point in his usual manner. "He wasn't too happy to see me. I questioned him about the break-in, and how he got his hands on a copy of your contract. He stuck to his story that it was emailed to him anonymously."

"Did you ask him if he knew that Ryder was harassing me?"

"He claims he didn't know anything about it," Detective

Hernandez replies. "But he didn't hide the fact that it wouldn't have bothered him if it had driven you out of town either."

"Charming," I say through gritted teeth. "Is there any way you can find out if he was in contact with Ryder recently— can you get a hold of his phone records or something?"

"That would require a warrant. And we'd need probable cause to convince a judge to grant one."

I let out a frustrated breath. "How much more probable cause do you need? Gareth Looney's in major debt, he stole a lucrative contract out from under me after he mysteriously got a hold of my offer, not to mention the fact that he admitted to you it wouldn't bother him if I left town. Doesn't any of that sound in the least bit suspicious to you?"

"It doesn't matter how it sounds. I can tell you straight out no judge would issue a warrant based on what you went over to me."

I rub a hand over my forehead. "Okay, how about this. I just had lunch with Margo. She insisted she hasn't talked to Gareth in years and that she had nothing to do with the harassment. I knew by her evasive manner she was lying about something so I followed her after she left the restaurant. Want to know where she went? Directly to Summit Solutions."

Detective Hernandez is silent for a moment and then asks, "Did you follow her inside?"

"No. I had to get back to work. In any case, I didn't want to let her know I'd seen her. She must have been going to warn Gareth about my suspicions. It's obvious she's in on the whole thing with him."

"Are you saying you think she might have helped Gareth murder Ryder?"

"No! Not the murder. She was obsessed with Ryder. If Gareth killed him, he kept it from her. She accused me of being behind it—made a petty stab about me having plenty of money to hire a hitman."

"All right," Detective Hernandez concedes with a sigh. "Leave it with me and I'll see what I can find out. If nothing else, you've given me enough to warrant looking into the nature of their relationship a little further."

"Please let me know as soon as you find out anything," I urge him. "I'm pulling up at my office right now so if you can't reach me on my cell, you can leave a message with my PA, Maria."

I manage to get back inside my office without being accosted by employees needing to talk to me about pressing software-related issues. Maria is still at lunch, so I pour myself a coffee and take a few minutes to compose myself before tackling the first of my follow-up calls with potential clients. The receptionist at AGA Precision Tooling takes my name and I wait on hold for several minutes before she comes back on the line, "I'm sorry, but Mr. Barlow has looked over your proposal and, regretfully, we're not interested at this time."

My stomach drops. "But I ... I don't understand. I just received an email from him yesterday stating that he was very interested in my proposal and would like to set up a time to meet with me to discuss the details."

There's an awkward pause before the receptionist clears her throat. "I apologize for the mix up. I'm simply relaying the message I was given. You're welcome to email Mr. Barlow if you have any further questions. Have a wonderful day, Mrs. McElroy."

I open my mouth to protest but she's hung up. I drop my

head into my hands, a sick feeling creeping over me. Did Gareth have something to do with this too? *No!* It's not possible. Hacking into a computer for financial gain is a felony. He wouldn't risk it. I'm being paranoid. It's just an unhappy coincidence. This kind of thing happens all the time in business. I need to pull myself together and move on to the next call.

Minutes later, I set my phone down on the desk in front of me and squeeze my shaking hands together in my lap. All three of the companies which were extremely enthusiastic about my proposal only a day or two ago have declined to sign a contract. I even managed to speak to one of the owners directly. He was apologetic but vague about his decision to go with another company *better suited* to their needs. It's exactly the kind of generic letdown that tells me there's something nefarious going on behind the scenes.

I know Gareth had a hand in this. I just can't figure out how he pulled it off. It's not like he could have sent out a mass email to every business in Austin disparaging me. And he doesn't know which companies I've sent proposals to. No one does, other than myself and the people who received them—and Maria, of course. I let that thought sit for a moment, hating myself for even considering the remote possibility that Maria would betray me. But, as unlikely as I deem it to be, it's an angle I need to consider. Despite how much I've come to depend on her in the span of a few short weeks, the reality is, I don't know Maria particularly well. I couldn't believe my luck when she accepted the position with my company. She stood head and shoulders above the other candidates, with her extensive experience and impressive qualifications. As a matter of fact, she was overly qualified—having worked for a major corporation in New York for the past several years—and I told her that straight up. I pay her well, but I wasn't able to match her previous salary. I hadn't questioned her reasoning when she said the flexible hours and location were perfect—she'd wanted to buy a place in Austin close to her elderly mother. Did she lie to me about that? Does she have some connection to Gareth? Could he be blackmailing her to turn over sensitive company information?

A knock on the door makes me jump almost out of my skin. I try to rearrange my face into a neutral expression when Maria sticks her head around the door. "How was your lunch date with Margo?"

"It was civil," I respond with a tight smile. I shuffle a few papers on my desk to indicate that I'm in the middle of something important. "I'm working on some new proposals this afternoon," I tell her. "If anyone calls, please take a message for me."

"Absolutely." She arches a brow. "Any word on the remaining proposals you sent out earlier this week?"

"Not yet," I answer, suppressing a shiver as I reach for my phone.

Maria nods. "I'll leave you to it, Boss. Let me know if you need anything."

The minute the door closes behind her, I suck in a jagged breath. My heart feels like it's on fire. Why did she ask about the proposals? Is she waiting to hear they pulled out so she can report back to Gareth? I can't deny the possibility, slim as it is, that Maria is moonlighting for Summit Solutions—stealing company secrets and sending over copies of my proposals. She could even have staged the break-in to cover her tracks.

I drum my fingers on my desk as I formulate a plan. I need to get into Maria's computer and find out what, if anything, she's been forwarding to Gareth. Proposals? Potential clients? Financials? I have no idea to what extent she might have exposed me, or the damage that's already been done. I even told Detective Hernandez to leave a message with her if he couldn't reach me. I shut my eyes and groan. Am I crazy suspecting everyone around me of being involved in a conspiracy to bring me down? Regardless, I need to know if there's a mole in my camp. As soon as Maria leaves for the day, I'll log into her computer. Realistically, I know I'm unlikely to find any concrete answers. If she is colluding with Gareth, it would be foolish to use her work computer to communicate with him. She's far too clever for that.

Reluctantly, I message Jack and Kathy and let them know I'm going to be tied up at work until late again this evening. Jack won't be happy about it, but we're barely speaking anyway. For the remainder of the afternoon I focus my efforts on drawing up a new proposal for a national client requesting a bid for a mobile application which promises to be almost as lucrative as the Huss Integrity deal.

One-by-one, my engineers shut down their computers for the day and check out. Maria is the last to leave. I remain working in my office for another thirty minutes after she checks out in case she comes waltzing back in for some reason or another, before going to the main door and locking it from the inside. I do a quick walk-through of the cubicles and offices to make sure I haven't missed anyone, and then seat myself at Maria's workspace. I have password access to all of my employees' computers, but to date I haven't needed to use it. After opening up Maria's Gmail account I click on the *sent folder* and do a quick search for Gareth's name and then for Summit Solutions. Neither search brings up any results. I try Margo's name next but come up empty-handed again.

Frustrated, I begin scrolling through the sent emails looking for anything unusual. I've gone through several hundred when my fingers freeze on the keyboard. I stare in disbelief at the recipient at the top of the screen.

Kathy_Welker58@gmail.com

25

My muscles lock as shock sets in. For a long moment I wrestle with emotions too deep to fathom. Even though I know without a shadow of a doubt that it's Kathy's email, I pull up my phone to double check my contacts anyway. The evidence is staring me in the face, but I still can't seem to grasp what I'm seeing. How does Maria know Kathy? I've never introduced them. Surrendering to whatever unwelcome revelation awaits, I click open the email and begin reading.

HI KATHY,

This is Maria Cassidy, Lauren's PA. I hope you don't think I'm being too forward, but I wanted to talk to you about Lauren. To cut to the chase, I'm extremely worried about her. All the stress she's been under lately is beginning to affect her work, to the extent that we're losing out on major contracts. I've been managing the situation as best I can in light of her frequent absences, but the engineers are starting to talk. Perhaps we could meet for lunch some day this week and discuss how we can help

her. You know her best. I'm available Thursday, or Friday. My
number is (737) 212-5564. Please don't mention to her that I
reached out to you.

   Kind regards,
   Maria

I FORCE myself to inhale and exhale a couple of times before
evaluating the contents. On the face of it, the email seems
harmless enough—compassionate even. But it irks me no
end that Maria went behind my back and contacted Kathy.
I've always considered Maria's initiative to be an asset. But
this time she's gone too far—crossed a line into my personal
life. She makes it sound as though I'm losing control of my
business and she needs to step in and save it. My engineers
know nothing about the status of potential contracts in the
pipeline—I haven't told them, at any rate. So far, I've been
feeding them enough work to keep them busy.

   Bristling, I reread the email, and this time a more
ominous thought occurs to me. Maria sent this two days ago.
How did she know we were losing out on contracts before I
did? Other than Huss Integrity, I hadn't heard back from the
other companies I presented proposals to until today. A cold
sweat breaks out along the back of my neck. Where is Maria
getting her information? And what underlying motive does
she have for wanting to meet up with Kathy?

   The other thing that's bothering me is that Kathy never
mentioned anything to me about Maria emailing her. It
feels disloyal. She should have asked me how I felt about my
PA wanting to take her out for lunch to discuss my inade-
quacies as a CEO. I would have told her straight out that it's
inappropriate.

   I cringe at the thought of my nanny and my PA

discussing my mental and emotional state behind my back —planning an intervention of sorts. Biting back my frustration, I power down Maria's computer and make my way back to my office to gather up my things. I have to confront Kathy about this tonight. I've known her long enough to believe she has only my best interests at heart, but she has no idea what Maria's true motives are. Nor do I, for that matter. If she's passing on information to Gareth, then it's dangerous to let her anywhere near my family or friends, not to mention my business. Come to think of it, she might have sent me the fake courier letter about Kathy. That would explain why no one saw it being delivered.

I grit my teeth as I peel out of the parking lot and head for home. I have to make it a priority to find out exactly who Maria is and what she's really doing at Capitol Technologies.

Jack looks miffed when I finally arrive home shortly after eight o'clock. "Lucas is asleep," he reports in a clipped tone. "He kept asking for you."

I give a shamefaced sigh. "I'm sorry, I was working on some important proposals."

Jack leans back against the kitchen counter and crosses his arms. It feels like a gesture of superiority, indicating that he's taking the high ground by being there for our son. "So important that you couldn't even call Lucas to say good night?"

"I said I'm sorry. I've had a very stressful day."

"Tell me about it," Jack grumbles.

I throw him a worried look. "What does that mean?"

"You tell me. I didn't want any more secrets, remember?"

I frown, wondering where he's going with this. My heartbeat picks up pace. Slipping my purse strap off my shoulder, I place it on the counter, trying to figure out how best to respond without letting this devolve into another silent deadlock. None of the secrets I've kept from Jack were good ones. What has he found out now?

He starts to say something but breaks off when Kathy shuffles into the kitchen in her slippers clutching an over-sized mug. "Lauren! You're home! I left a plate of lasagna in the warming drawer for you, and there's some Caesar salad in the fridge."

"My favorite," I say, forcing some enthusiasm into my voice.

She walks over to the sink and rinses the remnants of hot chocolate from her mug before placing it upside down in the dishwasher. "By the way, your not-so-neighborly neighbor, Stanley Hogg, called me over today to complain about Lucas riding his bike too close to his driveway." She presses her lips into a disapproving line. "I took the liberty of reminding him that he had no jurisdiction beyond the asphalt he personally paid for."

I give her a weak smile. "I'm sure you did a fine job putting him in his place."

"I think I'll watch a little television before I go to bed," she says, darting an uncertain glance between me and Jack. The tension emanating from us is hard to miss and she beats a hasty retreat to the family room leaving us alone once more.

"Where were we?" I ask with a brittle laugh.

Jack reaches into his back pocket and tosses a brochure on the counter.

"What's this?" I arch a questioning brow, resisting the urge to reach for it, as if that will somehow make whatever it is that's got Jack all worked up go away.

"It's a prospectus for a school," he replies in an overly calm tone.

I throw him a confused look. Is he looking into private schools for Lucas? Does he think our son will be safer there? I pick the leaflet up and read the name on the front. *Mountain View Girls Academy.*

"Look familiar?" Jack asks, anger seething between his lips.

My throat tightens as I begin reading the blurb on the cover:

AN EXPERIENTIAL LEARNING encounter teaching respect and responsibility. Is your child struggling with self-destructive or dangerous behaviors? Our vocational training and mentoring program will help transition your daughter to a successful life through unconditional support and guidance.

I GRIMACE INWARDLY at the irony of it. The brochure is new, but they haven't bothered to update the verbiage all these years later. "Where did you get this?" I ask, failing miserably to eliminate the tremor in my voice.

"Someone mailed it to my office," Jack answers. "Evidently, they wanted to make sure you didn't have a chance to dispose of it before I saw it."

I inhale a silent breath, wondering how much he knows.

"Go ahead. Open it up, Lauren," he says through gritted teeth. "There's more."

I'm tempted to toss the brochure in the trash and tell him to forget about it—deny knowing anything about it—but he has a strange look on his face that unsettles me.

Reluctantly, I open it and immediately spot the message scrawled across the double page in black magic marker: *Did Lauren tell you she was valedictorian of her class?*

Closing my eyes briefly, I try to collect my flailing thoughts. I didn't want Jack to find out, and certainly not like this, but someone has overruled me. "Why don't we ... sit down and talk about this?" I suggest, folding into a chair at the table. I feel sick inside, but there's no way out of this conversation now.

Jack remains standing, arms still firmly folded across his chest. "Go ahead. I'm listening." His face is a sealed mask of emotion. Any sympathy he had for my abandonment issues in my early years, has been eaten away by my lies.

"My parents gave me no choice," I begin. "They pulled me out of school and sent me to *Mountain High* for my senior year. It was an intervention to save my life, as far as they were concerned. I was addicted to some dangerous drugs. I'm ashamed of the decisions I made back then. But I can't reverse them. One of them is that I have to live with the stigma of knowing I graduated from a reform school for troubled teens."

A nerve twitches in Jack's cheek. "And what about me? How do I factor into this? I have to live with the reality that you lied to me about this as well. You told me you graduated from Bowman Rock High."

"And now you know the truth," I reply in a defeated tone.

Jack gives a sad shake of his head. "I don't know what to say, Lauren. I don't get why you hid all this from me. It makes me wonder what this whole thing with Ryder is really about. The revelations just keep coming. I'm afraid I'm going to find out something even worse about you."

"Like what?" I ask, my insides churning.

"I don't know. I'm afraid to think about it. Drugs, death threats, reform school—what's next? I'm beginning to understand why you're considered a person of interest in

Ryder's murder." He straightens up and stomps across to the door. "I'm going to bed," he grunts on his way out.

"Jack! Wait! Please!" I call after him.

My heart sinks as I listen to the sound of his footsteps retreating up the stairs. I drop my head on my arms, tears trickling out of the corners of my eyes as I crumple the brochure in my fist. How could he say something so cruel? And yet, he's so close to the truth. I can't take much more of this. I'm weighed down with secrets from the past which make me look guilty of things I had no involvement in. I'm more convinced than ever that Gareth was behind Ryder's murder, and he's trying to pin it on me. He threatened to reveal the details of my *murky past* as he put it. Who else would have sent the brochure to Jack? Somehow, Gareth has found out where I spent my senior year, which makes me wonder what else he's found out about. Is this the worst dirt he has on me, or did Ryder tell him everything?

"Lauren!" Kathy exclaims, shuffling back into the room. "What's the matter?" She pulls up a chair next to me and lays a hand on my shoulder. "Did you and Jack have a fight? I know he was worried about you working late in the office by yourself, what with the break-in and all."

I fish a tissue out of my pocket and blow my nose. It's easier to let Kathy believe that's what we were fighting about. I don't want to get sidetracked now that I have her alone. It's the perfect opportunity to bring up the email. "Jack was disappointed I didn't make it home to say good night to Lucas," I sniffle. "He made me feel like I was a bad mother for not calling."

Kathy squeezes my shoulder. "You're a great mother, and Lucas will be fine for one night. I think Jack's more worried about you than anything. He says you're not sleeping properly." She throws a glance at the warming drawer and sighs.

"You didn't eat yet, did you? You're not going to be able to sleep if you go to bed on an empty stomach. Let me fix you a plate."

"Thanks Kathy, but I'm not hungry anymore." I get to my feet and pour myself a glass of water before returning to the table. "Can I ask you something? Did you go to lunch with Maria Cassidy this week?"

Kathy blinks rapidly, clearly taken aback. She fidgets with the button on her sleeve. "What makes you say that?"

"Maria mentioned she was going to ask you, that's all," I say casually.

Kathy furrows her brow. "Oh, I didn't realize she'd told you."

I throw her a bemused look. "You are allowed to go to lunch, you know."

She gives me a sheepish grin. "I wasn't going to mention it, because she specifically asked me not to. We went yesterday, actually, to The Fisherman's Grill. Have you been there?"

I give a quick nod and smile, then wait for her to continue.

"Well, anyway, Maria's been worried about you, and she wanted to get my take on things." Kathy hesitates and rubs a finger over her knuckles. "I admit I was concerned when she told me things weren't going so well at work. She thought we should get together and brainstorm about how we could both make your life a little easier. You know you were right about her. She's a smart, young lady and very thoughtful."

"Yes, she is," I reply mechanically. "So, what else did you two talk about?"

Kathy shifts in her seat looking uncomfortable. "She wanted to know about your childhood, and of course we talked some about Ryder and how much I disapproved of him." She leans over and pats my arm. "Don't worry, I didn't tell her anything you hadn't already told her. And then of course she asked about the plane crash. She'd seen it on the news. She was curious ... like people are."

I frown down at a crumb on the table. *Looky-loos.* I wonder if Maria sought me out after reading about me in the paper. Maybe she's one of those people who thrive on being part of the drama—inserting themselves into situations for the thrill of it. Or maybe it's something more sinister. Either way, I'm beginning to suspect she had an ulterior motive for taking the job that didn't involve her elderly mother.

"Please don't take this the wrong way, Kathy," I say. "I know you're worried about me, but I'd rather keep my work and home life separate. Maria meant well, but I'm going to have a word with her too—it wasn't appropriate for her to call you up and discuss me and my business behind my back."

A pained expression comes over Kathy's face. "I'm sorry if I upset you. Believe me, pumpkin, I was only trying to help."

I force myself to smile at her. "I know. And I appreciate it."

She gets to her feet and hugs me with her usual warmth, but I don't reciprocate in kind. We smile awkwardly at each other, and I watch her exit the kitchen on her way to bed. Do I believe her? I'm not sure who I believe anymore. Or who I trust. Why did someone send me that note about Kathy? Were they trying to warn me, or simply mess with me?

I frown, thinking back to the brochure Jack received in the mail. Other than my parents, Kathy was the only one who knew I was shipped off to Mountain High my senior year—unexpectedly leaving her out of a job. An uneasy feeling creeps up my spine. It's odd that she called Jack up, unprompted, and offered to help with Lucas. My mind flips back to the day I picked Kathy up at the airport. I was early but she was already standing out at the curb with her bag. What if she didn't fly in from Lubbock that morning at all.

What if she's been in Austin all along?

26

I remain seated at the kitchen table staring out the window into the dark, long after everyone else has gone to bed. Weariness is seeping through my bones and my mind is beginning to play tricks on me. For a fleeting moment, I think I can make out the lumpy shape of a scarecrow at the bottom of the garden. I tense, breath on pause, but then the wind picks up and I realize it's only a bush swaying back and forth. Frustrated with myself, I get to my feet and yank the plantation shutters on the kitchen window closed. I feel like I'm going crazy, which is why I've resisted calling Detective Hernandez to tell him about the brochure, and the email exchange between my PA and my nanny.

At this point, I've suspected everyone around me, except for Jack. But he has his own suspicions about me, so it's not as though I have him in my camp either. The only person I can count on unconditionally is my six-year-old son—not that he can help with the mess I'm in. Tears stab my eyes like salted toothpicks. I don't know who to trust or who to turn to. It wouldn't shock me to discover that Gareth, Margo, and Ryder had teamed up to run me out of town, but it would be disturbing to find out that Maria was in on it with them from the beginning.

And then there's the letter warning me about Kathy. By far the biggest stab in the back would be to find out that she's somehow embroiled in everything that's been going on. Of course, that makes no sense. I've known her my entire life. I know everything there is to know about her. She went to school in West Lake Hills. She dropped out of Texas State University when she got pregnant. She gave her baby up for adoption and started nannying because she loves kids. I know my parents trusted her with my life. Kathy was there for me in all those moments when my own parents couldn't be. Cleaning and bandaging scraped knees, drying my tears, encouraging my hopes and dreams. She was so proud of me when I graduated college with a Bachelor of Science in software engineering. I think she always regretted dropping out herself. In my heart of hearts I don't believe Kathy has any part in this campaign of terror. She's as much a victim as I am, targeted in that courier letter, not because of who she is, but because of her association with me.

It's almost 2:30 a.m. by the time I make my way upstairs and crawl into bed. Jack is snoring lightly but it's enough of a rhythm to keep me awake. My brain stubbornly remains in overdrive, trying to analyze the possible motives of everyone who might be behind the harassment, and Ryder's murder—I have to believe the two are connected. I've already ruled out Kathy—she's an illogical choice. And how could Maria possibly be involved? It's not like Gareth could have planted her as an operative in my firm. I went through an executive PA service to find her. Still, there is the question of why someone with her qualifications would be willing to take a reduction in salary working for a startup.

Maybe I should call her previous employer back and ask a few more questions. Something about it's not right. My eyes flutter open and closed, my thoughts degenerating into scrambled code as sleep claims me.

Jack's alarm wakes me the following morning. I turn over and immediately fall back asleep until my own alarm goes off thirty minutes later. I groan as I crawl out of bed, my limbs heavy as lead. After a quick shower, I make my way downstairs to the kitchen. Jack has left for work early—no doubt to avoid me. Kathy gives me an uncertain smile as she pours a glass of orange juice for Lucas who's spooning Cheerios into his mouth with the speed of a package handler on an assembly line. He glances up at me. "Are you taking me to school today?"

"Don't talk with your mouth full, Lucas, and yes, I'll take you."

He reaches for his glass and takes a gulp of juice. "Are you sick, Mommy? Daddy said you weren't feeling well."

Kathy ducks away from the table with her hands full of dishes and busies herself at the sink.

"I'm fine, sweetie," I lie, catching Kathy's look of concern. "Just a little tired."

Fifteen minutes later, I'm walking Lucas out to the car when I spot Stanley Hogg hovering by his front door. I nod a greeting in his direction and then do a second take. Did he just beckon me over? I quickly dismiss the thought and turn my attention to buckling Lucas into the car. As I slam the back door closed, I chance another glance across the street. I wasn't imagining it. He's waving me over—angrily this time. Irritated, I open the passenger door and toss my purse on the seat. I'd better go over and listen to him gripe some more about Lucas riding his bike. Maybe I can smooth things over before things escalate. It's not like we're obnoxious neighbors who leave our trash can out after collection day. Our only crime, unless you count the dead body on our steps, is having a child—apparently, a pet peeve of his. "Wait here," I say to Lucas. "I need to talk to Mr. Hogg for a moment."

I stride across the street and hurry up the pathway to his front door, grimacing at the irony of it. It's the first time I've actually been invited onto his property.

"Good morning, Stanley," I say briskly, bracing myself for a lecture on residential biking etiquette. "We're about to leave for school. Did you need help with something?"

He throws a furtive glance up and down the street, and then nudges his door open a few more inches. Wetting his lips, he whispers, "He came back."

His voice is so low I'm not sure I catch what he says at first. "I'm sorry, can you repeat that?"

He scratches his scalp in an agitated fashion. "He came back," he rasps.

I don't know who he's referring to, but it's clear he's upset about it. Does he mean Detective Hernandez returned to ask him a few more questions? That would definitely rattle his cage. "I'm sorry, Stanley, I don't follow. Who are you talking about?"

His eyes zigzag around me. I can't help but notice that he's sweating profusely, and a flicker of sympathy goes through me. It's obviously difficult for him to make the effort to speak with me. Whatever is bothering him, it must be important. He stammers for a moment or two before getting the words out, "Him ...the man who left the body on your steps."

My heart slugs against my chest. "Are you sure it was him?"

He nods, pulls a handkerchief from his pocket and mops his forehead. "I recognized his limp."

I press my hands to my sides trying to quell the panic rising up inside me. "When? Where did you see him?"

"Yesterday, at noon," Stanley wheezes. "He walked past your house a couple of times, stared at it for the longest time like he was memorizing everything about it."

I rack my brains trying to assemble my thoughts. Jack and I were at work, Lucas was in school, and Kathy was having lunch with Maria. Did he know we were all out of the house at the time? I bite my lip, studying Stanley's face. Do I believe him? What motive would he have for making it up? He doesn't seem like the type to enjoy the attention.

"Thanks for letting me know," I say in a scratchy voice. "I need to call Detective Hernandez right away and fill him in. Do you think you could give him a description of the man?"

Stanley's eyes widen and he shakes his head. "I couldn't see his face from here."

He moves to push the door closed but I wedge my foot against it. "Please! Can you tell me anything else at all? What was he wearing?"

"A long coat." He casts a nervous glance behind him, as if expecting his wife to call out for him at any minute.

My eyes drift past his shoulder to the shadowy outline of the dead tree in the corner of the foyer. A lone umbrella dangles from the end of a branch. I swallow hard. I remember seeing a long coat hanging on it a few days ago.

The door shuts before I can ask Stanley what color of coat the man was wearing. But I think I know the answer.

The drive to Dawson Elementary seems to last an eternity with Lucas chattering nonstop and me making intermittent sounds to appear interested. I can't stop thinking about the coat that was hanging in Stanley Hogg's foyer.

And how he's always the one who opportunely spots my stalker. I shake my head to clear my increasingly erratic thoughts. It's ridiculous to imagine that my eccentric neighbor, who never leaves his house and doesn't know me from Adam, could be my stalker. Besides, he doesn't have a limp. The minute I drop Lucas off at school, I dial Detective Hernandez's number. He barks a greeting and asks how he can help in a tone that doesn't sound particularly helpful.

"My neighbor, Stanley Hogg, observed a man walking by my house yesterday," I begin.

"Hardly an uncommon sight," Detective Hernandez comments.

"Except that he stopped at my house and stared at it for a long time. I'm sure it was the same man Kathy spotted at the park. He was wearing an overcoat and walked with a limp."

Detective Hernandez sighs heavily on the other end of the line. "We talked to Mr. Hogg already. To put it kindly, he lives in his own world. It's possible he saw the man, but it's equally possible he imagined him, or he's making the whole incident up."

"But you can't dismiss it without following up on it," I protest. "It's a potential lead."

"I'll talk to the patrol officer assigned to your area—see if he noticed anything," Detective Hernandez says. "Did you get those cameras installed at your house yet?"

"My husband has someone lined up to come out on Tuesday."

"Good," Detective Hernandez replies. "I'll have another chat with Stanley Hogg when I get a chance."

I drive the rest of the way to Capitol Technologies mulling over the stranger in the overcoat. He's getting more brazen. Showing up at my house in broad daylight. So much for hanging out on the sidelines. Surely, he couldn't have known Kathy wouldn't be home. Unless ... Maria told him. I suck in a hard breath. It's time I had a conversation with her.

"Morning," I call to Faye as I breeze past the reception desk.

"Lauren! Wait!" she calls after me, one hand over the receiver of the phone she's holding.

I turn and frown, tapping my toe impatiently while she wraps up her conversation. She hangs up and reaches for an envelope on her desk. "This was taped to the front door when I opened up this morning," she says, passing it to me. "It's addressed to you from Maria."

"Maria? Where is she? Is she sick or something?" I ask, tamping down my frustration as I reach for the envelope. My plan was to have a heart-to-heart with her this morning —ask her outright if she has any connection to Gareth and Summit Solutions.

"I'm ... not sure," Faye replies, fidgeting with her glasses.

I fix my gaze on her and she averts her eyes, a blush creeping over her powdered cheeks. If I had to guess by the guilty look on her face, she's already held the envelope up to the light and read the contents of Maria's letter. Her evasive manner is making me more and more uneasy about what she might have discovered.

I make my way to my office nodding in passing to a couple of the engineers, trying to look put together and not like I'm crumbling into pieces.

Safely inside my office, I perch on the edge of my desk and rip open the envelope.

Dear Lauren,

I regretfully inform you that I am resigning from my position as executive assistant effective immediately for personal reasons. I realize this is unexpected and I apologize for leaving you in the lurch during this time of transition. Thank you for the opportu-

*nity to work at Capitol Technologies, and for your understanding
in this matter.*

    Sincerely,
    Maria Cassidy

I FLOP down in my chair and take several heaving breaths,
my emotions seesawing between despair and rage. I can't
believe this is happening. What am I going to do now? What
is this about? How can she just walk out without giving me
any notice—without even offering to train her replacement.
What does she mean by *personal reasons*? Is she jumping
ship because she thinks my business is going under? Or
does this have something to do with her elderly mother? I
thought we were friends. Why can't she tell me why she's
leaving?

I fight to keep my panic at bay, my suspicions about
Maria rising to the forefront once again. If she was working
with Gareth all along, she might have left with a USB of
confidential company information. My breath baulks in my
throat at the thought. Surely, she wouldn't dare. I could
prosecute her for breach of contract and data theft.

I tug a hand through my hair weighing the frightening
possibility. And then an entirely different thought occurs to
me. If she's innocent, Gareth might have found a way to get
to her. It would make sense that he'd want to eliminate my
best employee in his ongoing efforts to orchestrate the
demise of my company. I can't imagine what he could have
told her to make her leave in such a hurry. Did he threaten
her? My stomach twists as I consider the possibility that
Maria might be in danger because of me.

Gritting my teeth, I dig around in my purse for my
phone. I need to get a hold of her and make sure she's all

right. If she's betrayed my trust, I'll deal with that later. I tap the speed dial button and scrunch my eyes shut as I lean back in my chair. The phone rings twice and then a recording kicks in.

We're sorry. The number you have reached has been disconnected.

27

Goosebumps prick their way along my arms. I try Maria's number again to be sure it's really been disconnected, then hang up as soon as the recording begins. Shaking, I set down my phone and press a clenched fist to my mouth staring at the resignation letter looming up at me from my desk. Something about this isn't right. Maria would have told me to my face if she'd wanted to resign. That's the kind of take-the-bull-by-the-horns woman she is, forthright and intrepid to a fault. Not the type to tape a resignation letter to the front door and scuttle off in the early morning shadows like a coward. It makes no sense that she would disconnect her phone number either. My thoughts rapidly descend into a darker domain. What if I've put her life in danger by involving her in this situation? My stomach roils. Her only mistake was hiring on with me.

A sob slips through my lips. I can't just sit here wallowing in fear and despair. I need to track Maria down and make sure she's all right. I owe her that much. I'll figure out the rest later. With renewed resolve, I log into my employee database and scroll through multiple pages of personnel information until I locate Maria's contact info. I take a quick picture of her home address, wondering if it's legitimate. If she's there, I'll make her tell me the truth. If Gareth put her up to this, it's time she confessed. And if she's being coerced—if Gareth found some dirt on her and forced her to resign—I'll get to the bottom of it. As I reach for my purse, it occurs to me that the security camera footage might show who taped the resignation letter to the door.

Trying to exude an air of calm, I make my way through the open-plan office, where the software engineers are hard at work, to the mechanical room that houses the network video recorder. I'm still hoping the rest of my staff are unaware of the chaos I'm dealing with. This is as much a probationary period for Capitol Technologies as it is for them. Once word gets out that Maria has resigned, it's sure to fuel all kinds of rumors unless I can nip this in the bud.

My fingers shake as I retrieve the footage and play it back. I watch as each of my employees arrive in reverse order. I continue rewinding the clip until I see a lone, unfamiliar figure standing in front of the door. The timestamp is 5:34 a.m.—too early to be anyone arriving for work. I freeze the clip and focus with mounting frustration on the grainy image of someone dressed in a trench coat and holding an umbrella up to the camera to obscure their face. It's impossible to tell if it's Maria or not, although, if I had to guess, I'd say this person is several inches taller than her. I'm not even sure if it's a man or a woman. After watching the footage through again, I copy it onto a USB and slip it into my purse. I'll take it to Detective Hernandez. The police have ways of enhancing images—maybe they can even determine a person's height from an image like this. My gut tells me it's not Maria—why would she hide her face from the camera after signing her name to the letter?

I let out a surprised yelp when one of my software engineers bounds into the room. He comes to a sudden halt when he sees me, a bemused look on his face. "Hey, Lauren, didn't realize you were working in here. I just need to do an update on the servers, but I can come back another time, if you like."

"No! Go right ahead," I answer with a tight smile. "I'm all done in here."

I swiftly exit the room before he can ask me any questions about what I was doing or offer me assistance. I'm not ready to announce Maria's resignation, yet—not until I've figured out what's behind her sudden departure. On my way out, I stop at the reception desk to relay a few instructions to Faye. "I need you to manage my calls for the next hour or two. Redirect anything technical to the engineers and put the rest through to my voicemail if you can't be of any immediate assistance."

"No problem," she replies, tilting her head in a concerned manner. "Is ... everything all right with Maria?"

I let my shoulders sag, knowing I'm only delaying the inevitable. For all I know, Maria might have texted some of the staff already. "She's resigned. I'll need you to handle her mail and inbox, for now. Don't mention anything to the rest of the staff, yet. I'll know more later and then I'll make an official announcement." I push open the door and exit the lobby before she can press me for more details.

On the drive to the police station, I go over in my mind the pieces I'm going to have to pick up from the fallout of Maria's sudden departure. Before I tackle anything else, I need to get the ball rolling on finding a replacement PA. However this plays out, I don't hold out much hope of Maria coming back to work for Capitol Technologies. I send Faye a quick message asking her to start the recruitment process immediately.

Detective Hernandez's reception is growing cooler every time he sees me. I'm not sure if he still considers me a suspect in Ryder's murder, or if he thinks I'm falling apart at the seams from stress and losing the plot. Either way, the cordial air he greeted me with the first time we met has long since evaporated. "Lauren," he says, working his jaw. "What can I do for you?"

I place the USB drive on the table between us. "My PA, Maria, resigned this morning. At least I think she did. My receptionist found a resignation letter taped to the front door of my company when she arrived to open up this morning. According to the security footage—which I made you a copy of—it was placed there at 5:34 a.m." I reach into my purse and retrieve the letter. "It's pretty generic," I say pushing it across the desk to him. "No explanation given. I tried calling Maria to discuss it, but her number's been disconnected."

Detective Hernandez unfolds the letter and scans it, then gives a disinterested grunt. "It's not illegal in the state of Texas to give notice or disconnect your phone number."

I lean forward and skewer him with my gaze. "Don't you think it's just the slightest bit odd that my PA quit without warning, and her phone's been disconnected, considering everything else that's been happening to my business?" I tap my nail on the USB lying on the desk. "Take a look at this. It's the security footage of someone taping the letter to the glass entrance door. Why would they hide beneath an umbrella when it's not raining, unless it was to block their face from the camera? I don't think it was Maria who dropped the letter off at all."

Detective Hernandez flattens his lips and inserts the USB into his computer.

I study his reaction as he watches the fuzzy video footage, but his expression gives nothing away.

"That person appears to be taller than Maria," I comment.

Detective Hernandez scratches the stubble on his cheek. "How tall is she?"

"She's five-foot-seven. Can you determine a person's height from an image like that?"

He sighs and removes the USB drive before passing it back to me. "It wouldn't help. She might have got someone else to drop the letter off if she didn't want to run into her colleagues."

"Or maybe something has happened to her," I counter, raising my voice. "This vendetta against me is already affecting everyone around me, at home and at work. My son's in danger, my husband, even my nanny—doesn't it stand to reason that my PA might be in danger too?"

Detective Hernandez cracks his knuckles. "If you're concerned, I can do a welfare check on her. Do you have an address?"

I dive into my purse again and pull out my phone. "It's 5716 Acorn Grove Lane," I say, reading it off. "Can you send someone now, please?"

Detective Hernandez stands and adjusts his holster. "This is a busy precinct. We have a lot more pressing crime to deal with in Austin than following up on disgruntled employees."

"Her name's Maria, and she's not a disgruntled employ-ee," I retort. "If anything, she loved her job. This is completely out of character for her." I get to my feet and lock eyes with him. "You and I both know there's still a murderer out there. If her body turns up on my front steps tomorrow morning, it will be on your head."

I turn and stomp out of the office, hoping the look of shock on Detective Hernandez's face will be enough to spur him into action sooner rather than later. Back in my car, I plug in my seatbelt and make a split-second decision. I can't wait for the police to act. I'll drive out to Maria's house right now. The least I can do is make sure she's unharmed, even if it turns out that she's left me in the lurch for personal reasons—or worse, that she's sold me out to Gareth Looney.

I plug her address into my GPS and settle in for the forty-minute drive, my mind churning over every possible scenario. I keep oscillating between perfectly reasonable explanations for Maria's sudden resignation—her elderly mother fell and needs full-time care—to the worst outcome imaginable, that Maria's been murdered, and the evidence points to me, again. The closer I get to her house, the more I begin to second guess the wisdom of driving out here to look for her. What if the police arrive just as I'm creeping around peering in through the windows? If they find evidence of foul play, my presence is going to look suspicious—a criminal returning to the scene of the crime. I should probably call Gabriel and let him talk me out of this before I incriminate myself and end up handcuffed in the back of a squad car.

Even the fact that I went to the police station and asked Detective Hernandez to do a welfare check might look suspicious, as if I'm inserting myself into the investigation—like Jack keeps warning me not to do. I dread to think what he would say if he knew what I was up to. Sweat beads along my hairline. The alternative is to turn around and drive back to my office while I still have time. But I won't be able to live with myself if I do. I can't forget all the late nights Maria put in at my side, unpacking boxes and setting up computers—living off pizza and caffeine right alongside me. Hardly the actions of someone who's out to destroy me. My thoughts gravitate toward Gareth. He's the only person who clearly stands to benefit from toppling my business.

"Hey Siri," I say through gritted teeth, "Call Gareth Looney."

Calling Gareth Looney at work, the iOS personal assistant responds.

"I didn't expect to hear from you again," Gareth answers.

"You wouldn't be except for the fact that my PA, Maria, resigned this morning," I say. "She's gone missing."

"And I can help you how, exactly?" he asks haughtily.

"I'm done playing games, Gareth. I know you're doing everything in your power to crush my business. Did you put Maria up to this? Have you offered her some outrageous signing bonus to go to work for you, or what?"

"You're really out of your mind, you know that," Gareth growls. "I've never met your PA and I'm not currently hiring, so if she does come knocking on my door, she'll be wasting her time."

"You're the only one who stands to benefit from crushing my business," I snap back. "I know it, and the police know it, and believe me, they're keeping close tabs on you. I have footage of someone other than Maria taping her resignation letter to the foyer door of my firm. So if you're involved in any way, you're not going to get away with it, Gareth."

"And you won't get away with threatening me like you did Ryder," he replies with a derisive snort. "I'm recording this conversation by the way."

I grimace as I turn on my blinker and make a right turn onto the street where Maria lives. "Well, record this, Gareth.

We're not just competitors anymore, we're gladiators in a fight to the death," I fire at him, before hanging up.

I clench the steering wheel tightly, instantly regretting my foolish outburst. What was I thinking? Would that count as a threat in a court of law? Shaking, I slow to a crawl, checking each consecutive house number until I come to Maria's place.

It's not hard to spot. The front door is smashed in and there's a cop car parked outside.

28

The thundering of fear in my chest crescendos as I put the car in park and turn off the ignition. For several agonizing minutes, I sit frozen behind the wheel watching Maria's front door, waiting for a cop to appear. I desperately want to know what they've found inside, but at the same time I want nothing more than to drive away before I hear something that's going to make my world come crashing down again. I wrap my arms around the steering wheel and rest my chin on it, wondering how I'm going to break it to the rest of the staff if something's happened to Maria.

Minutes later, I'm startled out of my reverie by the arrival of two more cop cars. The knot in my stomach tightens. If they've called for backup, it's a clear indication they've discovered something untoward in the house. Panic rises up inside me as they draw closer. Do I look suspicious sitting here outside Maria's house? I quickly dismiss the thought. I wasn't trespassing, and I haven't contaminated a potential crime scene. Besides, I'm the one who called Detective Hernandez and asked him to do a welfare check in the first place. I have every right to be here. More important, I should be here as Maria's employer, and friend.

The squad cars pull up behind me and I watch in my rearview mirror as Detective Hernandez climbs out of the first vehicle. He confers briefly with the officer who parked behind him, and then makes his way over to me. "Didn't expect to see you here," he says drily. "I told you I would request a welfare check."

"And, apparently, they've found something suspicious," I respond, more sharply than I intend. The fact is, I'm trying not to burst into tears. "Did they ... find her?"

Detective Hernandez purses his lips. "Wait in your car and I'll be back out to brief you in a few minutes." Without further explanation, he strides up to the front door and disappears inside the house. I rub my cold hands together, unable to shake the queasy feeling creeping from the pit of my stomach all the way up my throat. My imagination is landing on one horrible scenario after another. They must have found something inside—blood perhaps, or a weapon? Why else would the cop conducting the welfare check have called Detective Hernandez to the scene? I wonder if he found the door smashed in, or if he had to kick it in to gain entry? Something sinister has happened to Maria—that much I'm sure of.

Out of the blue, a late model Honda Accord comes screeching around the corner. It's not Maria's car, but I hold my breath anyway, hoping she'll jump out and demand to know what's happening at her house. A moment later, the vehicle wheels into Maria's driveway. A balding man with a gray mustache and an angry scowl steps out. He makes a beeline for the front door, leaning over to inspect the damage before stomping into the house. Curious, I roll down my window, hoping to overhear something, but I can't make out his muffled exchange with the officers. Moments later, he comes walking back out gesticulating wildly, accompanied by a somber-looking Detective Hernandez. "When's the last time you saw your tenant?" the detective asks.

"A few days ago. I asked her if she'd received a letter from my lawyer. She's been nothing but trouble since the day she moved in," the bald man grumbles. "She hasn't paid rent in months. I told her I was starting eviction proceedings so of course she ups and disappears in the middle of the night. I'll never see my money at this rate."

I slowly let out the breath I was holding. By the sound of things, they didn't find a body, or a blood-splattered murder scene. I'm surprised to learn Maria was only renting the house. I thought she said she'd bought a place of her own when she moved back to Austin to be near her elderly mother. Even more shocking is the news that she hadn't been paying her rent. She mightn't have been making as much as she did in New York, but I was paying her a decent salary by Austin standards—enough to live off comfortably. None of this is making any sense. She never hinted to me she was having money problems. I climb out of my car and approach the landlord to introduce myself. "Hi, I'm Lauren McElroy, Maria's boss," I say, stretching out a hand.

"Chris Beringer," he grunts in response, keeping his own hands stuffed in his pockets. His beady eyes run over my tailored suit. "Are you here to take care of her back rent? She told me her boss hadn't paid her in weeks."

My mouth falls open, my composure momentarily thrown off balance. "I can assure you Maria was paid bi-monthly, the same as everyone else in my firm." I throw Detective Hernandez a mortified look. I hope he doesn't believe for one minute that I was cheating my employees.

Not that his opinion of me can sink much lower. I know I can't be held liable by the landlord for Maria's back rent, but I'm irate to learn she lied about me withholding her wages. I pride myself on taking care of my employees and I'd pull money out of savings to make payroll if I had to before I stiffed them.

I'm not sure how much to divulge about what's going on to Maria's landlord. Gabriel would probably advise me to say nothing so, for once, I keep my mouth shut, and leave Detective Hernandez to do his job.

"I can only imagine what a new front door's going to cost," Chris grumbles. "I'm gonna need her stuff out of here by Friday. I've got to line up my handyman to hang a new door so I can get this place leased to someone else ASAP. The mortgage won't pay itself."

"I'm afraid that won't be possible until we complete our investigation," Detective Hernandez clarifies.

Chris gives a disgusted shake of his head as he walks off, already talking on his phone to someone about the repairs.

I turn to Detective Hernandez. "Was the front door smashed in when the first officer got here?"

He gives a curt nod. "Apparently so. It looks like there could have been a struggle of some kind in the family room. A few items were knocked over. Hard to say if anything was taken—nothing obvious at any rate."

"Nothing obvious, how about Maria?" I exclaim. "If there are signs of a struggle, she might have been taken some-where against her will. By the sound of things, she was in some kind of trouble. Maybe she's running from people she owed money to."

"Based on what her landlord had to say, she might have skipped town knowing eviction was imminent. She could have staged the break-in to cover her tracks," Detective

Hernandez says. "But we're dusting the place for fingerprints just in case. In the meantime, if you hear from her, please get in touch with us right away." He tilts his chin toward the landlord, standing off to one side. "That goes for you too."

Chris Beringer throws his hands up in the air and walks back to his Honda, still muttering angrily into the phone.

I return to my car and drive back to my office in a daze, still trying to assimilate what I've learned. The fact that Maria lied about not being paid in weeks stings but, at the same time, if she was in some kind of financial trouble, I'm not going to take it personally—not until I know for sure she's safe, at least. She might have been stretched thin financially trying to help her elderly mother for all I know. She was aware I was struggling to secure contracts, so maybe she didn't feel comfortable asking me for an advance. Of course, there's also the very real possibility that Maria's not who I thought she was at all.

The third possibility is the most disturbing. That the man who killed Ryder has struck again.

29

Faye looks up at me expectantly the minute I walk back into the office. "How did it go?" she asks in an urgent whisper. "Did you find Maria?"

I shake my head, trying to decide how much to reveal to her. Probably best to say as little as possible now that Maria's disappearance is under investigation. "Not yet. She wasn't at home. I asked the police to do a welfare check. They said they'll look into it and keep me updated."

"Really?" Faye's eyes widen. "I can't say I blame you for notifying the police. Maria's always so straight to the point and blunt about everything. I would have expected her to have walked right into your office and told you to your face if she was quitting—and then to up and disappear like that. Very odd."

I give a distracted nod. "Keep it to yourself for now," I remind her, before hurrying off down the hall in the direction of my office. I don't want to air my suspicions—not until I know exactly what I'm dealing with. It's hard to believe Maria would bail on me like she did, but I have yet to answer the question swirling around inside my head—whether or not I knew the real Maria.

Safely ensconced in my office, I brew some coffee and sit down at my desk, resigned to another long night tackling my mounting workload. For now, at least, there's nothing more I can do to locate Maria. I need to trust Detective Hernandez to get to the bottom of her disappearance, sooner rather than later, for everyone's sake. I pull my keyboard toward me and begin working my way through my emails. Without Maria to screen them beforehand, I'm left to wade through everything from unwanted spam to legitimate queries from prospective clients. I'm about two-thirds of the way through deleting, filing, and processing everything in my inbox when I come across an email from an unidentified sender. The subject line reads: *Urgent Employee Information.* I click on it, expecting a tedious update to Worker's Comp. benefits or something along those lines. My throat constricts as I begin to read.

YOU'RE PATHETIC, *Lauren,*

Turns out you don't know your employees very well at all. Maria was a surprise, wasn't she? And there's more coming. Don't say I didn't warn you. Watch out for Kathy. She's a dark horse, that one. Took me a while to figure it out.

Talk soon,

Your favorite scarecrow

MY STOMACH BEGINS to churn its contents in a roiling sea of acid. I scan through the email again searching for clues; familiar phrases, misspellings—anything that might point to who wrote it. I'm guessing it's the same person who sent the letter warning me about Kathy. It's frightening to think they know so much about the people in my life. I pick at the skin around my nails as I consider this latest message. *Watch out for Kathy.* Should I be scared of my childhood nanny, or is she in danger from the person who sent this? Fear ricochets up and down my spine. What if Kathy's gone missing too? Without a second's hesitation, I whip out my phone and shoot her a quick text:

I'll be working late again tonight. Jack will be home to take care of Lucas.

I tap my foot impatiently on the floor as I wait for a reply. To my relief, she responds almost immediately:

I'll leave you a plate of food in the warming drawer. Just heading out to visit Jan for a bit before I pick Lucas up from school.

I sink my head back against the chair and exhale in relief. I was imagining rushing home to discover Kathy had disappeared too. I realize I'm being irrational, but I can't help it. My brain feels like it's on fire. The last few days have been unbearably stressful, exhausting, and terrifying, and I'm teetering dangerously close to the edge of a trifecta collapse. Gritting my teeth, I force my attention back to my work. My phone pings with an incoming text and I glance at it to see Jack's name on the screen.

Digi-view Security had a cancellation. They want to install the cameras today at 1:30 p.m. instead of Tuesday. Can you be there? I have a client meeting.

I groan and rub my hands over my face. I really need to be here this afternoon to keep everything running smoothly in Maria's absence. But I'm also desperate to get those cameras installed at the house. I check the time on my iPhone—almost twelve-thirty. I can make it if I leave in the next thirty minutes.

Sure. Email me the paperwork, I message Jack back.

I finish cleaning out my inbox and then head out to the foyer to let Faye know I'll be gone for a couple of hours.

She throws me a worried look. "Is this about Maria?"

"No. I just have a few errands to take care of," I say with a vague wave of my hand. It's not exactly a crime to put in security cameras at my house but I'd rather not have my employees speculating on why I'm having them installed. The story about a body being found on my steps hasn't broken, yet, and I'm hoping to keep it that way. Detective Hernandez has assured us they won't release an address to the press, especially in an ongoing investigation, but it wouldn't be hard for some bloodhound reporter interested in the story to do a little digging. Stanley Hogg may not be too keen in talking to the press, but some of my other neighbors might prove more than willing if it earned them a spot on the evening news.

I reach my house five minutes before the security firm shows up. Two men dressed in matching navy blue golf shirts with the Digi-view logo embroidered on their left breast pockets step out of the van. For the briefest of moments I question if this is a set up by my stalker. Maybe they aren't really employees of the security firm at all. My throat goes dry as panic moves in like a biting wind. Why did they suddenly reschedule our appointment? Did Jack even ask? I take a few quick, calming breaths to clear my head and then muster my courage and introduce myself as the homeowner. To my relief, the two men get to work at once installing the cameras, apparently with no hidden agenda to kill me and drive off with my body in their van. After supplying them with water bottles, I leave the front door ajar and go back inside the house to wait until they finish up. I'm too distracted to concentrate on work so I don't bother setting up my laptop as I'd intended. Instead, I empty the dryer and fold the load of clothes Kathy put in earlier. I carry a pile of clean clothing upstairs to my bedroom, throwing a curious look at the door to the guest room in passing.

It occurs to me that I could use this time to take a quick look around in Kathy's room and see if I spot anything suspicious, although I've no idea what that might be. I hate myself for even contemplating the idea of violating Kathy's space, but it would give me some peace of mind if I knew for sure she wasn't hiding anything from me. *She's a dark horse, that one.* This latest email has unnerved me—left me wondering. I waste no time putting away the clean clothes in my bedroom before heading back to Kathy's room.

With one last anxious glance down the stairs to make sure the installers are still outside, I reach for the door handle and gingerly push it open, surveying the space as if it were sacred. And, in a way, it is. My nanny's room was always off limits to me as a child—her one refuge in our home. There's still time to change my mind and back out before I intrude on her space. But I'm past the point of respecting obsolete boundaries from my childhood. I'm desperate for answers and, if they're here, I intend to find them. Stepping inside, it comes as no surprise to see that the room is neat as a pin, the bed made, and the corners expertly tucked in, just like she taught me. A pair of reading glasses sits atop a romance novel on the nightstand, next to an empty tumbler.

I spot her suitcase tucked beneath the bed and I reach for it, swallowing the remorse already surging up my throat. Before I can change my mind, I yank on the zipper, sick to my stomach at the thought of Kathy walking in on me in the act of rummaging through her belongings. I take a flimsy breath and flip open the lid. It's empty, apart from a pair of tennis shoes and a charging cord. I slide my hand into the inner pocket to make sure there's nothing inside. My fingers land on something soft and silky, and I pull it out, gasping out loud when I recognize my mother's Hermes scarf.

I stare at it for a long moment, trying to make sense of what I'm seeing. I would know this scarf anywhere because I was with my mother when she bought it and I remember being shocked at the exorbitant cost of something so hideous. I rub it between my fingers, tendrils of dread curling in my stomach. It was my mother's favorite scarf. I don't remember her giving it to Kathy. My heart clatters at the unwelcome thought that Kathy might have stolen it. But then why would she bring it here with her? Unless she forgot it was in her case.

Kathy's not who you think she is.

I frantically stuff the scarf back inside the pocket, zip up the suitcase, and shove it under the bed again. My hands are shaking. Is that why Kathy offered to come here? Is she helping Gareth? Is this about money? Does she think my family owes her something more than her wages and the generous severance package they gave her when they moved to San Antonio? I just can't wrap my head around it. Kathy's never given any indication that she resented the money our family made. She knew better than most the sacrifices it took, and she always celebrated our successes along the way.

I glance inside the bathroom, eying her small makeup bag and the travel toiletries neatly lined up next to her toothbrush, before walking over to the bedroom closet and sliding open the mirrored door. I study the small assortment of Kathy's clothes hanging on the rail. There's nothing incriminating—nothing else that belonged to my mother as far as I can see.

I'm about to slide the door closed again when I spot something dangling in the shadowy depths of the closet. I reach for the hanger, and then freeze.

Fear ripples through me as my gaze lands on a long, gray overcoat.

30

Vibrating with terror, I clap a hand over my mouth to trap the scream that threatens to erupt. I can't believe what I'm seeing. Is this some kind of sick joke? What is Kathy doing with a long, gray overcoat—a man's overcoat, no less—in her closet? Does she know it's here? Could someone have planted it in her room to spook me, to convince me that I should be afraid of Kathy? I heave a ragged breath, as the room spins and churns around me. Was it Kathy all along who approached Lucas in our drive-way? Am I crazy for thinking what I'm thinking—that my childhood nanny could be part of an elaborate plot to take down my business? This can't be the same coat, can it? Surely there must be a perfectly reasonable explanation for it hanging in Kathy's closet. I frown, thinking back through the various sightings of my stalker. What about the man watching Lucas at the park—did Kathy make him up? In retrospect, it's pretty convenient that Lucas didn't see him.

When I've recovered from the shock enough to think straight, I remove the coat from the closet to examine it in more detail. I rub the material between my fingers—it's a classic cotton twill. Double breasted, with a high collar to keep the rain off—not that we've had much lately. But the collar also works well to conceal the wearer's features. I root around in the pockets and come across a pair of cheap, plastic sunglasses. Stomach in knots, I do another search of the closet, but there's no sign of a hat, or a walking stick.

Maybe I'm jumping to the wrong conclusion, and this is just a coincidence. Except I know in my heart that the explanation can't be that simple. Either someone is trying to set Kathy up, or she's turned on me for some reason I'm not clear on. I take a closer look at the overcoat. It's definitely a man's coat. Was it really Kathy who walked past my house multiple times and stared at it long enough for Stanley to notice—a deliberate ploy so he would alert me? Kathy's tall enough to pass as a man, tall enough to be the person in the security footage taping Maria's resignation letter to the foyer door. My brain fogs with fear at the thought. Did she hurt Maria, or is she working with her?

Lucas said it was an older man who gave him the straw, but it could just as easily have been an older woman behind the sunglasses, with her collar turned up and hat pulled down. I lean the palm of my hand against the frame of the closet, my breathing shallow and hard. That means Kathy must have written the notes warning me about herself, knowing it would make it look like she was being targeted too. I can't deny the evidence staring me in the face, but the question hanging over my head is why Kathy would do something like this to me, and to my six-year-old son. She loves children—it's completely out of character for her to deceive an innocent child.

My thoughts drift to the Hermes scarf tucked away in

her suitcase. Everything always seems to come back to money. Is she hurting for funds? Maybe Gareth approached her and made her an offer she couldn't refuse. It's possible she never thought it would go this far—that it would be only a few stunts to scare me. I shake my head in disbelief. That's not the Kathy I know—she would never have stooped to something this low. Nothing would have induced her to voluntarily participate in such a blatant act of betrayal after all those years of faithful service.

A vortex of anger builds inside me when Gareth's sneering face comes to mind. However he did it, it's becoming apparent that he's managed to pollute or strong-arm everyone in my circle, in a malicious bid to ruin me. He was always envious of the financial start I had in life, but I had no control of the hand I was dealt. He should have been grateful for the IQ he was endowed with that put him on the fast track to success. Instead, he's gambling away his good fortune with his addictive behavior, risking his life and freedom in the process, and destroying mine.

A man's voice drifts up the stairs and I startle almost out of my skin. I hurriedly hang the overcoat back in the recesses of the closet and slide the mirrored door closed. I catch a glimpse of my hollow, shell-shocked face and wonder briefly where the self-assertive CEO of Capitol Technologies has gone. "Coming!" I call, before jogging back downstairs to where the two men from Digi-view Security are waiting at the front door for me to check out the installation and sign the paperwork. I scarcely pay attention as one of them launches into a lengthy explanation of how to operate the cameras, troubleshoot problems, and set and deactivate the alarm system. They leave me with a brochure, a hefty receipt and an 800 number to call if I have any questions. The minute they drive off, I reach for my phone and call Jack. "I need you to pick up Lucas from school today. Kathy's visiting an old friend and I'm tied up at the office."

"That's inconvenient," Jack replies tersely. "I'm tied up too."

"Define tied up," I snark back. "Maria's gone missing. The police did a welfare check at her house. The front door was smashed in, and they suspect foul play. I've got my hands full trying to hold things together at the company right now. Cancel your clients if you have to."

After a significant pause, Jack asks, "What kind of foul play are we talking about?"

"I don't know any specifics. Detective Hernandez is going to keep me posted. I've got to go. Can you pick Lucas up or not?"

"Yeah, I'll get him," Jack replies, his tone subdued.

I hang up and breathe a sigh of relief as I shoot Kathy a quick text letting her know that she doesn't have to pick up Lucas today. I don't want her alone with him after what I discovered in her room. In fact, I don't want anyone going anywhere near my son, other than myself or Jack, not until I've ruled out any connection between them and this campaign of terror, mayhem, and murder being waged against me. I consider calling Detective Hernandez to let him know about the overcoat I found in my house, but something holds me back. He might suspect I planted it. Stupidly, I handled it and now my fingerprints are all over it.

Whatever Kathy has or hasn't done, I owe it to her to give her a chance to explain herself first. It's possible she was hurting for money and was too proud to ask me for help. Maybe she turned to Gareth and now she's being forced to pay on her debts in ways she never contemplated. Whatever the case, I don't want to rat on her to Detective Hernandez if it turns out she was merely a pawn in Gareth's cunning game. It will be enough justice for me if she agrees to testify against him.

Like a master puppeteer, he's orchestrated everything and everyone around to crush me. I have to find a way to prove he killed Ryder before I'm charged with first-degree murder.

31

It turns out I needn't have agonized about calling Detective Hernandez after all because he calls me a few minutes after I arrive back at Capitol Technologies. "I'd like you to come down to the station for an interview at 3:00 p.m.," he announces, dispensing with even the most minimal of greetings.

"I'm up to my ears in work," I say, biting back my frustration. "Can't you come by my office if you have more questions?"

"I'd like to conduct a taped interview," he responds.

My heart begins to pound. To say he's not being forthcoming is an understatement, which tells me things are about to take an ugly turn, as Jack predicted. "Is this about Maria? Have you found her?"

"No. It's regarding Ryder Montoya."

I grip the phone a little tighter. "Do I need to bring my lawyer?"

"Entirely up to you," Detective Hernandez replies flatly. "I'll expect you at three this afternoon."

I clench my fists on my desk, the buzzing of my thoughts

an almost unbearable sensation in my head. *Entirely up to you.* Definitely code for: *if I were you, I'd lawyer up.* Gabriel assured me the police have no case against me, but they might be trying to piece one together. Maybe they've found what they consider to be more substantial evidence. I can't imagine what that would be. Perhaps they found Maria alive and well, and she told them I killed Ryder. If she's colluding with Gareth, for whatever reason, she's most likely pushing that narrative. She lied to her landlord about me, why not to the police?

Regardless, there's no point in sitting here speculating. I need a game plan. The first thing I have to make sure of is that Gabriel can accompany me to the station. I dial his office, jogging my leg up and down impatiently beneath the desk until his receptionist answers. Once I explain the situation, she puts me straight through to Gabriel.

"It's happening," I say grimly. "Detective Hernandez wants to interview me at three o'clock this afternoon at the station. Can you be there?"

"I can probably move some things around," he replies gravely. "You'd better bring me up to speed on what's been happening."

I rub the tip of my finger across my eyelid as I try to think back to the last update I gave Gabriel. I thought about calling him multiple times over the course of the past two days but neglected to do so. I hope it doesn't come back to haunt me now that I'm dumping everything on him at the last minute. "My PA, Maria Cassidy, has gone missing," I begin. "The police did a welfare check at her house and found her door kicked in and possible evidence of a struggle. One of my employees found a resignation letter signed by her taped to the main entry door this morning, but I can't tell from looking at the security footage if it was actually

Maria who left it there. I turned a copy over to Detective Hernandez to see if he can enhance it somehow."

Gabriel sighs heavily. "I wish you'd discussed it with me beforehand. You shouldn't have volunteered any evidence to the police without my consent."

"I was just trying to help them find Maria. I'm worried about her. I don't know if she's conspiring with Gareth or not, but she could be in danger either way. He's extremely clever and devious."

"Which is why, as your counsel, I'm advising you to stay in the background from now on. You have enough to contend with fielding questions about your ex's murder. Have the police given you any updates on the investigation?"

"No," I say glumly. "But I'm pretty sure I just shot back up to the top of their suspect list. I'm the only common denominator between Maria's disappearance and Ryder's murder."

"I'm sure the police are equally interested in looking into Gareth Looney's finances and illegal gambling activities," Gabriel responds. "A dire financial state can lead to desperate measures, including murder." He clears his throat. "I need to wrap up a few things here. Any other developments I should know about before I meet you at the station?"

"Yes, one other thing. I received another email from an unknown IP address. It was cautioning me about Kathy again, something about her being a dark horse. It also mentioned Maria, gloating about how she'd blindsided me."

"Forward it to me," Gabriel says, briskly. "I'll look at it before the interview. I'll see you at the station."

I end the call and turn to stare out the window at the bustling street below my office. I considered telling him about the overcoat I found in Kathy's room, but I knew what he would say—that I'm not in a position to show mercy when my own innocence is being questioned. But I'm not ready to turn her in—at least not until I confront her about the coat and scarf and listen to what she has to say about them. It's not like Detective Hernandez is going to arrest me this afternoon. He would have done it by now if he had any solid evidence.

I spend the next couple of hours following up on some projects with my engineers and leaving instructions with Faye on how to handle some of the more pressing administrative tasks I need taken care of. On the way to my car, I stop by a deli and order a turkey sandwich to go. I'm not hungry but I'll force myself to eat a few bites en route. I don't need the distraction of listening to my stomach rumbling while I'm being questioned.

I connect my phone to my car stereo and scroll through Spotify, settling on some acoustic guitar music to calm my nerves as I drive. I know how to conduct myself in high stress situations, but this is pushing me to the brink of insanity. My gut tells me Detective Hernandez will throw some hardball questions my way this time, and I don't want to appear to be guiltily fumbling my way through my responses.

Gabriel meets me outside the station dressed in a tailored wool suit, the very picture of authority and confidence. I breathe out a sigh of relief, thankful I shelled out the money to retain his services. The situation could have dire consequences for my company's reputation if it's not handled properly. But I have every reason to believe Gabriel can make this all go away. I'm innocent, after all.

"Now remember," he says, "this is a voluntary interview. You're not under arrest. If I tell you not to answer something, just say *no comment*. It's not an indication of guilt, it's your legal right to avoid saying something adverse to your situation."

I nod my understanding and lead the way inside.

We're seated at a rectangular metal table in a chilly interview room painted a dusky shade of blue. Detective Hernandez introduces the officer observing the interview and then, true to form, gets right down to business, asking me to say and spell my first and last name for the tape. He reads me my Miranda rights and then passes me a form to initial and sign. I throw a tentative glance at Gabriel, and he gives a nod of approval.

"I'd like to go back to the first time you allegedly threatened Ryder, as witnessed by your friend, Margo McGowan," Detective Hernandez begins. "Can you tell me exactly what happened that night?"

"I—"

"Don't answer that," Gabriel cuts in. He twists his lips. "It's hearsay."

Detective Hernandez's steely gaze travels over Gabriel, as if sizing up how worthy an opponent he's facing off with.

"Let's move on to the phone call you initiated the day before Ryder was murdered," Detective Hernandez continues. "Walk me through what was said."

I raise a shoulder in a half-hearted shrug. "Like I told you already, I asked him to stop harassing me."

"Did you bring up any specific incidents you believed Ryder was responsible for?"

"Yes. He pretended he didn't know what I was talking about."

Detective Hernandez leans an elbow on the table, tapping a finger to his chin as he scrutinizes me. "Is that when you threatened him with a restraining order?"

I glance at Gabriel, and he gives a firm shake of his head.

"Uh, no comment," I mumble, twisting the toe of my shoe into the vinyl flooring.

"Just so we're clear here, detective," Gabriel cuts in, throwing him a reproving look, "my client is the one who was threatened by Mr. Montoya."

Unfazed, Detective Hernandez moves on. "You mentioned when we last spoke that you felt you had made things worse by calling Ryder and confronting him. Can you elaborate?"

"He got extremely angry during the course of the call. And later that day, the scarecrows appeared in my back yard."

Detective Hernandez nods thoughtfully. "He was a very volatile man, by all accounts."

"Is that a question?" Gabriel asks.

Detective Hernandez ignores him, cocking an eyebrow at me as though inviting me to say something.

Gabriel turns to me, adjusting the sleeve of his jacket. "You don't have to respond to that."

"No comment," I say.

Detective Hernandez glances down at his notes again. "You mentioned Ryder being very possessive, that he said he would never let you leave him. Why did he have such a strong hold on you?"

I shrug. "I was a teenager at the time, addicted to the drugs he supplied me with."

"It was more than that though, wasn't it?" Detective Hernandez presses. "You told your husband that Ryder said you owed him your loyalty. Why would he say such a thing?"

My eyes widen. I press my knees tightly together beneath the table, shaking with rage. Why did Jack discuss a private conversation with the police? Does my own husband think I had something to do with bumping Ryder off?

Detective Hernandez tents his fingers and places both elbows on the table. "I did a little digging into Ryder's checkered past. You told me he'd been in and out of prison over the years, but you neglected to tell me about his first stint behind bars when he was only seventeen." He fixes a frozen smile on his face. "Correct me if I'm wrong, but I believe you were dating him at the time?"

A cold sweat breaks out on the back of my neck.

"This is irrelevant," Gabriel breaks in. "Unless you're charging my client, this interview's over."

Detective Hernandez narrows his eyes at him. "How does obstruction of justice sound?"

Gabriel frowns and leans back in his seat, folding his arms across his chest.

Detective Hernandez pivots back to me. "You told your husband Ryder went to juvenile hall."

I shrug. "Juvenile hall, prison, what's the difference?"

"The difference is that he wasn't incarcerated for selling meth on the Bowman High School campus at all, was he? He went to prison for arson."

I breathe slowly in and out, taking Gabriel's advice to exercise my right to remain silent.

"Is that why you owed Ryder your loyalty? Because you were with him that night and he didn't turn you in?" Detective Hernandez bows his head briefly and then looks back up at me, pinning me with a stare that turns my blood to ice. "Was it you who set fire to the barn where two people died?"

32

I freeze, waiting to hear Gabriel's dismayed gasp—or the sudden thump as he leaps to his feet—but the only discernible reaction is an overpowering silence emanating through the room like noxious fumes. I can't even hear the sound of my own breathing—*am* I still breathing? I stare fixedly at the recording device as the room blurs around me, vaguely aware that Gabriel is saying something to Detective Hernandez. And now he's pulling me to my feet by my elbow and ushering me out of the room with a firm grip. Detective Hernandez's gaze follows me the entire way. He can't know for sure—it was a shot in the dark—but I can tell by the expression on his face that he thinks he hit the mark. Has he shared his suspicions with Jack? My knees give way at the thought, and I reach a hand out to the wall to support myself, but Gabriel swoops in and saves me the effort.

"I got you. Just keep walking," he mutters fiercely in my ear, as we exit the police station. One hand on my back, he escorts me over to a black Mercedes sedan, grille blades shimmering in the sun, and opens the passenger door. "Get in," he says brusquely.

I obey without question. He doesn't even need to say the words, *we need to talk*. They hang in the air between us like an undetonated bomb. I can't help wondering if Detective Hernandez figured it out on his own, or if Ryder told Margo or Gareth, and one of them passed the information along.

Gabriel climbs in on the driver's side and slams the door shut. "Ready to tell me what that was all about?" His voice is deliberately low and even, as polished and professional as the sumptuous interior of his luxury car. At the end of the day, this is just another job for him, even if it feels like the end of my life as I know it.

I turn and look out the passenger window, my insides twisting at the thought of revisiting that night. I've never breathed a word about it to anyone, other than Ryder—and only to swear a pact that we'd never talk about it again.

"Lauren, I can't represent you properly if you keep critical information from me," Gabriel says in a long-suffering tone.

"All right, yes! I was there!" I let loose, tears springing to my eyes. "Am I going to be arrested?"

Gabriel rubs a hand across his forehead. "The statute of limitations renders that impossible, but it makes it look like you had a motive to kill Ryder. Hernandez is speculating you did it to keep him from talking. Let's face it, a front-page headline about the CEO of Capitol Technologies committing arson resulting in two deaths would annihilate your business."

I let out a despairing sigh and curl my hands into fists in my lap. "I tried to break up with Ryder that night at the pumpkin patch. I'd had enough. But ... it ended up the same way it always did. He said he was sorry and begged me not to leave him, plied me with drugs. Next thing you know, we were driving around, high as kites, which wasn't uncommon for us." I pause, the overpowering smell of the expensive leather interior of Gabriel's Mercedes making my stomach churn. "We wound up getting lost and driving down some country lane. We sat in the car drinking vodka for a while. Then Ryder spotted this raggedy old scarecrow in a field next to a barn. He had the bright idea we should set it on fire. I didn't want to, but he pulled me out of the car anyway." A tiny sob escapes my lips. "I was so drunk he was half-carrying me down the lane. When we reached the scarecrow, Ryder pressed a lighter into my hands. He told me to do it, that it would be symbolic, a way of burning all my fears. My hands were shaking too hard, so he flicked the lighter and then held my fingers over his and set fire to the scarecrow."

"Did you set the barn on fire too?" Gabriel asks, frowning.

"No! It was an accident." I search his eyes in vain for any indication he believes me. "It was windy that night, branches blowing every which way. But we were too high to give any thought to the danger."

Gabriel fingers his jaw thoughtfully, staring straight ahead. "And ... the two people who died? Were they in the barn?"

I give a chagrined shake of my head. "No, there was only a horse inside. It went berserk when it smelled the smoke, neighing and kicking at its stall. Ryder and I ... we panicked and took off." I bite down on my lip, the coppery taste of blood mingling with my saliva as the overwhelming dark-ness of that awful night comes rushing back. "I ... I didn't find out until the following day that two people had died—the elderly couple who owned the farm. They saw the flames from their house and ran down to the barn to try and rescue their horse." My breath hitches in my chest. "The horse made it out safely, but the roof collapsed on them."

After a somber silence, Gabriel asks, "How did the police find out it was you and Ryder who started the fire?"

"Some neighbor reported seeing our car near the farm. They were able to give a description and a partial license plate—supposedly, we were swerving all over the road. The cops tracked Ryder to his house and arrested him—it was his car." I press my lips tightly together. "He swore I played no part in setting the scarecrow on fire. He told the cops I was passed out in the car."

Gabriel raises puzzled brows. "Why did he protect you?"

"Because I'd already turned eighteen by then and he was only seventeen. He figured he'd get sent to juvenile hall for a few months and that would be the end of it. He told me I would owe him for the rest of my life. He made me swear I'd wait for him in return for his silence. It felt like a threat, to be honest. In some ways, I was almost relieved when my parents sent me away and he couldn't contact me anymore."

Gabriel taps the side of the steering wheel, seemingly lost in thought.

"So now what?" I venture to ask. "Do I need to tell Detective Hernandez what I told you?"

Gabriel purses his lips. "No. He has no evidence you were involved in Ryder's murder. He's scratching for a link, and he thinks he's found something to spook you into confessing, that's all."

"What if he arrests me?"

"He won't. The best he can do is hold you for forty-eight hours, and it would serve no purpose. He'll wait until he has enough evidence for an arrest."

"The only evidence he'll find is circumstantial," I say defensively. "I didn't kill Ryder."

Gabriel gives a curt nod, his face impassive. "In the meantime, keep your nose clean and your head down. They're going to be watching you. Don't call Detective Hernandez, for any reason, unless you clear it with me first." He glances at his watch. "I need to get going. I have an appointment back at the office."

I open the door and climb out, taking a minute to steady my shaking legs. To his credit, Gabriel watches to make sure I get back to my own car safely before pulling out of the parking lot.

I sit with my troubled thoughts for several minutes before starting the engine. I can't help feeling mortified that Gabriel knows my shameful secret. The successful CEO persona I presented to him is eroding faster than sand as the dark waves of my past lap ever closer. Gabriel doesn't sound so convinced anymore that I won't end up being arrested. If it's only a matter of time, I have to move quickly. Somehow, I need to prove I didn't kill Ryder.

My phone pings and I glance distractedly at a text from Jack.

I'm taking Lucas to a matinee. We'll grab dinner after and have some guy time. Figured you'd be working late anyway.

I realize *guy time* is just a euphemism for time away from me, but I'm glad he's offering to spend it with Lucas. I know I've neglected our son of late—only half-listening when he's prattling on about what happened in school that day, or the intricate workings of his latest craft project. The last thing I want is for him to feel like I did as a kid—that his nanny is his surrogate parent.

I hit the *like* emoji for Jack's text. It gives me a few hours alone to work out what I'm going to do. I'm tempted to tell him about my interview at the station, but I'm still too angry with him for blabbing to Detective Hernandez about things I told him in confidence. And I'm worried about what the detective might have told him in return. We'll talk about it tonight after I've rehearsed in my mind exactly what I want to say. An emotional tirade will accomplish nothing other than alienating him further.

After thinking it over, I decide against returning to the office. Faye's bound to be working late after everything I added to her plate, and I can't face the thought of trying to fend off any more of her probing questions. Half an hour later, I pull into my driveway. Thankfully, there's no sign of Kathy's rental car. She's probably still at Jan's. I can't help feeling relieved that I'll have some time to myself to organize my thoughts before I'm forced to confront her.

I toss my purse and keys on the console table in the foyer and throw a hesitant glance around. The house is eerily silent, the only sound the quiet tread of my own feet. I'm about to head to the kitchen to make some tea when I hesitate, one hand on the post at the bottom of the stairs. I should take another look at the coat in Kathy's room before she gets back. I'm already beginning to question my wild theory that it's connected in any way to the mysterious stalker. So what if it's a man's coat? It could be hers. Kathy's a tall, broad-shouldered woman—maybe she found it more comfortable.

I climb the stairs, breathing a little harder as my adrenalin spikes. Outside the guest room, I stall, questioning again what I'm doing and if I really want to go through with this. But I'm growing increasingly desperate for answers as my freedom hangs in the balance. Gritting my teeth, I push down on the handle and slip inside. I pad across the carpet and slide the mirrored closet door open. Reaching into the recesses of the closet, my fingers close around the cotton twill overcoat. My heart hammers a manic beat. I cast a harried glance over my shoulder at the door to make sure no one has crept up on me unawares, and then reach for the hanger. I study the coat for a moment—gray, double-breasted, just like I remembered it—and then lay it down on the bed. Filled with a looming sense of dread, I pull out my phone and snap a quick picture. I'll show it to Lucas and ask him if it looks like the same coat the stranger was wearing. I'll send a copy to Gabriel too and ask him if he thinks I should let Detective Hernandez know about it. But not until I've had it out with Kathy first. If she is the stranger in the gray coat, I want to know what she's playing at.

I twist the material in my fist, my stomach suddenly heaving at the possibility that Kathy, my beloved nanny, the one person who was always there for me, might be aiding and abetting Gareth. Darting into the bathroom, I lean over the toilet, wincing at the bitter acid in my throat. My head pounds like crashing waves. I can barely think straight, white spots floating before my eyes. After a few minutes, I straighten up, feeling a little less queasy, although my head is full of static and the floor feels like it's moving beneath me. I could really use a cup of tea now—extra sugar. I exit the bathroom and come to a sudden halt. Goosebumps creep to the surface of my skin and begin prickling along the back of my neck. Kathy's statuesque frame fills the doorway to the bedroom. She rests a hand on the casing, an enigmatic look on her face. "Is ... everything all right, Lauren?"

My eyelids twitch in terror, as it hits me like a bullet that I'm alone in the house, trapped in this room with a woman I no longer trust. I search for the words to explain myself. "I ...

I was just checking the plumbing. We have a leak in our bathroom."

Kathy frowns. "Can't say I've noticed any problems." Her eyes flick to the bed and her frown deepens.

I follow her gaze to the coat, my chest tightening to the point of bursting. "Is it yours, Kathy?" I blurt out. "I need you to tell me the truth. Is Gareth Looney paying you?"

Her head swivels in my direction, her face flooding with a look of utter bewilderment. "What are you talking about?"

I march over to the bed, grab the coat and shake it. "Is this yours? Was it you all along, stalking me?"

Kathy lets out a horrified gasp. "What? No! Of course not!"

"Then who was it?" I sob. "*Who*?"

"Right behind you," a low-pitched voice says.

33

I spin around and stare in shock at a tall figure dressed in a petrol blue technician shirt with a black balaclava pulled down over his face. The embroidered logo on his shirt reads *Atlas Plumbing, Heating & Air*. Random thoughts fire through my confused brain. I haven't called anyone out. Is he here to rob us? I take a step backward, instinctively spreading my arms out like a butterfly to try and shield Kathy from the intruder. "Who ... who are you?" I stutter.

"Maybe you should ask your nanny that," he replies. His tone is disarmingly flippant, but I don't miss the angry gleam in his eyes as his lips move. Apart from the holes in the balaclava, I can see nothing of his face, which only makes him seem more dangerous. A trickle of sweat runs down the back of my neck. Could this be the stranger who killed Ryder? I pivot, searching Kathy's eyes for any indication that she knows this man. But her face is a crumpled mask of terror.

"Kathy," I whisper urgently to her. "Do you know him? If

Gareth coerced you into something, I can help you. But you have to tell me what's going on."

"Yeah, *Kathy*," the man scoffs. "Why don't you introduce this entitled bloodsucker to your son?"

Kathy's bottom lip begins to tremble. The blood drains from her face and her hand shoots to her chest. For one awful moment, I'm afraid she's going to succumb to a heart attack right in front of me.

"Kathy! Are you all right?" I reach out to grab her before she collapses.

She brushes me aside. "Titus?" she rasps. "How ... how did you find me?"

My eyes dart in confusion between Kathy and the tall, big-boned stranger. "He's ... your son?" I squeeze out. "But—"

"The one and only," Titus cuts in. "Her firstborn son, abandoned at birth—"

"You were never abandoned!" Kathy cries out. "I gave you up for adoption so you'd have the best possible start in life. I was nineteen with no means of support. I wasn't giving up on you—I gave you everything I had. I gave you life, and a family to love you."

My breath comes in short, hard pulses. *Nineteen*. Titus was the baby Kathy dropped out of college to have.

"Well it wasn't enough, you owe me, *mother*," he growls. "Like I wrote you, it's hard finding a job out of prison. I needed money and you couldn't even come through for me then."

Kathy's throat bobs. "That was ten years ago. And I sent you five-hundred dollars."

Titus throws back his head and laughs. "How far did you think that would get me?" He gestures contemptuously at me. "You were working for this rich cat's family, and you couldn't even give me enough to get me back on my feet."

"How ... how did you find me?" Kathy asks.

I shiver as the thin lips in the hole in the balaclava curve slowly upward. "Lucky break. I had a cell mate who was very helpful in that regard. He was a small-time druggie loser. He liked to rant about this wealthy punk girlfriend he had who'd got him locked up and then bailed on him."

I reach out to steady myself on the edge of the bed, my fingers inadvertently touching the overcoat. I recoil from it as if it's contaminated. Did Titus plant it in Kathy's room? My stomach muscles lock at the thought that he's been in my house before, roaming freely around—perhaps he's even been watching us while we sleep.

"He covered for her on some arson and manslaughter charge," Titus goes on, in a deceptively genial manner, like he's telling a fireside story and relishing commanding our rapt attention. "Once he figured out that she'd ditched him, he tried to tell his lawyer it was her that did it, but no-one was interested in a druggie changing his story after he'd already confessed and been convicted."

Kathy turns to me, shock and disbelief contorting her face.

Titus cracks his knuckles, clearly enjoying my agony. "He jabbered non-stop about how he was going to hunt her down and teach her a lesson for what she did to him as soon as he was released. He was just too stupid to pull it off. So, after I got out, I offered to help."

"Were you the one who gave my son the straw?" I ask.

He lets out a mirthless laugh full of menace that's meant to serve as an answer.

"How did this get in here?" I demand, gesturing at the coat on the bed. My eyes flit between Kathy and Titus once more as I try to piece it together. Is Titus the reason Kathy needed money? Was she helping him all along?

"I have no idea. I had nothing to do with it," Kathy says. "I swear to you, Lauren. I've never even met my son. He wrote me a begging letter before his release from prison and I sent him what money I could spare and told him not to contact me again."

"You could say breaking and entering is what I specialize in," Titus interjects. He flashes Kathy a wicked grin. "Framing you was purely for my own amusement, *mother*. I figured you ought to pay for your lack of interest in your only child."

She gives a sad shake of her head. "I knew I should never have sent you that money. You had everything going for you —a wonderful adoptive family. There was no reason for you to end up in prison."

I chew on my lip, wondering if breaking and entering was all Titus was in prison for. "Did you kill Ryder?" I ask.

He gives a contemptuous snort. "Ryder's own stupidity killed him. He was all in on the plan to teach you a lesson until he found out you had a kid around the same age as his son. Then, all of a sudden, he got cold feet. Typical small time druggie loser—they're all big talkers."

Titus limps toward me, confirming my suspicion that he was the man Stanley Hogg saw dumping Ryder's body on my front steps. "When people get cold feet, they become loose ends, if you get my drift."

"What do you want?" I ask, taking a hasty step backward and bumping up against Kathy. Instinctively, we reach for each other's hands.

"Five-hundred-grand will make me and the scarecrow horror show your raving ex dreamed up go away." He lets rip with a caustic laugh.

"She's not going to give you a penny!" Kathy huffs.

"It's out of the question," I add, my voice surprisingly

calm. "Even if I wanted to, I couldn't give you that kind of cash. My money's tied up in my firm's assets."

Titus sets his teeth with a snap, a gleam of anger in his eyes. "Don't give me the software heiress sob story. I know Capitol Technologies took in a million-and-a-half in deposits on several multi-million-dollar contracts last week."

My lips part in astonishment. How is he privy to confidential company information? For that matter, how does he even know the name of my company? I grimace inwardly as gears begin clicking in my brain. "You're working for Gareth Looney, aren't you?" I fire accusingly at him.

"I don't work for anyone," he says with an air of reproachful condescension. "They work for me."

"Who's they?" I demand.

Titus flattens his lips. "Gareth Looney owes some friends of mine big money. Ryder said he knew him, and he might be able to help us get our cash. So, I offered him a deal. I agreed to send some business his way, if he squared up on his gambling debts, with a fat commission for me, of course."

"How did you send—" My voice trails off when it dawns on me. "Maria was working for you too, wasn't she?"

I can almost sense him grinning with satisfaction behind his mask. I don't know why he's bothering with it now that we know who he is. Maybe he thinks it makes him more intimidating.

"Maria's brilliant, isn't she?" Titus says, a hint of pride in his voice. "You seriously underestimated my girlfriend."

Kathy gasps out loud and grips my arm like a vise.

I breathe steadily in and out, trying to absorb the impact of what feels like a dagger to my heart. Maria was the mole all along. I cringe at how generously I praised her to everyone around. She was capable all right—only her capabilities were all in the criminal department as it turns out. I suppose her references from New York were fake too.

Titus pulls a phone from his shirt pocket. "Speaking of Maria, she's waiting in your office for my call. And you're going to play nice and walk her through that half-a-million-dollar transfer."

34

"You'll never get away with this," I say, reaching surreptitiously for the phone in my back pocket. Seemingly out of nowhere, Titus produces a gun and aims it directly at my head. I freeze, my pulse thundering in my ears. A scream rips from Kathy's throat as she staggers toward the bathroom. Titus pounces on her, dragging his left leg. "Shut up!" he hisses, before slugging her on the side of the head with the barrel of his gun. She slumps to the ground with a muted grunt.

Titus holds out a gloved hand to me. "Give me your phone. *Now!*" Hesitantly, I reach behind and slide my phone from my pocket. I pass it to him, knowing it's my only lifeline to get out of here alive. I'm not stupid enough to think Titus won't shoot me as soon as the transfer goes through—Kathy too. He can't leave any witnesses alive. We may not have seen his face, but we know who he is. I do a quick calculation in my head. Jack and Lucas aren't due back for another couple of hours, at least. No one's going to show up to save us. I have to think fast. I drop to my knees next to

Kathy and check her pulse to make sure she's still breathing. "She needs medical attention," I say. "You need to call an ambulance."

"The sooner you cooperate, the sooner she'll get help," Titus replies, jamming my phone into the back pocket of his cargo pants. "I'm putting Maria on speaker now and you're going to give her the password to your company bank accounts. Don't ask her any questions, and don't attempt to engage her in conversation." He swivels the gun around and points it at Kathy. "Because if you do, nanny goes belly up. Understood?"

I give a slight nod, racking my brains to try and find a way out of this precarious situation. If I were alone, it would be a different matter. But I can't risk a reckless escape move that might seal Kathy's fate in her helpless state. I need to keep my head about me and wait for an opportunity to over-power Titus and gain the upper hand. My only advantage is that I'm quicker and lighter on my feet. Whatever injury Titus sustained, it's left him with a considerable limp.

"You there?" Titus barks into his phone, before setting it down on the bed.

"Swiveling in the queen bee's chair as we speak," Maria replies, her voice dripping with condescension.

Her words riddle through me like machine gun fire. Anger, rage, sadness, and pain swirl like a tornado in my chest at the very sound of her voice—a voice I trusted, consulted with, laughed with—a duplicitous voice that was repeating everything back to Titus. I feel like a fool to think I believed we had bonded as ambitious women in a field dominated by men. And I feel a burning sense of visceral loss at a friendship that never was anything but a double-dealing sham.

Titus narrows his eyes at me, his breathing hard and heavy. "What are you waiting for? Give her the number."

"I... I don't know my account numbers by heart," I say. "I need my phone to get into my password manager."

Titus clenches his jaw and raises the gun again. "Don't lie to me! Just give her the number!"

"I'm telling you the truth!" I protest. "I have multiple passwords for multiple business accounts. I can't possibly remember them all. They're in my password manager. If you give me my phone, I'll get you the number."

He skewers me with a look so cold it feels like an ice pick going through my chest, before lowering the gun and retrieving my phone from his pocket. "Hold on a minute, Maria," he says, before addressing me again. "Passcode to get into your phone?"

"It's 5491," I recite, trying to nail a docile tone, despite my disappointment that he's not dumb enough to give me the phone.

He punches the four digits in carefully with a gloved finger and frowns at the screen. "Which one's the password manager?"

"The blue app with the keyhole in the center," I reply.

"Master password?" he asks, his eyes flicking constantly between me and the screen, as if he's anticipating a sudden move on my part. I'm tempted, but I need to buy myself more time. I can't strike unless I'm sure of victory—and that's not going to happen as long as Titus has a gun at his disposal. I wet my lips nervously as I hatch a makeshift plan that's sure to incur his wrath. The lockout threshold on my password manager is set to three attempts. After that, there's a thirty-minute wait before I can get back in—thirty more minutes of life to strategize about how to get out of here. I just have to make it sound convincing, so Titus doesn't think I'm deliberately trying to thwart him. "It's, uh #!#7193HYC!#!" I say, rambling the password off.

"Whoa! Slow down and start over," he orders me. "Maria, write this down."

I repeat the code, with an air of exaggerated huffiness.

Titus types it in as I talk and then throws me a menacing look. "That ain't right. Maria, read back to her what she said."

Maria enunciates each character. "#!#7193HYC!#!"

Titus jerks his chin at me. "Well?"

"Sorry, I ... I forgot the T after the C for Capitol Technologies," I say sheepishly.

Titus gives a disgusted grunt. "Walk me through it again, Maria," he orders her, focusing his attention back on my phone. A minute later he growls and aims the gun at Kathy's head. "Incorrect password. I swear I'll take her out right now if you keep this up."

"No! Please, stop!" I cry out. "You're making me so nervous I'm botching it, that's all. Let me think about it for a minute." I press my fingertips to my temples. "I'm mixing it up at the end. It's #!#, not !#!"

"Go again, Maria," Titus barks.

I hold my breath as she reads the password off to him again with the correction. Seconds later, Titus glares across at me. "It's locked me out. Why's it locked me out?"

"You must have mistyped it," I say with a deferential shrug. "You should have taken your gloves off. I told—" I break off at a sudden punch to the head that momentarily splinters my vision.

"You did that on purpose, didn't you?" Titus yells in my face. "How long am I locked out for?"

"Just ... thirty minutes," I stammer, rubbing the side of

my head. "I gave you the right number. You should have let me do it."

Titus contemplates me for a long moment and then grabs my chin and jerks it up until I'm looking directly into his dark eyes. "You're going to type the password next time while I hold a gun to nanny's head over there. So if you slip up, *oops*—guess what? Nanny no more."

35

Titus lifts his phone to his ear and engages in a hushed conversation with Maria as he leans against the wall next to the bedroom door, essentially keeping an eye on me while guarding the only exit to freedom at the same time. There's no possibility of making a run for it, and I wouldn't leave Kathy alone with her lunatic son anyway. My only hope of getting us out of here is to get a hold of that gun somehow.

There's a sudden rustling at my side and Kathy moans softly. I reach over and grasp her hand in mine. "Kathy, it's me, Lauren. Can you hear me?"

"Is ... he ... still ... here?" She squeezes each word out like she's forcing it through a tube, which makes me think she's in a lot of pain, but the fact that she's fully aware of what's going on is reassuring.

"Yes," I whisper back to her, one eye on Titus who's watching us like a hawk, while continuing his conversation with Maria. Gingerly, I help Kathy up into a more comfortable sitting position. "I'm going to get us out of here," I murmur to her. "I'm working on it."

She gives my hand a quick squeeze but says nothing. She's not naive enough to think the odds of us getting out of here alive are in our favor.

Titus shuffles restlessly in place at his sentry position, intermittently scratching the back of his neck and checking the time on his phone. His overly casual demeanor has given way to a heightened state of anxiety, like a twitching addict growing more desperate for a fix. What should have been a ten-minute job has stretched into a forty-minute marathon—at a minimum. The more time he spends here, the more he runs the risk that someone will come to the door, or Jack and Lucas will arrive home. The thought fills me with more dread than hope. Titus is unlikely to show mercy to anyone who gets in his way.

"Yeah, yeah, I'll call you back," he says to Maria before slipping the phone into his shirt pocket.

Engage with him, I say to myself, scratching to remember any advice I've picked up from crime podcasts over the years. *Humanize yourself, repeat your name as often as possible, find some common ground.*

"How did you get your limp?" I ask, keeping my voice low and neutral.

His dark eyes peer contemptuously at me through the holes in the balaclava. I'm tempted to ask him why he's still wearing it. It seems pointless, but I suppose it would make it harder to identify him in a police lineup.

"Got my kneecap blown out for asking too many questions," he says with a hint of amusement in his voice. He peers with an air of deliberation down the barrel of the gun, moving it slowly from Kathy to me and back again in a silent game of eeny meeny miny mo. I swallow the jagged lump in my throat, unnerved by his reckless indifference as he stands in front of us toying with our lives. Logically, it wouldn't make sense for him to kill us before he gets his money, but guns go off accidentally all the time.

I try to calculate in my head how much time has passed since I locked him out of my password manager. It feels like an eternity, but it's probably only been about ten minutes so far. Titus lets out a frustrated grunt and adjusts his stance for the umpteenth time. Clearly, his injury still nags at him. A shiver passes over me at the thought of how he incurred it. If what he said is true, it says a lot about the circles he moves in, and what he might be capable of doing himself.

"Cat got your tongue, or what?" he says with an amused snort. "Is that the only question you have for me? Don't you want to know what I was in the slammer for all those years?" He hesitates, his lips curling into another sinister smile. "Maybe you want to know what it's like on the inside. A rich chick like you would never make it. Lucky for you your boyfriend took the hit for that one." He pushes himself away from the wall and gestures with the gun to Kathy. "Did you know your entitled ward was the one who lit that place up and burned it to the ground? She's nothing but a moneyed murderess."

Kathy tightens her lips, rubbing her knuckles in her lap.

"So me and her aren't all that different after all," Titus goes on. "But you elected to raise her instead of me—how'd that work out?"

I grit my teeth and turn to Kathy. "It was Ryder who set the scarecrow on fire, not me. But I take full responsibility for the choice I made to be there with him that night. I chose to get in the car even though I knew he was an abusive bully. I chose to get high and drink until I was so out of my face that I had no control over what I was doing, or what he forced me to do." I pause and suck in a deep breath. "In a sense, Titus is right. I'm partly responsible for the death of two people, morally if not legally." I turn to Titus. "But that's where the similarities end. I made a U-turn and walked away from my destructive lifestyle. And I live with regret and remorse every day over what happened. Evidently, you haven't changed your ways, and you're not losing any sleep over your choices."

Titus laughs derisively. "Got me all psychoanalyzed, have you? Ryder always said you were full of yourself, but you know what, I like a woman who knows what she wants and goes for it. So I guess we have that in common too."

"You're wrong about—" My voice trails off at the distant wail of a police siren.

Titus's head jerks sideways. Time seems to constrict as I sense his body moving in the direction of the window. Adrenalin surges through me.

"Stay down!" he yells at us as he takes a lumbering step toward the window.

But I'm already catapulting through the air and barreling into the back of his good knee. He lurches forward under the unexpected force of my weight. His wonky leg gives out beneath him and he crashes to the floor with a bellow of pain. I scramble to my knees, intent on wrestling the gun from him, but he's dropped it in the fall. A fisted black glove grabs hold of my shirt and yanks me toward him. I gasp at the sudden force. He's so much stronger than I anticipated. My hair spills over my face as I struggle to free myself from his powerful grip. I throw a desperate glance around, but there's no sign of the gun anywhere.

His massive hands reach around my neck, and he begins to squeeze. Panic grips me as my necklace snaps, beads pinging across the hardwood floor. I know how this ends. Unconsciousness within seconds, death within minutes. The terror that takes hold of me is matched only by the searing pain in my throat. I flail in desperation, trying to claw his gloved fingers off me, but they're like steel digging so hard into my skin it feels as though they're about to punch through. I kick at him with all the strength I can muster but he flips me over like I'm nothing, and sits on top of me, the weight of his body crushing me as he continues to squeeze. The pain is excruciating, and I almost wish I could die and be released from it.

Just as the final curtain of blackness is closing in, there's a sudden crash and Titus's fingers miraculously release their death grip. I roll to my side, wheezing as I suck in breath after sweet breath. Through muddied vision, I catch a glimpse of Kathy standing over Titus, the remnants of a decorative antique urn scattered around him. He's momentarily stunned, but on the move again. He powers to his feet with a roar and reaches for Kathy.

"Get off me, you coward!" she screams, wrenching the balaclava from his head. Hoary hair full of static stands to attention above eyes that are dark orbs of rage. His thin lips writhe in serpent-like fury as his arms shoot out and lock around Kathy's neck.

I stare in trancelike horror as she twists beneath his grip in desperation. Still gasping for air myself, I can almost feel the pain exploding inside her head. Willing myself into action, I blink to clear my vision, catching a glimpse of the gun. As unobtrusively as possible, I reach my hand beneath the bed and fumble for it. Carefully, I pull it toward me, going over in my mind how to take control of the situation. *Let her go or I'll shoot.* Should I say it calmly or try screaming it? Will my voice amount to anything more than a croak right now? Maybe I shouldn't say anything. It might just give him the chance to disarm me. It might be better to shoot without warning. I get to my feet and raise the gun, vaguely aware that the wailing of sirens is noticeably louder now. I wonder briefly where they're going. I wish there was a way to flag them down and save me from this terrible decision.

Suddenly aware of my concentrated gaze, Titus glances in my direction. His eyes glitter with rage when he sees the gun in my hand.

"Let her go, Titus," I rasp. "Or I'll blow out your other kneecap."

He hesitates, weighing the threat for its merit, before flinging Kathy away from him like a rag doll. She stumbles backward, clutching her throat and heaving oxygen into her lungs like she's been trapped underwater for minutes. Titus takes an unsteady step in my direction, a warped smile on his face. "You couldn't pull the trigger if your life depended on it."

I open my mouth to respond but flinch at a sudden loud banging on the front door, followed by a crash and a flurry of voices. Someone shouts, *police*, and then I hear the thud of boots pounding up the stairs. The expression on Titus's face hardens, and I see the split-second decision he makes before he springs into action. He's not going back to prison. Time seems to stand still and all I can think about is Ryder screaming at me to flick the wheel of the lighter while I stand there shaking, wishing I was someplace else. But I'm not a teenager anymore, and, despite my sweating palms, I'm focused and resolute in the decision I'm making this time. I take aim, exhale and squeeze the trigger as Titus lunges. Everything happens in an explosion of slow-motion sensations—a bright flash, an instantaneous ear-splitting crack, an acrid smell. My body jolts, and I reel backward on my heels as the bullet discharges. Titus buckles, his face contorting in agony. It's all over before I've even consciously processed what's happened.

I drop the gun on the bed, trembling uncontrollably, a grab bag of emotions hurtling through me. The adrenalin that spiked a moment earlier, seeps from me like air from a burst balloon, leaving me weak and nauseous.

Seconds later, the door to the guest room bursts open and I find myself staring down the barrel of a gun for the second time before everything goes black.

36

Bits and pieces of what's happening around me waft in and out of my consciousness but it's like a dream I can't wake up from. When I finally blink awake, I find myself staring up at a stark white ceiling. I frown, wondering when I agreed to let Jack paint our bedroom, but as my groggy eyes travel around the room, I soon realize I'm lying prostrate in a hospital bed.

I shut my eyes again, the blinding whiteness too much for my throbbing head to contend with. Gingerly, I press my taut, parched lips together. It's painful to swallow, and I feel as if I've been tied to the back of a car and dragged along a paved road for a mile or two. I shift sideways in the bed, wondering how long I've been asleep. A fuzzy memory of staring down the barrel of a gun filters into my brain. A loud crack flashes back to mind, followed by an intense burning smell. A wave of panic engulfs me. Was I shot? Tentatively, I start patting my body searching for evidence of a wound.

"Lauren, can you hear me?"

The voice registers in a hallucinatory sort of way, but it doesn't sound familiar.

"Do you know where you are, Lauren?"

My eyes shoot open again and I find myself staring up at a smiling nurse in blue scrubs. I flick my tongue over my lips and grind out the word, "Hospital." My voice is gritty, barely recognizable even to myself.

"Very good, Lauren. My name is Janet and I'll be looking after you." The nurse promptly raises the head of my bed, and then reaches for a plastic water cup with a straw and holds it to my lips. I suck on it gratefully, the cool liquid instantly soothing the raw lining of my throat. Clips from the past few hours flash before me. "Kathy, my nanny," I croak. "Is she all right—Kathy Welker?"

"She's fine," Janet reassures me with another smile. "She's in the waiting room with your husband and son."

"Thank you," I manage, sinking back on the pillows, the tension in my limbs ratcheting down a notch.

"I'll let your family know you're awake," Janet says, a cheerful spring to her step as she exits the room.

Moments later, Lucas comes running in and flings his arms around me. "Mommy! Is your head all better now?"

I throw a confused look at Jack and Kathy who follow him in. "My head?" I rasp, to no one in particular.

"You hit your head on the bedframe in the guest room when you passed out—right when the police burst through the door," Kathy explains with a chuckle. "You always did have impeccable timing." She walks over to my bed and pats my hand reassuringly. "You saved our lives, pumpkin."

"Your... neck," I murmur. "It looks painful."

Instinctively, Kathy's fingers shoot to the purplish bruising on her throat. "Not any more painful than yours, I'd venture to say. I have an egg-sized lump on the side of my head too, but they checked me out and discharged me."

Jack leans over and presses his lips to my forehead. "We're all glad you're okay," he says.

I study his expression, questioning the underlying meaning of his words. Why didn't he say *I'm* glad you're okay? My head's hurting too much to try and make sense of it. Jack always tells me I over-analyze everything, so maybe I shouldn't read too much into it. But my gut's telling me he's intentionally distancing himself, and even my brush with death won't erase the rift in our relationship so easily.

"How about I take Lucas down to the cafeteria for a snack?" Kathy suggests, looking meaningfully between me and Jack.

"No!" we both answer in unison.

"I want Lucas to stay here and tell me all about his day," I whisper, smoothing a hand over his soft cheek.

Thankfully, that's all it takes for Lucas to launch into an exhaustive account of Mrs. Bernardi's new pet turtle, his soccer game at recess, and the animated movie Jack took him to see after school. I soon get lost in the details, but Lucas doesn't seem to notice that my attention has drifted— or that the adults in the room are actively avoiding meeting each other's eyes.

When Lucas has finally worn himself out, Jack offers to take him home, leaving me alone with Kathy.

"I'm so sorry, pumpkin," she begins.

The briny tang of tears tickles my nose. "For what? I'm the one who dragged you into this."

She sighs. "For Titus, of course."

"You have nothing to be sorry for. You're not responsible for the choices he made."

Kathy pulls her lips into a rueful grimace. "I shouldn't have responded to his letter. I wasn't going to, at first. But then I thought what harm could it do? Maybe five-hundred dollars would be all it would take for him to turn his life around. He said his adoptive parents had washed their hands of him, and I felt guilt-ridden. I know how difficult it is for people to get a job after they've been released from prison. Having a little bit of money in your pocket helps. At least I thought it would. He probably just used it for drugs or something. And now look where he's at, right back behind bars where he started."

"What are they charging him with?"

Kathy shakes her head. "I don't know the details. Detective Hernandez promised to keep us updated."

I tense at the mention of Detective Hernandez. "How did the police know Titus was in my house?"

Kathy eyes me with a knowing look on her face. "You have your one-man neighborhood watch committee to thank for that. Stanley Hogg saw the plumbing van pull up outside your house. He watched the driver go up to the front door and recognized his limp immediately. He was even more suspicious when the man opened the door and walked right in without knocking. He told the police he regretted not speaking up before, and he wasn't going to make the same mistake twice."

"Good old Stanley Hogg," I say, with a gravelly chuckle. "I owe him my life."

"We both do," Kathy adds. "We need to find some way to thank him. I smell a baking marathon on the horizon."

I glance up as a shadow darkens the doorway.

"What's all this about a baking marathon?" Detective Hernandez asks in a gruff, good-humored way. Despite his disarming tone, I can't help feeling a certain level of apprehension at the sight of him. Gabriel assured me I couldn't be prosecuted for something from eighteen years ago, but my guilty conscience is not convinced quite yet.

"Come in and sit down," Kathy says, pulling up a chair for him. "We were just talking about what charges Titus will face. Maybe you can enlighten us."

Detective Hernandez takes off his jacket and hangs it on the back of his chair. "I'll never understand why they keep this place so hot," he grumbles, blowing out a sharp breath. His gaze comes to rest on me. "How are you doing, Lauren?"

"I've been better. I hurt all over and I guess I hit my head on top of everything else."

"You cracked it pretty hard, all right." Detective Hernandez's eyes gleam with amusement. "We thought you'd passed out from fright at the sight of all those uniforms."

I give a mortified chortle. "Apparently, my nanny's made of sturdier stock than I am. She got whacked on the side of the head with a gun and somehow she got discharged before me."

"I got lucky, that's all," Kathy responds with a pleased grin.

"Do you have any updates for us?" I ask Detective Hernandez.

He squeezes his jaw contemplatively. "As of an hour ago, Titus has been formally charged with two counts of attempted murder, and one count of murder. There are likely be some additional charges once we complete our interviews with him. He's already got a lengthy rap sheet—armed robbery and aggravated assault. He even held his adoptive parents at gunpoint after he'd milked them dry, and they refused to bail him out anymore. They didn't press charges, although they might be regretting that now."

"Those poor people," Kathy says quietly.

"Is he talking?" I ask. "Did he tell you about Gareth's involvement?"

Detective Hernandez grunts. "Gareth Looney's in a world

of trouble. Summit Solutions is being investigated for fraud. Let's hope for his sake he gets himself a good lawyer, or he could find himself implicated in the murder of Ryder Montoya too. Margo McGowan's been cleared. She had no involvement in any of it—she genuinely thought you'd hired a hit man to take Ryder out, and Gareth encouraged her delusion. She went to confront him after you told her at lunch that you suspected he'd hired Ryder to harass you. Gareth convinced her you were spreading lies about him to cover up your own guilt."

"What about Maria?" I ask, wincing at how painful just saying her name out loud is.

"We picked her up. She was still in your office waiting on Titus to call her back."

"How did she explain her presence to my receptionist, Faye?" I ask, frowning at him curiously.

"She told Faye that her elderly mother made her feel guilty about working and she'd made a spur of the moment decision to quit, but that you'd talked her into returning."

I clench my hands into fists beneath the sheets. "I'm not surprised to hear she waltzed right back into Capitol Technologies unabashed. She's a very accomplished liar. I'm pretty sure she sabotaged several of my contracts with potential clients."

Detective Hernandez rests his elbows on the arms of his chair. "She won't be able to lie her way out of this one. She's left a digital trail of evidence. We have the burner phones she and Titus used in our possession."

I press my lips together, mustering the courage to ask the question that's been bothering me. "Did she ... seem remorseful?"

"No, not at all." Detective Hernandez straightens up in his chair, a somber look on his face. "But she did ask me to give you a message. She wanted to know if she'd been worth her dowry. Does that mean anything to you?"

Tears sting my eyes. I'd really considered Maria more of a peer then an assistant, and I was already planning on promoting her. All the time, I was her clueless sidekick. It's a hard pill to swallow. "It was a joke we had about the fee I paid to an executive PA service to find her," I explain, with a beleaguered sigh. "Just goes to show that paying a premium means absolutely nothing. You know, I watched a crime show once about a female lawyer who moved into a luxury gated apartment complex with full-time security because she wanted to make sure she would be safe in case any of the criminals she had prosecuted came after her. She ended up being attacked in her own apartment one night. She was raped and had her throat slit and was left for dead. The scary part was that it turned out to be a security guard who was employed by the complex who did it, not some lowlife criminal from the streets."

Detective Hernandez stares at me for a long moment and then clears his throat. "If I've learned anything from this business, it's that everyone's capable of almost anything given the right circumstances." He gets to his feet and slides his arms into his jacket. "I'll keep you in the loop with any developments. By the way, your lawyer's been in touch with me. He wanted to clarify a few things. I told him you're no longer a person of interest."

He holds my gaze for a moment and I think I know what he's trying to tell me. I'm no longer a person of interest in *anyone's* death.

37

Two days later, I return to work, more determined than ever to make Capitol Technologies a roaring success. In my absence, Faye got busy and lined up several qualified candidates for the PA position, and I've just finished up my fourth and final interview of the day. I didn't use the executive PA service this time, but I feel good about my decision to handle the vetting process myself. I've already decided which of the candidates I'm going to offer the job to, provided his references check out. But the best part of the day was a late afternoon phone call from Dan Huss. He informed me that under the circumstances, he had decided to go with Capitol Technologies after all. He was vague about what *under the circumstances* meant, but it's obvious he's intent on shielding his company's reputation now that Summit Solutions is under investigation for fraud.

I glance at my watch and jump to my feet when I realize how late it is. I promised Lucas I would make it home in time for dinner tonight as he's helping Kathy cook something special for my first day back at work. Kathy's offered to stay on for as long as I need her, and that might be indefinitely. I apologized tearfully to her for ever doubting her loyalty, and she graciously wiped away my tears and told me she understood my suspicion. As it turns out, she had found my mother's scarf in the pocket of one of the coats I gave to her to donate to the women's shelter. She recognized it as my mother's favorite and pulled it out to return it to me, but it had slipped her mind with everything that was going on.

Things are still strained between Jack and me and we haven't had a chance, yet, to sit down together and talk things through like we need to. Kathy still thinks he's the best thing to have happened to me, and she's doing everything in her power to encourage us to patch this breach in our relationship.

I've always thought "patch" is a weird word to use when it comes to mending relationships. The whole idea of a patch seems more akin to faking it 'till you make it—hiding the weak spots with something that covers up the problem. But I think Jack and I both realize that would be a mistake. If we're going to save our marriage, it's going to take some serious therapy and hard work on both of our parts. Jack has a lot to forgive, and I have a lot to face up to. I've spent most of my life blaming my parents for the choices I made instead of admitting that I was mostly coasting on their success through my teen years. At the end of the day, I was no different than Titus—playing the parental blame game rather than being thankful for what I had. In a world where kids are routinely beaten, neglected, starved, and even murdered by their own parents, having workaholic or adoptive parents doesn't come close to real hardship, let alone justify going down a self-absorbed path of addiction or criminality.

"I'm home!" I call, pushing open the front door.

"Mommy!" Lucas cries as he hurtles toward me. "Guess what!"

"I don't know," I say, shrugging out of my jacket. "Did you score a goal at soccer practice?"

"I didn't have soccer practice today," he corrects me, tilting his head at me reprovingly. "I helped Kathy bake a cream cheese coffee cake for Mr. Hogg. Because it's important to be nice to our neighbors, isn't it, Mommy?"

I pull him toward me and squeeze him tightly. "Yes. You're absolutely right. How about we take it over to him in a few minutes?"

"Okay," Lucas agrees, skipping his way to the kitchen.

Kathy smiles at me from the sink, elbows deep in soapy dish water. "How was work, pumpkin?"

"Good—excellent, actually," I say. "We got the Huss Integrity contract back. And I interviewed four candidates for the PA position."

Kathy cocks an interested eyebrow. "And?"

"I think I'm going to hire one of them. He's young, doesn't have a ton of experience, but he's super sharp. And of course the best part is that there's no dowry involved this time," I add with a wry grin.

Kathy rolls her eyes. "Dowries and prenups. Start of every bad relationship if you ask me."

I laugh, but the sound echoes around inside me. Jack and I could have used an emotional prenup agreeing not to begin our marriage on a bed of buried lies. Digging out from this mess is going to be tougher than being honest at the outset would have been.

"I was just about to get dinner started," Kathy remarks, drying her hands off.

"That coffee cake smells delicious," I say. "Lucas and I

better take it over to Mr. Hogg before dinner, or we might dig into it ourselves."

"Don't worry, we made one for us too," Kathy says, giving Lucas a conspiratorial wink.

"Can I ride my bike, please?" Lucas asks, his eyes wide and pleading as he peers up at me.

I open my mouth to tell him *no* but then stop myself. Why ever not? Lucas is six years old and he's going to have another twelve years of riding his bike around this neighborhood, if we end up staying. Stanley Hogg might as well get used to it now if we're to be neighbors. "Sure thing," I say, ruffling Lucas's hair. "Put your helmet on."

Ten minutes later, I'm shuffling from one foot to the other outside Stanley Hogg's front door, trying to ignore my misgivings about showing up uninvited. Lucas stands next to me, his helmet slipping over his eyes, struggling to hold the cake in his arms. His bike is parked along the curb, per my instructions. Just as Stanley has to accept the fact that the road is public property, Lucas needs to understand that other people's driveways are not his playground.

"Hi, Mr. Hogg. I made you a cake," Lucas says, thrusting it at him as soon as the door opens.

Stanley takes a startled step backward and casts a tense glance up and down the street like this might be some kind of a trap, before reaching out a hairy hand to accept the plate.

"We wanted to thank you for what you did—alerting the police," I add. "You saved my life, and Kathy's."

He gives an embarrassed shrug, his gaze dropping to Lucas. "Thanks for the cake, son."

"You're welcome," Lucas singsongs back to him.

My gaze meanders over Stanley's shoulder to the dead tree in the shadowy corner of his foyer. I realize now that what I initially thought was an overcoat is actually an old gray dressing gown. A wave of sadness washes over me. It's a pitiful reflection of how confined Stanley's life has become within these walls. He may be a cranky old man, but he has a lot on his plate, undertaking the never-ending and repetitive tasks of caregiving for a wife who can't think for herself anymore. No wonder he comes across as numb and hostile at times. He's probably depressed, and that's what makes him angry about every little infraction in the tiny sphere of life he still has some control over. I can't fault him for his hyper-vigilance. If it hadn't been for his fastidious attention to every movement on the block, I wouldn't be standing here on his steps today. I'd be at some funeral home awaiting burial, and Titus would have been facing two murder charges—three, if he'd managed to kill Kathy too.

"I recognized his limp," Stanley pipes up, almost as though he's been reading my thoughts. "I knew it wasn't right, that plumbing and heating van." He leans a little closer and lowers his voice. "That's how they do it, you know —get inside your house—they pose as some service or another. It's easy to walk into any building you want, if you put on a hard hat and act like you know where you're going."

I give a sober nod as if I'm agreeing with every word he says. And, in a way, I am. I know better than most how easy it was for an imposter to slip into Capitol Technologies and make it seem like they were meant to be there all along.

"Stan-ley, where are you?" a thin voice calls out.

"There's my cue." Stanley's eyes meet mine and he gives a sliver of a smile. "Coffee cake's her favorite. Not that she'll remember."

He closes the door, gently this time, and I can't help feeling it's a bashful invitation to call again sometime.

fter I bathe Lucas and put him to bed, I head back down to the kitchen to make some chamomile tea. Kathy has finished cleaning up and already turned in for the night. I stand at the window, staring out into the backyard at nothing in particular until the air begins to vibrate inside the kettle, the whistling calling me back to the moment. I'm disappointed Jack didn't make it home for dinner, but not all that surprised. It tells me he's conflicted about how he feels, still trying to process it all. He texted to let me know he had a late appointment, but I'm not sure what kind of appointment it could have been because he doesn't see clients in the evenings.

My mind immediately went into overdrive analyzing the possibilities. Did he go out with friends to drown his sorrows? Was it an appointment with a divorce lawyer? *No*— not this soon. Jack's not that reckless. That's the difference between the two of us. He's conservative, but I've always been attracted to risk like a moth to the light. Which is why his life has been a steady progression to ever greater heights of success whereas mine has been a wild ride filled with too many roll-of-the-dice moments to count.

My thoughts drift to Margo. I really should reach out to her again. Now that Ryder's murderer has been apprehended, she might be more receptive to my overtures. She might even accept my apology for my sickening and cowardly behavior all those years ago. She didn't deserve to be the brunt of so many vicious jokes, which only cemented her insecurities and led her down a dangerous path of anorexia and a string of superfluous surgeries. If she had died somewhere along the way, her death would have been on my conscience now too. If she gives me an opportunity to make amends, I'll take it.

I retrieve my phone from my purse and scroll through my contacts to Margo's number. My finger hovers over it for several minutes before I press it. Margo answers with a dull, *hello*—the kind of black-and-blue tone indicating she's been kicked around so much she's only going through the motions.

"Hi, Margo, it's Lauren."

"I heard they made an arrest," she says heatedly. "Saint Lauren is off the hook. If you're calling to gloat that I got it wrong, don't bother."

"I'm not," I reply. "You still have every right to hate me, Margo. There are a lot of things I'm guilty of. I failed you as a friend. The way I treated you in high school was wrong—it was appalling—and I'm ashamed of what a self-centered cow I was. Everything you said about me was right. I had parents who were able to provide for me in every way imaginable, and, instead of using that for good, I chose to resent them and take my anger out on other people, including you. For what it's worth, I'm truly sorry Ryder's dead, for your son's sake, if for no other reason."

Margo lets out a long, drawn-out sigh. "I suppose now neither of us gets him, we're even."

After a heartbeat, I ask, "Does that mean we can call a truce—maybe get the boys together sometime?"

"I'd ... like that. Sometime," Margo agrees, her voice quivering.

"You have my number," I say. "Call me when you're ready."

We hang up and I feel a weight slide from my shoulders like ice melting off a roof in the morning sun. Margo and I may not have a lot in common, but what we do share is important. We're both mothers who are fiercely protective of their children. Margo's got a difficult road ahead of her raising a fatherless son. I intend to be there for her as much as she wants me to be. I won't let the pain of our past overshadow the potential of a future friendship.

I tense at the sound of the front door opening, and shut my eyes briefly, trying to rein in my thoughts. I've been going over in my mind, off and on all day, what I want to say to Jack, and how I want to say it. But I'm afraid my emotions will betray me in the moment, and I'll simply break down and beg him not to leave.

"Hey," he greets me flatly when he walks into the kitchen. He heads straight to the refrigerator and helps himself to a Pellegrino.

"There are leftovers if you're hungry," I offer.

He gulps down some water and then shakes his head. "I ate already."

"Jack, we need to talk," I say, pulling out a chair at the table.

He hesitates, and for one awful moment I think he's going to refuse and walk out, but then he drops into the chair next to me, one hand squeezing the bottle of Pellegrino. "Yeah, we do."

"I know you're disappointed in me, maybe even disgusted," I begin, "and I don't blame you. You have every right to feel like that, but we have to find a way forward from here."

"We don't *have* to do anything," Jack corrects me. He fixes an earnest gaze on me. "We didn't have to get married. We got married because we wanted to. Because we loved and trusted each other. It's not that I expect you to tell me every little detail of your life before you met me, but you left out some pretty consequential things. Things that put our son's life in danger. Put *your* life in danger."

"Believe me, Jack, if I had had any idea things would turn out the way they did, I would have told you about Ryder a long time ago. I thought he was a fixture in my past—it didn't seem to serve any purpose to tell you about him."

"You should have told me about the arson. Two people died, Lauren. That's a pretty significant thing to have been involved in. I can't imagine the guilt you've been carrying around." He twists the cap on and off his bottle of water, staring at a spot in the corner of the room. "It's not what you did, shocking as it is. It's the lies that are tearing me apart."

"I know, and I'm sorry," I repeat, choking back a sob. "I wish I'd been completely honest with you, but I was terrified I'd lose you. You're so squeaky clean and by the book and never make a misstep. It's intimidating. I wanted you to view me as a successful woman you could be proud of, not a screw up."

Jack rubs his forehead. "Marriage is about being intimate even when it's scary to say things out loud. It's supposed to be us against our circumstances, not us colliding." He pulls his brows together. "I honestly don't know if we're going to make it as a couple. Maybe I should move out."

I throw him a look of alarm. "Don't say that!"

"I need time to heal from all the lies," Jack replies. "You don't get to erase them with a casual, *sorry*. It's not as simple as replacing a battery and then everything powers back up. I know we made a promise to do this for better or for worse, but I feel like a freight train just went over my heart."

"I realize I did a first-class job of messing up, but we can still make it if we want to," I implore. "Maybe this is our *for worse* moment, but it doesn't mean to say our *for better* moment isn't just around the corner. If you pack a martyr bag and leave, you'll never know, will you?"

Jack's lips twist in a ghost of a smile. "Are you suggesting I might finally be making a misstep by indulging in petty behavior?"

"I'm not *suggesting*, I'm *telling* you you're going to trip up on your own sanctimoniousness."

He laughs and reaches for my hand, rubbing it gently between his thumb and forefinger. "You're my ride-or-die friend, Lauren. All spunk and spirit. I don't want to lose you."

We both startle at a sudden sound in the doorway. "Did you lose Mommy?" Lucas asks, stifling a yawn as he shuffles into the kitchen in his fuzzy dinosaur slippers.

Jack chuckles. "No, son. I was scared I might have, but—" He trails off, his eyes searching mine. "I don't think I did, after all."

"You can have my good luck straw, if you want," Lucas offers, climbing up into Jack's lap and snuggling against his chest.

Jack's eyes lock with mine again. "Something tells me I won't be needing it," he says. "Maybe I'll just keep a hold of my favorite wife's hand instead."

"*And* your favorite son's," Lucas adds in a tone of mock outrage.

"That's right," Jack agrees, leaning across him and cradling my face gently in his hands. "Because I don't ever want to lose my favorite son, *or* my favorite wife."

———

A QUICK FAVOR

Dear Reader,

I hope you enjoyed reading *Right Behind You* as much as I enjoyed writing it. Thank you for taking the time to check out my books and I would appreciate it from the bottom of my heart if you would leave a review on Amazon or Goodreads as it makes a HUGE difference in helping new readers find the series. Thank you!

To be the first to hear about my upcoming book releases, sales, and fun giveaways, join my newsletter at

**https://normahinkens.-
com/newsletter**

and follow me on Twitter, Instagram and Facebook. Feel free to email me at norma@normahinkens.com with any feedback or comments. I LOVE hearing from readers. YOU are the reason I keep writing!

All my best,

Norma

WRONG EXIT

*Check out **Wrong Exit**, the first book in the **Treacherous Trips** Collection!*

Her life is about to change. But first she must survive the road trip.

Driving the I-40 coast to coast was never on newlywed Cora Dalton's bucket list. Until the day she finds out she has inherited a house in New York from an eccentric grandmother she has never met. Terrified of flying, Cora talks her best friend, Adele into accompanying her on a rip-roaring fun, ten-day road trip.

But when they pick up a teenage runaway at a gas station with a dark and disturbing past, things begin to go awry. Someone is following them—someone determined to finish a job they started. When their passenger inexplicably disappears at their motel one night, Cora finds a diary in the back seat of her car. Everything in it points to murder.

But never believe what you read. The truth lies between the lines.

- An edge-of-your-seat thriller with an earth-shattering final twist! -

WHAT TO READ NEXT

Ready for another thrilling read with shocking twists and a
mind-blowing murder plot?

Explore my entire lineup of thrillers on Amazon or at
https://normahinkens.com/thrillers

———

Do you enjoy reading across genres? I also write young
adult science fiction and fantasy thrillers. You can find out
more about those titles at
https://normahinkens.com/YAbooks

BIOGRAPHY

NYT and USA Today bestselling author N. L. Hinkens writes twisty psychological suspense thrillers with unexpected endings. She's a travel junkie, coffee hound, and idea wrangler, in no particular order. She grew up in Ireland—land of legends and storytelling—and now resides in the US. Her work has won the Grand Prize Next Generation Indie Book Award for fiction, as well as numerous other awards. Check out her newsletter for hot new releases, stellar giveaways, exclusive content, behind the scenes and more.

https://normahinkens.com/newsletter

Follow her on Facebook for funnies, giveaways, cool stuff & more!

https://normahinkens.com/Facebook

BOOKS BY N. L. HINKENS

SHOP THE ENTIRE CATALOG HERE

https://normahinkens.com/thrillers

<u>VILLAINOUS VACATIONS COLLECTION</u>

- The Cabin Below
- You Will Never Leave
- Her Last Steps

<u>DOMESTIC DECEPTIONS COLLECTION</u>

- Never Tell Them
- I Know What You Did
- The Other Woman

<u>PAYBACK PASTS COLLECTION</u>

- The Class Reunion
- The Lies She Told
- Right Behind You

<u>TREACHEROUS TRIPS COLLECTION</u>

- Wrong Exit
- The Invitation
- While She Slept

<u>WICKED WAYS COLLECTION</u>

- All But Safe

- What You Wish For

NOVELLAS

- The Silent Surrogate

BOOKS BY NORMA HINKENS

I also write young adult science fiction and fantasy thrillers under Norma Hinkens.

https://normahinkens.com/YAbooks

THE UNDERGROUNDERS SERIES
POST-APOCALYPTIC

- Immurement
- Embattlement
- Judgement

THE EXPULSION PROJECT
SCIENCE FICTION

- Girl of Fire
- Girl of Stone
- Girl of Blood

THE KEEPERS CHRONICLES
EPIC FANTASY

- Opal of Light
- Onyx of Darkness
- Opus of Doom

FOLLOW NORMA